Praise for *Coming of Age at the End of Days*

"[The novel's] swift plot, combined with a few stunning twists, keep the story skipping along."　　—*San Francisco Chronicle*

"LaPlante skillfully builds a protagonist whose decisions spring from a deep apathy for her surroundings. *Coming of Age at the End of Days* paints a surreal profile of suburban California where religious groups worship in abandoned malls and Laundromats, and where modern Silicon Valley clashes oddly with the apocalyptic visions of dark prophets ... A vivid portrayal ... thoughtful and challenging."　　—*LitReactor*

"The push and pull of relationships and complexity of unstable personalities create a compelling read. Tension and suspense are heightened through short chapters, terse matter-of-fact prose, and what is left unsaid ... Hard to put down."　　—*Library Journal*

"LaPlante masterfully weaves a distressing plot in which complex, sympathetic characters, each with a complete and absorbing past, are brought to the brink of destruction and then seemingly asked: What kind of life, and death, will you choose? The reader's imagination will be won by this brilliant, thought-provoking and memorable novel. It perfectly captures the dynamics of family relationships and friendships, loyalties and priorities, and the nuanced workings of an unusual mind."　　—*Shelf Awareness*

"[This novel] raises questions about mental fragility, vulnerability, and a variety of paths toward wholeness, many of which will find resonance among readers ... [this is] the kind of book that will inspire fierce debate."　　—*Bookreporter*

"With a satirist's eye and fleet, insightful prose, LaPlante delivers gratifying . . . twists in one girl's search for salvation."

—*Kirkus Reviews*

"LaPlante has a talent for depicting family dynamics and for making the environments her characters inhabit reflect their inner states." —*Booklist*

"An electrifying and beautifully rendered page-turner, *Coming of Age at the End of Days* is a richly evocative look at what it means to find yourself in a world that can feel so hopelessly lost."

—Kimberly McCreight, *New York Times* bestselling author of *Reconstructing Amelia*

"LaPlante's psychological thriller [is] a thought-provoking bildungsroman . . . rich themes of faith and doubt, vision and blindness, emerge compellingly." —*Publishers Weekly*

COMING OF AGE
AT THE END
OF DAYS

Fiction by Alice LaPlante

Turn of Mind

A Circle of Wives

COMING OF AGE
AT THE END
OF DAYS

Alice LaPlante

Grove Press
New York

First published by Grove Atlantic, August 2015

Published simultaneously in Canada
Printed in the United States of America

FIRST PAPERBACK EDITION, August 2016

ISBN 978-0-8021-2501-9
eISBN 978-0-8021-9134-2

Grove Press
an imprint of Grove Atlantic
154 West 14th Street
New York, NY 10011

Distributed by Publishers Group West

groveatlantic.com

16 17 18 19   10 9 8 7 6 5 4 3 2 1

For Sarah, with all my love

In those days men will seek death and will not find it;
they will desire to die, and death will flee from them.

—Revelation 9:6

I give her sadness,
And the gift of pain,
The new-moon madness,
And a love of rain.

—Dorothy Parker, "Godmother"

Prologue

ANNA DREAMS OF THE RED HEIFER night after night.

In the dream, the Red Heifer is moving carefully, even delicately, through the aisles of the Walgreens on El Camino. Past the diapers, the Benadryl, and the deodorant, gazing at the wares with its large wet eyes. A value shopper.

Nothing much happens in the first part of the dream. People walk by as if a brilliantly hued bovine in a suburban drugstore is the most natural thing in the world. No one questions its presence, much less its right to exist at all. Except Anna. She follows the Red Heifer as it ambles through the automatic doors into the blinding California sun. She knows the Red Heifer is important. And she feels responsible. If she can just keep it in sight. Prevent it from falling into the wrong hands. But she loses the Red Heifer in the parking lot. She searches, increasingly frantic. Where did it go? Not out onto the street— Anna hears no screeching brakes, no blaring horns. Vehicles roar past. The Red Heifer has simply vanished.

Then, only silence. The traffic ceases. Cars freeze, line up motionless in every direction, although the stoplights continue to cycle through greens, yellows, and reds. The cars are empty. No humans inhabit this world any longer. And Anna, knowing that she has failed, is full of woe. She invariably wakes in tears. Because she must accept responsibility. Because she knows, deep down, that she helped bring this on. That she's one of them. A true believer.

PART I

In the Beginning

1

ANNA LIVES IN SUNNYVALE, CALIFORNIA, in a housing development built in the sixties. In a subdivision that supplanted a citrus grove in what was then called the Valley of Heart's Delight. In an uninspired house that was a forerunner of the barracks that would soon obliterate all the fields and orchards and give rise to a new name for the region: Silicon Valley.

Anna's street has twenty-five houses on it, but just four house models: a rancher, a colonial, a Cape Cod, and a split-level. Over the years people have added decks and landscaping, enlarged the windows and converted garages, but the skeletons of the original structures remain. When a light goes on upstairs in the colonial diagonally across the street, the mirror image of Anna's own home, Anna knows that Janie Poole, thirteen years old, has taken refuge in the bathroom to avoid the squalling of her newborn twin brothers. If the hall on the bottom floor of the split-level next door is suddenly illuminated in the late evening, Mr. Johnson is helping Mrs. Johnson to the master bedroom after she's enjoyed one scotch too many. There are no secrets, no mysteries, in this suburban enclave.

The Sunnyvale Post Office knows Anna's block as the Street of Children's Names. A year before Anna was born, the city dug up and re-poured the sidewalks. The glistening gray virgin squares proved too tempting to the neighborhood children, who carved their names in the still-wet concrete. Their engravings remain today, are writ large along the block. Each letter covers an entire pavement panel, and over the years the residents have come to call the houses by the children's names rather than their numerical addresses. Anna lives in *S-A-R-A-H* with her mother and father. The Goldschmidts live in *K-A-R-I-S*. Jim Fulson, the only child of that epic effort still living on the block, can be found across the street in *C-A-R-O-L-I-N-E*. The foul Hendersons next door to him in *C-L-A-I-R-E*.

Most lights are out by midnight on the Street of Children's Names. Everyone in bed by 11:30 PM. Except Anna. She ghosts in the early morning. No respite. Up at 3 AM, unable to sleep. Too agitated to lie in bed. An uncalm insomnia. Her mother tries everything—chamomile tea, hot milk, even pills. Those Anna flushes down the toilet. She knows there must be a reason for her to be awake at such an hour. She is waiting for answers. Until then, she is resigned to witness the death of each successive night. To acknowledge the arrival of each new day. To prepare for whatever follows.

2

ANNA IS SIXTEEN WHEN THE darkness descends.

She had hints that it was coming. Interludes of deep sadness over the past twelve months. Mourning, almost, triggered by the smallest things. An expression flitting across her father's face as he gazed at her mother. A glimpse of a small boy waiting alone at a bus stop. But the sadness always dissipated, she would always come to, and find herself again. Until now.

The morning it all changes, the problem starts with the mirror, still plastered with pink Disney princess stickers, smudged from practice kisses. She looks at her reflection and retches. A sudden, violent aversion. What. Is. That. Thing.

Only the previous evening, she'd stood naked in front of her mirror—just so—appreciating her shoulders, her breasts, her waist, admiring her long blonde hair. Her recent makeup purchases were scattered on the bureau: cheap Maybelline, L'Oréal from Walgreens. *Because I'm worth it.* Those were the articles of faith of her peers, their most fervent beliefs, and Anna had been trying to subscribe to them, trying to *blend in.* "People like us, we pretend. We fake it, until we're into our twenties," her mother told her. "Then we come into our own. Then our weirdnesses become our strengths." Anna had had one of her flashes of despair at this, but her mother hadn't noticed, was looking straight ahead while driving, her hands steady on the wheel. Their most intimate talks, of which this was one, occurred while her mother was preoccupied with other things.

Anna can't bear to look at herself now. She covers her mirror and turns all the photos of herself to the walls. Her mother gives up turning them back after the fifth day. Both she and Anna's father are openly concerned. Whispering stops whenever Anna walks into the room. She begins wearing her Stanford sweatshirt everywhere, the peaked hood drawn tight around her head, over her ears, pulled down to cover her forehead. Anna's mother tries to make light of it. "Hello, Grumpy," she says. "Or is it Bashful?" but Anna is as receptive to human interaction as a slab of meat.

Depression, they call it. Such a flat name for such a ferocious and uncompromising beast. Anna prefers the medieval term. *Melancholia. Black bile.* A foul humor that steals into your joints, paralyzes your muscles, immobilizes your bones. But it also clears your vision, reveals the truth that everything is tainted, and that you are worse than untouchable. An obscenity.

At school, first: *What's wrong, Anna?* Then increasingly, sullenly, even from her friends: *What's your problem?* A couple of phone calls. A dramatic attempt at intervention. Then, nothing. Three weeks later Anna is where she needs to be: alone.

But Anna's body is the true enemy. A heaviness of limbs. She can barely lift her head from the pillow in the morning. *Melancholia.* Transforming her into a machine for manufacturing despair. It is hard to breathe. Why breathe.

Anna cycles through the rote motions of an automaton. Her day shaped by invisible orders by an invisible commandant. Wear this. Eat this. Look this way. Now look down. Shake your head *no*. Say not a word. Turn. Turn and leave the room.

Then, one morning, at the breakfast table. Staring at the milk carton. Then. There it is. Her path forward. *Expiration date.* Heat spreads across Anna's face. Her fingers tingle. Her expiration date. Anna does not yet know the exact day and time. But it is coming. It will come. She will be released from pain.

3

IT IS AROUND THIS TIME that Anna's mother decides to start a reading regime at bedtime. Anna feebly protests—"I'm sixteen!"—but lacks the energy to prevail. Her mother is adamant. She chooses an old Bible that once belonged to Anna's grandmother. "This gives us some time together," she says. "Besides, you're not truly educated if you don't know your biblical stories. You won't understand literary references. Or great works of art or music. Or what religious nutcases are talking about in election years." Until this point, Anna has learned nothing about God. "Religions are the work of the devil," her mother is fond of saying, without irony. In the throes of her melancholia, and ultimately grateful for any attention her mother deigns to give her, Anna acquiesces when her mother opens the book and begins to read.

In the beginning God created the heaven and the earth . . .

So Anna learns about the creation of the world, about Adam and Eve, but as metaphors, not truths. The snake stands for temptation. The apple for knowledge that humans should not possess. Anna doesn't blame Eve for coveting it. She would have coveted it, too.

Anna finds she enjoys thinking that powers exist greater than herself. She recognizes Satan's determination and ruthless single-mindedness. Both her parents have it, each in their own way. They usually gaze past Anna to focus intently on some other object—her mother, the pianist, on her music; her father, the amateur scientist, on his study of earthquakes. Anna knows she doesn't come first with either of them. But Satan? The sweet cajoling that convinced Eve to eat the fruit—Anna would like to be subjected to that intense wooing.

Anna's mother is particularly scornful when explaining original sin, but it makes sense to Anna, this idea that she was born in shadow, and that some redemptive act is required to make her endurable.

Despite her mother's commentary, Anna is rapt during the nightly readings, riveted by the stories of Daniel, and Joseph, and David.

They have become a welcome ritual, the only occasions Anna gets precious time alone with her mother. Her mother doesn't even mind being touched now; they sit side by side propped up by pillows on Anna's double bed, together holding the heavy book so both can see the printed words. Anna's mother reads them out loud, slowly. When they reach Revelation, Anna sits straight, grips her mother's arm. She finds the answers she has been unknowingly searching for. She recognizes it when she hears it.

I have the keys to hell and of death.

Anna looks up pictures of hell on the Internet. She finds Bosch's *The Last Judgment*. Bosch's vision of hell delights her, the strange horned and great-snouted creatures wrestling with the humans in the crevices of dark mountains. The nakedness here excites her, rouses her from her lethargy. This is a hell she can believe in. This is a place she can get to whenever she chooses to go. She doesn't see the strange creatures as metaphors, but as truths, and the chaos in the painting reflects that inside her. Here would be a place she would fit in.

Where their worm dieth not, and the fire is not quenched.

Yes, Anna can believe in this.

4

DISMAYED AS MUCH BY ANNA'S fixation on Revelation as by her depression, Anna's parents and her therapist try to trace Anna's current state back to its roots. The friendless early days at school. Her tendency to be a loner. For Anna is different. This has always been the case. At six, she was clumsy and earnest. Children are ruthless conformists, and Anna diverged from the norm just enough to affront the sensibilities of the other first graders, who firmly closed ranks against her. They didn't invite Anna to their homes, to the park, to the ice-cream parlor after school. Anna was aware that things happened between her classmates, that bonds were being forged, but she never had a way in.

Anna's mother didn't help. Wouldn't approach the other mothers, the social arbiters of the elementary school, the keepers of the playdate schedules. When approached herself—a rare occurrence—Anna's mother pulled back, rejected advances. She couldn't play tennis in the afternoon, her job as a piano tuner wouldn't allow it. She didn't have time for coffee in the morning after drop-off, that was her piano practice time. At pickup, when the other mothers gossiped in clusters at the front of the school, Anna's mother sat in her car listening to the music of Erik Satie, her eyes closed, her fingers moving as if over a keyboard. Or she talked on the phone to her best friend Martha, to her technician buddies at the music academy where she helped maintain the pianos. Whenever Anna and her mother bumped into little groups of classmates around town, at the park, or at the public swimming pool, Anna knew not to intrude upon those closed circles, she would move herself to a different swing set, or eat her ice cream outside. Anna's mother was oblivious to all this, didn't even recognize the other mothers, who long ago stopped attempting to break through her reserve.

Even back then, Anna had trouble sleeping. So at night she often slipped out of her room and down the hall to the living room, hid behind the couch while her parents, unmindful, went about their evening routine.

Anna was soothed by watching her father at his computer, charting and graphing geological seismic activity, her mother at the piano, noting fingerings on a piece of music. Her mother at that time was engrossed in Satie's *Gymnopédies,* the unhurried and dissonant melodies so heavy and grave that Anna's heart slowed its beating to match their measured calm. She lay behind the couch growing languid and somnolent, and eventually would crawl back to bed and sleep.

A year passed, then two. But Anna still had trouble fitting in, was still the same loner she'd been in first grade. Just be patient, the pediatrician told her parents. This is just a phase. Anna's mother would push her out the door when the other neighborhood children were playing tag in the street. But even here she felt awkward, unwelcome. Her parents would see her futilely chasing a crowd of mocking boys and girls around home base, a weak and spindly tree. She'd come into the house in tears. Her father told her that anger was greater than sadness. He told Anna to stand up for herself. But Anna, at eight, knew she was being patronized, knew how ineffectual her father was.

One day an older boy from across the street called to Anna as she hovered awkwardly around the periphery of yet another game of tag.

"Hey there," he said. "You. Yes, you." Anna pointed to herself uncertainly. "Come over here." He was standing in front of C-A-R-O-L-I-N-E. "It's Annie, right?"

Anna stopped to listen but kept her eye on the girl who was It, ready to run should she become prey.

"I want to show you something," the boy said. He was fourteen, maybe fifteen, almost man-sized, belonging to that most mysterious of places, *high school*. He opened his right hand and showed Anna a fistful of small rocks that he'd gathered from the border of the flowerbeds of C-A-R-O-L-I-N-E, where he lived. He settled himself cross-legged about five feet from a tree, and motioned for Anna to sit next to him. He piled the rocks in a small pyramid between them.

"Do what I do," and the boy picked up a rock and threw it at the tree. It bounced harmlessly off the trunk. "Just get mad. Throw some stones. Get it out of your system. Then you can show those other kids what's what." Anna looked at the tree, then at the boy. Her face revealed nothing, she'd already learned from her mother how to hide her thoughts. Anna picked up a rock and threw. She missed.

"No, you have to hit it," said the boy, and he did so again. Anna tried and this time the rock made a satisfying *thud* when it struck wood.

The boy pointed to the branches that were swaying back and forth in the wind, causing the trees to bend and nearly touch each other. "See, they all talk to each other. Right now, they're whispering up and down the street that no one better mess with you, or else."

The boy smiled at Anna, but stopped when he saw her face. This time she let her expression show. She was not stupid. She knew she was being infantilized.

"Ridiculous," Anna said, speaking for the first time, using one of her father's favorite words.

The boy saw that he had failed. He was no dummy, either. "Can I go back to the game now?" Anna asked.

The boy had other plans. He scrambled to his feet. "I'll show you something, I'll show you something I've never shown anyone else," he said. He was speaking in a very low voice. He took Anna by the hand and led her to his house. They waved to a woman that Anna assumed was his mother, who was kneeling in the yard planting red flowers. Geraniums, Anna knew from the sharp, unpleasant smell that her mother hated. The boy opened the garage door and took Anna inside the garage's dark coolness. It was very neat. Like most of the residents on the Street of Children's Names, the boy's family didn't park cars in their garage, but used it as storage space. A refrigerator. A stand-alone freezer. Tools hanging on the wall. Boxes stacked into a tower, edges perfectly aligned. The boy dragged a lawn mower from the corner to the middle of the floor. His hands shook as he turned the mower on its side, exposing the mechanical un-derbelly. "Look at this," the boy said. *"Look at this."* A tremor in his voice. He reached out and nearly touched the bright blade.

Anna heard him swallowing. "When you turn this on, it shreds anything that comes near. Toes, fingers. Once, I ran over a baby bird," he said. "This is a very dangerous piece of equipment." But from the way he said the word *dangerous* Anna understood he meant *evil*. She recognized terror when she saw it.

"I have to mow the lawn every Saturday," the boy said. "It used to bother me. But now I come here, I turn the lawn mower over. I touch the blade like this." And he reached out with his index finger, pressed the tip of it against the blade. He closed his eyes. With a quick, hard motion he pulled his finger across the blade. It sliced. It drew blood. Just a little. The boy had been careful. He held out his finger to Anna so she could see the red line in the flesh. Next to it, pale white lines from earlier cuts. Battle scars. "After I do this, it's okay. I can mow the lawn," he told Anna, and she could see this was true: his fear had dissipated, his hands were now steady.

A ritual. Anna understood rituals. She believed in them. Her mother, before performing a piece, always stroked the piano keys as if petting a cat. Before going to sleep at night, Anna herself turned a full circle in bed, like she'd seen some dogs do. These rituals were potent. "You throw those rocks," the boy said. "Or something. You'll figure it out. You're a smart kid."

The boy flipped the lawn mower over and led Anna back outside. "You can do this," he said, and this time he was not patronizing her. His name was Jim Fulson. He lived in C-A-R-O-L-I-N-E.

"Thank you, Jim Fulson," Anna said, and this made him laugh.

"You're welcome, Annie Franklin," and he took her hand for a minute in a warm squeeze. They both looked at the tree the other children were congregating against as it shuddered in the wind. "You're on your way now. There's no looking back," Jim Fulson said. Anna had believed him.

5

ANNA SEES DR. CUMMINGS WEEKLY. Dr. Cummings is compassion-
ate. She understands. She is wise in the ways of girls. Especially
teenagers. Especially good girls gone suddenly bad. Who, like
Anna, rotted overnight. Who have begun to noticeably stink. *In
cases like this we advise swift and early intervention.*

Dr. Cummings gives Anna her space. She respects Anna's
silences. Dr. Cummings empowers Anna, believes she can in
fact be empowered. Though she will sometimes need to be
hard on Anna. She knows how to read the tea leaves. If Anna's
skirts are too short, Dr. Cummings will understand she is too
eager for male approval. If Anna doesn't use makeup, Dr. Cummings will know she is sending signals to other girls. That she's
not a threat. That she deserves their sympathy and pity, not their
natural instinct to reject the *Other,* the outsider, from the flock.
Showing belly, like a dog would, Dr. Cummings laughs. Most of
Dr. Cummings's metaphors involve animals, her analyses lead
to one conclusion: Power games are being played by the pack.
*Dog eat dog. Top cat. Slippery as an eel. Playing possum. Barracuda
behavior.* The morals of these stories come down to this: Anna
should accept that *her problem,* as Dr. Cummings calls it, is due

to a simple misalignment with her herd. "Hunt with the pack," Dr. Cummings says. "Do it physically, with enthusiasm. Even if it's just an act at first. All else will occur naturally. The heart and the mind always follow the body." As she utters this heresy, she smiles, waits for Anna to challenge her.

Anna tells her nothing.

Her mother sits in the waiting room, listening to Hindemith. Her eyes closed. As Anna's mother will only wear opentoed sandals, even in winter, waiting patients voyeuristically watch her toes curl and uncurl in an agony of sensory pleasure. So engrossed is she that Anna picks the check her mother had already written and signed out of her lap and carries it back to Dr. Cummings without her mother noticing. "Next week," Dr. Cummings says, and her voice is warm, inviting. Anna has disappointed her again. Anna has nothing for her, or anyone, hasn't for nearly five months now. Anna nods and exits to rouse her mother from her silent ecstasy.

They continue feeding Anna pills. Small round white ones. Large pink oval ones. But Anna knows better than to take them. She shakes the pills in her hand, watches the colors bounce before she disposes of them when her mother isn't looking. Dr. Cummings is beginning to talk about wiring Anna to a machine, shooting her through with electricity. "It's very safe these days," she tells Anna's parents, who are horrified by the idea. "And it's the most effective method overall, the efficacy is remarkable, really." She talks about *prognosis, outcomes, likelihoods.* She talks about *risk factors. Safety measures.* Anna's parents raid her closet, take her belts. They hide all the razors. She doesn't mind, she's hidden her other implements away. Anna knows her time will come, that opportunities will manifest themselves.

For I am passionately in love with death. Where did Anna hear this? She doesn't remember. But the phrase resonates.

Dr. Cummings begins issuing commands. "Go through the motions. Get out of bed. Get dressed. Take a shower and wash your hair. You'll feel better." Anna disagrees. It is better to remain dormant. Avoid the sunlight. Avoid her mother's music. Even staring at the spot on the wall next to her bed is too much for Anna to process some mornings. She shuts her eyes and shudders, waits for the familiar plummeting feeling that inevitably follows.

One day, at her mother's insistence, Anna tries. She takes her cello out of its case. She presses the index finger of her left hand onto the D string, but she can't pin it tightly enough against the fingerboard, her nails are too long, she hasn't cut them in months. Her mother brings her the nail clippers and stands by until Anna has trimmed all ten nails, takes the clippers away again. Once more, Anna places her finger on the string, this time making contact between her flesh and the wood of the fingerboard, the string cutting into her tender skin no longer hardened by calluses. She picks up the bow with her right hand, it feels heavy and clumsy, and she only draws it halfway across the string before losing strength. She had quit her teacher, quit the school orchestra, quit the quartet she'd been playing in since freshman year. Everyone had at first been kind, but most people lose patience quickly, Anna discovered, when you stop responding to social cues. People feel insulted, take it personally.

Her mother chose an easy piece for them to play together, the Haydn concerto in C major, first movement. Yet Anna's hands are sweating, her fingers slide off the strings. Her bow shears off without drawing a solid note.

"Try again," her mother says. Her hands connected to piano keys, connected down through the floor up through Anna's cello to Anna herself. There is a connection there. Anna feels it, attempts to gather her resources. She is drawing the bow across the strings, she is moving her fingers. She keeps playing because of the connection. She is playing badly, but when she stops that connection will be lost. She would sit here forever with her bow on the strings if she could, her umbilical cord to her mother, holding on for dear life.

6

FIGHTS NOW OCCUR FREQUENTLY IN Anna's family, fights of a sort never seen before in their household. Anna is at the center of them. Anna is somehow the instigator, she can do it without saying a word, her joyless presence alone has the power to drive her parents into a frenzy of mutual recriminations while she slips quietly away to her room.

Her father, always volatile, becomes insufferable. So Anna's mother says. He is no longer gentle when talking to Anna, openly berates her for *not trying*. He seems determined to break Anna. Unusual, her mother says, whatever his moods, it's unlike him to deliberately hurt her.

Anna remembers a previous exception to this. Five years ago. Anna's eleventh birthday. She was in the passenger seat, next to her father, who was driving. "We need to tell you something," Anna's father said. He said *we* but he was the only other person in the car.

As usual, Anna's father was going too fast—55 in a 35 zone. He considered the posted speed limit to be the absolute minimum acceptable velocity, drove faster when agitated or elated. Anna's mother was at work, tuning the rarely played baby grand pianos of Hillsborough, Woodside, Portola Valley. Anna's father had taken the day off to celebrate with Anna. They were on their way to the miniature-golf course in San Carlos where they were going to play two games, then hit the arcade. This was their birthday tradition.

But Anna's father was not himself. He had been like this all morning. Anna's parents had one of their unusual fights the previous evening. No shouting, Anna's mother is difficult to engage in that way, she always shrugs off the inconvenience of anger by humming atonally or fingering a melody on the piano. It drives Anna's father mad. Always quick to anger, he usually cooled down fast, but not this time. He'd slammed his door so hard getting into the car that Anna's teeth jarred. He didn't say anything until they were on 101.

"You were conceived in a petri dish," he told Anna just as they passed Moffett Field, past the huge empty dirigible hangar. "You were not conceived in love."

The words came out hard.

He'd promised to stop at the In-N-Out Burger in Mountain View for cheeseburgers and chocolate shakes, but he drove right by the exit.

"You're eleven, you're old enough to understand," her father told Anna. "You're old enough to take it."

So she was a test-tube baby. Anna was startled, but not upset. She mulled over this in silence. They had learned about it in biology. The very first test-tube baby had given birth to a test-tube baby herself not long ago. Anna had liked the symmetry of that. Finally, Anna asked what her father would consider a stupid question. She can see from his face. "Where?" But she wanted to know. She is hoping for some exotic locale. Perhaps she is Spanish? Zimbabwean? She'd always checked the citizen box for U.S citizen, always put down her birthplace as *San Jose* on official forms.

"You were created in a lab in Daly City, California," her father said. She was put off by his disdainful tone, by the unspoken *idiot* at the end of his sentence. *Idiot. Idiot. Idiot.*

"Don't you want to know why?" her father asked.

"Okay, why?"

"I was sterile. I had the mumps in college. It's rare to get it that late, but it happens. And it nukes your testes." He wasn't embarrassed to say this, and Anna wasn't embarrassed to hear. Her parents openly joked about the insipid pleasures of marital coitus. Her mother was prepared to buy Anna birth control whenever she asked. Sex sounded like a bodily necessity that settled the nerves and produced happy endorphins.

The story her father wanted to tell came out gradually. He was growing calmer now, and Anna suspected that he was regretting his anger. He always did. Anna loved her father. He still sang silly songs for her when he suspected she was blue.

Bananas in pajamas are coming down the stairs
Bananas in pajamas are coming down in pairs
Bananas in pajamas are chasing teddy bears

Her father's voice became noticeably softer, more hesitant. But still he continued on. He kept stopping to look at Anna to gauge how she was taking it. She leaned forward in her seat, hungry for details.

Anna was one of six eggs extracted from her mother and fertilized with a stranger's sperm. Her parents chose her for her looks and her agility, from a dish containing six five-day-old blastocysts. She was the fastest-growing, and the biggest. She was ready to burst from her shell. She was the one they chose. She was the chosen one.

Anna asked what she most wanted to know. Her father was waiting for it. "So who's my father?"

"I am." His voice again raised. He pressed on the accelerator. They'd reached Redwood City, drawing near to their destination, but he sped up rather than preparing to exit, was swiftly passing all other vehicles. "And don't think about chasing after your so-called real father. I'm your real father. This is not like an adoption, where you can search through records when you're eighteen. Your mother and I agreed to destroy the documentation. We thought you should know the truth, but we didn't want you harboring some romantic idea of finding the sperm donor."

Anna said nothing. She wondered who her father was arguing with. It wasn't her.

The sperm donor was a fantasy picked out of a database by her mother, Anna's father told her. The sperm donor had been chosen, too. He was chosen for his photograph, for his physical beauty and resemblance to a boy Anna's mother had once been infatuated with. He was also chosen because he was a gifted musician, because on his bio sheet he wrote that he loved Mahler, just as her mother's first lover had.

"You knew this?" Anna asked.

"Of course not. Your mother told me she picked a donor who was as intelligent and good-looking as I was. I couldn't see the resemblance. But she insisted."

"Maybe she was telling the truth."

"Maybe I was cuckolded, plain and simple." The speed-ometer was above 90. Her father did not want her reassurances. Usually he was less difficult to placate, the balm for his rages typically within easy reach. "Of course it hasn't mattered," he said. "Not one bit. I sulked for a few days after she told me. This was a month before you were born. I drank heavily for two weeks after that. And then I forgave all. By the time you arrived I had accepted it." He did not sound forgiving. He did not sound accepting. He pressed harder on the accelerator: 100 miles per hour.

"I see a cop," Anna said. She didn't, but her father im-mediately braked and checked his mirrors. One more speeding ticket and he could lose his license.

Anna thinks of her five siblings, frozen on that day. Ac-cording to her father, so advanced is the technology and so ambiguous the laws and ethics, the embryos are probably still frozen and viable. Her brothers and sisters, locked in an indus-trial freezer in Daly City. She could claim them. She could even give birth to her own kin someday.

But she was chosen. Her parents wanted her, Anna. If a younger sister or brother were ever defrosted, implanted, and nurtured until birth, she could taunt them with that fact. *Mom and Dad loved* me *best.* The simple truth.

7

ANNA'S MOTHER ROUSES HER ONE Saturday morning to go to the farmer's market. At her mother's insistence, Anna changes out of the T-shirt and shorts she has been wearing for four days. That the sun is shining when they step outdoors is an active reproach. Anna instructs her feet to step, one in front of the other. See, others do it. A brilliant Saturday morning, and the parking lot of Anna's old middle school is covered with tents full of vegetables and fruit. A man is playing fiddle, accompanied by a vocalist on guitar. The singer has the microphone amped too high and leans in too close, his words are impossible to distinguish, he seems to be wailing in some ancient tongue. The adults are clapping and smiling broadly but small children are distressed by the noise, some beginning to cry.

The farmers running the stands all know Anna's mother. She is in her element. She can be relied upon to know which kale is the freshest, which apples are truly organic, whether the fish at the fish stand is local or flown in from Seattle. Other shoppers listen to her banter with the farmers. Anna tires of towering over her dark, petite mother, of listening to the talk of mulches and soil and irrigation. She retreats to the periphery of the market with the smokers, blinking against the light and gagging a little amidst the fumes. It's hard to breathe. But it's always hard to breathe.

"Smell this, sweetie," her mother comes over, holding up a bouquet of cilantro. But Anna can't detect anything special. Anna's mother puts her hand on Anna's arm. She has been doing this a lot lately, Anna suspects on orders from Dr. Cummings. The hand never lingers, but drops off after a few nonresponsive seconds.

Against health regulations, a small white dog is off leash and is running around the market, yapping at ankles. Anna's mother hates dogs, hates the way they smell, that they invade your personal space. She swats at the dog as if at a fly. "Shoo." But this creature is less a dog than a little lamb, complete with soft woolly hair and long floppy ears. It is adorable. People are exclaiming. Even Anna can see why.

The dog approaches Anna, bumps its way around her ankles. She feels sinewy muscles and bones, sharp edges. She contemplates the creature, and then, exuding enormous effort, reaches down and attempts to touch it. But it shies away, scampers off to another person. It knows. Everyone, every thing knows. She is untouchable.

Her mother assigns her tasks. "You get the tomatoes and the potatoes, I'll get the apples and lettuce." She gives Anna twenty dollars, then hesitates, takes it out of Anna's limp hand, and puts it in Anna's front pocket for safety. She gives Anna a push and Anna wills her feet to move. She enters a stall piled high with potatoes. Small, large, oblong, misshapen, purple, gray, white. Other shoppers are picking up specimens, marveling at their color and quality and unusual shapes, but Anna simply takes a plastic bag and dully begins filling it. Then it happens. That cruelest of all things. A flash of normality. A glimpse of life as other people are experiencing it. For an instant the scene changes from sepia to full color, Anna is assaulted by the bright hues, the earthy smells, she feels the buzzing energy of the crowd. Anna puts her hands on a pile of orange-tinted potatoes, feels their coolness, their strange bumps and rough hollows. She holds one up to her cheek, sniffs it. And for a minute Anna thinks sheer willpower can do it, can vanquish the melancholia. A simple mindset adjustment, a quick wrenching of perspective, and she could be out of misery and into the light. It is all her fault. She has simply been looking at things the wrong way round. The world really isn't so sad, so dead. It has all been a terrible mistake. Hers. Then, just as suddenly, the vision passes. Back to sepia, back to pain, even more pain after such a moment of grace. Anna drops the half-filled bag of potatoes on the ground and leaves the stall, manages to find a place on the curb between the tomato stand and an Indian spice concession and sits down. Her sense of smell has dulled again although she sees, as if in pantomime, passersby stopped mid-step by the aromas. She puts her head in her hands and does what she so often does these days: weeps.

Her fit lasts three, maybe four minutes. Anna decides to find her mother, but as she stands she knocks over a tray of heirloom tomatoes. They roll across the pavement, strange-hued fruits of purple and yellow and green, colors that tomatoes have no right being. How angry Anna is suddenly, at this, and everything else. A woman blunders and steps on one of the tomatoes, others are being squashed under the wheels of baby strollers. It looks like a battleground on which dozens of tiny slaughters had been perpetrated. Anna's mother appears, embarrassed. She tries to force money on the farmer, who is kindly refusing payment. "These things happen," he says. "Take care of the little girl." He means Anna, who has turned her back, the hood of her Stanford sweatshirt tight over her head.

"Oh, Annie," says her mother, and leads Anna away from the crowd, away from the market. "Oh Annie."

Anna takes a bag of basil and a sack of apples from her mother without looking at her. Her hands brush against the basil leaves, releasing their sharp pungent aroma. Anna barely notices. She yearns for something, something she believes her mother can give her. She is also terrified. Unable to articulate either her need or her terror, she treads heavily after her mother, her head held low to keep the sun's rays off her face. Her sweatshirt is insufferably hot, but she doesn't dare remove it. That would mean exposure, and shame so fiery it would singe her insides. Her mother is too far away. Her mother is too near to her. Within reach of her fingers if she, Anna, reached out with her free hand. She could touch that shoulder, caress its petite, fragile bones, send a message. Somehow that is the most chilling thought of all.

Because the bags are heavy, Anna's mother leads her toward the forbidden shortcut, across the municipal golf course: *No pedestrians allowed*. The day is windless. Anna's mother takes off her shoes, puts them in a bag on top of some broccoli.

"When I was pregnant with you, I played the wrong music." Anna's mother is talking as if they had been in the middle of a conversation. "They tell you that Mozart will make your child smart and happy, but I was just discovering the Impressionists then, was bored with Mozart. I riled you up with my choices. I could feel you churning inside me. Agitating. At the time I thought it was a good thing, I was educating your ears, stimulating you. But when you came out, you looked so sad. Can a baby look sad? You did. I was sad, too. So sad it was over. We'd been so close. And now I had to share you."

Her mother has never talked to her like this before. Anna is startled. Sweat is trickling down her back, between her breasts, but still she keeps her sweatshirt zipped, the hood over her head. She doesn't trust her voice to respond. She slows her steps to increase the distance between herself and her mother. It's safer that way.

"I tried golfing once," her mother says, seemingly apropos of nothing. Then Anna sees two elderly men playing on the ninth hole. Anna and her mother guiltily skirt to the left, around a grove of fir trees. They've frequently taken this forbidden path. Sometimes clubs are shaken at them, once a ball was thrown. The heat is making them both somnolent, how they keep walking is a miracle. Anna has a thirsty ache in her throat. Dr. Cummings blames the medications, but Anna knows that's impossible. Her thirst is due to something else, something deep that is insatiable.

Anna stumbles in the grass because she's not lifting her feet high enough.

"At least take your shoes off," her mother says, and when she does, Anna is surprised at how pleasantly cool the grass is. They run into trouble at the sixth hole, where two middle-aged women stare icily at the friendly wave Anna's mother gives.

One hundred feet farther, they stop to rest under an oak tree that must be two hundred years old—it is massive, with far-reaching limbs.

"You don't know what a huge presence you are in our lives," her mother says, again as if picking up a conversation in progress. "Even if you're in your room with the door closed, we can *feel* you."

To this Anna has no answer. There are no answers.

"Oh Annie," her mother says finally, not looking at her. "Do you see any way out of this?" Anna's mother is sitting with her back against the tree, is picking blades of grass and shredding them. To which Anna says nothing. She sits about four feet from her mother. She uncrosses and extends her legs, lies back on the grass. She could almost go to sleep. The heavy summer air.

Then suddenly the sprinklers go on. Anna's skin is so hot she can almost hear the sizzle as the cold water kisses her face, her hands, her feet. It's such a fine mist that it isn't uncomfortable, is welcome, even. Anna's mother gives a little cry of happiness, and moving away from the tree, stretches out on the grass, her arms opened wide, her hair spread around her head. Drops sparkle on the dark strands.

Her mother begins humming. Anna doesn't recognize the tune, but it is haunting and dissonant. It doesn't match the bright day. It is more in line with Anna's mood than anything she has ever heard. An appropriate soundtrack to her inner life. Then her mother starts singing the words. Anna doesn't understand German, but she recognizes the syllables of misery.

Nun will die Sonn' so hell aufgeh'n
als sei kein Unglück die Nacht gescheh'n.

Anna's mother stops. She's lying motionless, staring straight up at the sky, not smiling.

"What is that?"

"Mahler. *Kindertotenlieder.*"

"What does that mean?"

"Songs on the Deaths of Children."

"And the words?"

Her mother hesitates. "I can only approximate," she says. Anna waits.

When she sees that Anna is going to persist, her mother gives in.

Now the sun wants to rise as brightly
as if nothing terrible had happened during the night.

"Yes," says Anna.

"What?" asks her mother.

"That's it. He got it. He got it right."

Her mother suddenly sits up, startling Anna.

"Oh, Annie," she says once more, "we're not going to lose you, are we?" She reaches over and puts her hand on Anna's shoulder. It weighs heavily there.

"To say you are precious to us is such an understatement," Anna's mother says. Her eyes are dry but Anna knows how that can be, how the heat of emotion can scorch your tear ducts, cause any moisture to evaporate.

Her mother pulls away. "I realize I'm taking a risk by saying this. I realize that simply saying these words out loud is dangerous. So Dr. Cummings warns. Not to put any ideas in your head."

Anna doesn't answer. She thinks she would like the pain to stop. She thinks she *will* stop the pain, eventually. *For I am passionately in love with death.*

What surprises Anna is the anger. It comes in flashes, at times when she has a plausible weapon in her hand. A dissecting knife in the biology lab. The steering wheel of a car. She'd only had her license two months when she entered the darkness. She is truly dangerous on the road. Her parents don't understand or they would forbid her the car keys. Instead, they encourage her to take the car out, encourage anything that will take her away from her bed. Sometimes Anna just drives around and around the block, for twenty, thirty minutes, her anger steadily mounting.

"Are we going to lose you?" Anna's mother asks again, and her voice quavers.

You already have, thinks Anna.

PART II
Revelation

8

ANNA WASN'T THE ONLY PERSON on her street living in self-exile that year. Not the only person hiding from the sun and eschewing human contact. Anna would catch a glimpse sometimes from her bedroom window. She'd have to wait. She'd have to be patient. Then there he'd be. Jim Fulson, in *C-A-R-O-L-I-N-E*. Former football star. He had ridden off victorious to UCLA six years ago amidst a virtual parade of admirers, but returned home without fanfare five years later in apparent disgrace, taking up residence in his parents' rec room. A shadow. Anna would see him mowing the lawn by moonlight, or on a ladder after dark fixing something on the roof, an electric lantern hanging from the chimney.

While waiting at the bus stop, in front of *C-A-R-O-L-I-N-E,* Anna studies the windows of the rec room, tries to catch a glimpse of Jim Fulson, some sign of life. Occasionally, a flicker behind the curtain. On a rare foggy day, a dull light shines through. Usually nothing. But she has a feeling. She doesn't like turning her back on *C-A-R-O-L-I-N-E*. Whatever happens, whenever it happens, she wants to know. She wants to bear witness.

Anna's neighborhood has never been chummy, so no one knows Jim Fulson's complete story. No one gossips over fences. No one organizes block parties or jumbo garage sales. Nothing ever brings the longtime residents together except a common loathing of the foul Hendersons, a childless couple who live down the block from Anna. They snobbishly refuse to speak to the newer residents, who spend their weekends stripping houses down to wooden skeletons and then layering only the most eco-friendly and luxurious amenities on top. Huge bamboo forests now separate houses, the traditional metal chainlink fencing long gone, and the older iron swing sets replaced by brightly colored molded plastic play modules.

Then, in February of Anna's junior year of high school, the Goldschmidts move in next door. Lars, a pale fifteen-year-old, his mother and father. They are different from the beginning. For starters, they bring so little with them. They don't even use a moving van. Instead, they drive up in their Honda Civic, followed by a battered truck that spits out a few pieces of furniture and boxes of kitchen stuff onto the lawn. Some of the items sit for hours before gradually being hauled inside, so the neighbors grow intimate with the Goldschmidts' possessions long before meeting them. Salvation Army–quality mismatched chairs and a plastic table. Mattresses, but as far as the neighbors can tell, no bed frames. The one couch and two armchairs are carried into the living room. The Goldschmidts hadn't bothered to pack their clothes—they possess so few they had simply thrown them into the back of their own small car. The wardrobes of three people wouldn't even fill a single bedroom closet. There are no curtains. They simply pin up bedsheets their first night in the house.

Both the Goldschmidts work. They leave the house at 8 AM, nod to the other neighbors as they get into their Civic and drive off each morning. Professional jobs, if you judged by their attire. He in pressed trousers, a long-sleeved white shirt and tie, she in a skirt—always a skirt, never pants—with a neutral-colored blouse and black blazer or sweater. Anna's mother points out that Mrs. Goldschmidt possesses exactly three skirts, two blouses, and one pair of black shoes. "She just mixes and matches them very cleverly," Anna's mother tells Anna.

Even before meeting the Goldschmidts, the neighbors know something is off. No sign of a television. At night you can only see the glow of lamps through the sheets, the shadows of Lars and his parents as they move from one room to the next. They turn their lights off early. Before 9 PM. And then on again early while it is still dark, before anyone else on the street wakes. Except Anna, of course. She watches their shadows in the predawn darkness and feels a small pinprick of interest. The Goldschmidts and Jim Fulson. The only solid objects to permeate the fortress of pain she inhabits.

9

MORE THAN TWO MONTHS PASS before Anna makes contact with the Goldschmidts. A Tuesday morning. A beautiful spring day in Northern California. Like everything else, it oppresses Anna. *For I am passionately in love with death*. She still exists. She has taken no action over these long months. She is a coward after all.

Anna did get out of bed this morning. She did put on clothes. She did urinate. She did not brush her teeth. She did not floss. She did not look in the mirror. She did approach the breakfast table when her mother called. She did not eat. Her mother dragged a comb through her hair as Anna sat in front of a bowl of Cheerios and milk, then pushed her out the door at 8:02, only to run after Anna to stuff lunch money that won't be used into the pocket of her jeans.

Anna is standing at the bus stop. The bus is late. The only other person waiting is Lars Goldschmidt. Anna knows him only by sight. Although they've stood here together every morning since he moved in next door, they've never exchanged a word.

Nothing is different. Nothing has changed from yesterday, or the day before. Yet Anna finds herself examining Lars's slight frame and refined features, allowing herself to really see him for the first time. She's surprised to be interested. She admires his fastidiousness, his delicacy. His wrists are so thin she could snap them between her thumb and forefinger. Her fingers itch to try.

Then he lifts his face to look directly into hers. Anna wants to avoid his gaze, but finds she cannot. At 5'9", she's at least four inches taller, and, at 135 pounds, perhaps a third again as heavy as him. A bruiser, in comparison. Lars begins speaking, but Anna doesn't catch his meaning. She shakes her head.

Lars repeats his words.

"I said, how long do we wait when the bus is late? Before we assume it isn't coming?"

His voice is deeper than expected. Such manly tones from this hollow shell of a boy. He doesn't seem to know what to do with his hands. They dangle awkwardly at his side. Then he lifts them and carefully adjusts a strand of longish darkish hair infringing on his eyes. He pauses, moves it another millimeter to the left. He tightens a strap on his backpack. Such fussy conscientiousness. Anna feels a twinge. He is so pitifully small. Anna has overheard things in school about what is happening in the locker room and before and after classes, just outside of teachers' sight lines: ugly names, punches, pummelings, taunts. Yet Lars always emerges with an air of calm equanimity. No sign of anxiety or resentment. Anna admires such resilience, such apparent invulnerability of the spirit, however bruised the flesh might be.

"If the bus hasn't arrived by now, it's not coming," Anna says. "Time to consider alternate transportation."

Her voice comes out louder and harsher than she intends. Lars has already forced her to break two of her self-imposed rules. No direct eye contact. No speech except when absolutely necessary.

Lars then asks her a question, but it takes Anna several moments to realize what a strange question it is.

"Do you want to go to church with us?"

"What?" she asks him.

He smiles. "Church," he says. "I think you might like it." His voice has real warmth, so at odds with the rest of his cold shrimplike self. Has the sun ever fingered his pale flesh?

"I don't go to church," Anna says. "We never have."

He waits to see if she is going to say anything else. "I think you'd like it," he repeats. "I think you'd be surprised." He pauses. "You have much to offer." And then, oddly: "We could use you."

Use Anna, this lump of useless meat? She has nothing to say to that. She turns back toward her house, to ask her mother for a ride to school. But before Anna can take a step, Lars begins speaking once more. Anna doesn't, can't, take in the substance of his words. Yet somehow she hears him and her body thrills.

"And I looked, and behold a pale horse."

"What did you say?" Anna asks. She stops trying to move away from Lars. She is caught by the terrible, wonderful image that his words evoke. She remembers the phrase from Revelation, the pale horse, ghostly animal, bone thin, its limbs and head improbably stretched. "What did you say?" she repeats. She wants to hear him say the words again in his electrifying voice.

"Its rider was named Death."

Anna has seen that rider. That rider is always in Anna's mind. Tall and fierce, her body as elongated as her horse's, as ghostly white. Her hair long and streaming behind. She holds a small child, as fair as she, on her lap. Her arms tight around the child's waist. Both are naked.

Incredibly, then, Lars laughs, such a contagious burst of genuine animal *noise* that Anna almost laughs, too. She stops herself. She is suddenly aware of the stillness of the morning street. All who work have left for work. Schoolchildren have saddled bikes and pedaled off. Younger ones have been strapped into cars and driven to playgroups. The park at the end of the Street of Children's Names will not start to fill for another hour. They are alone. Lars is telling Anna secrets. He is telling her things she already knows.

"And power was given unto them," Lars says, *"over the fourth part of the earth, to kill . . ."*

Anna understands what's coming.

"With sword," he says. *"And with hunger, and . . ."*

"With death," Anna says. The seven years of scarcity and hunger that followed seven years of fertility and plenty. The fools who wasted the surplus. The wise ones who held back, denying themselves because they understood what lay ahead.

Lars reaches out with his left hand and touches Anna on the arm. Just once. He pulls away. Then he comes at her again. She's still unprepared, still shocked. This time he takes an unresisting hand away from Anna's side. *"And their infants will be dashed in pieces before their eyes,"* he says. *"Their houses will be plundered and their wives ravished."*

Vile words, vile thoughts. A vision of hell on earth. Yet music is there, also. Anna's hand being held, sweetly. An unresolvable paradox. She takes her hand back. She resolves to regain control. She resolves to leave. To end this.

And then it happens. Anna's hands begin to tremble. A twinge that starts in her chest ignites and spreads to her face, out to her limbs, her fingers and toes. She's still clutching her book bag, but barely. She's still standing, but only just. Fighting to remain upright. She loses the battle. She falls. She's now lying on the ground on the grass next to the sidewalk, Lars kneeling beside her. He is touching her again. He is stroking her arm. He is speaking words she can't hear. Then the sun darkens. The empty street pulses with a reddish hue. A buzz as if an army of cicadas was descending, an interior pulsing of the earth. The light fades, all feeling fades. She is losing contact. She understands that her world is now inexorably divided in two: before and after.

"For His sake," says Lars, leaning over Anna, taking her hand again. "To Him alone." As weak as Anna is, she shudders as Lars finishes. *"For we are counted as sheep to be slaughtered."*

When Anna returns to herself, Lars is smiling. Anna sits up, far enough above the ground to read the entire name carved into the sidewalk in front of her, the large unsteady letters. C-A-R-O-L-I-N-E. *I live in* S-A-R-A-H, *Lars in* K-A-R-I-S. As the world comes into focus, Anna turns to look at the house behind her. She sees the curtains on the downstairs windows of C-A-R-O-L-I-N-E move slightly, a hand adjusting them. Then everything tips back into place.

Yet the familiar, dull suburban neighborhood is now anything but. All is strange, magnificent. The indifferently constructed houses dazzle. The spindly maples extend a rich dark canopy over her head. Even the clouds that threaten rain are glorious, their full, pregnant darkness illuminated from the sun hidden within their depths. They have a holy purpose.

Everything does. Everything its own purpose and place. Clutching Lars's hands with hers, Anna knows she is both cursed and blessed. For she has been smitten.

Anna's mother senses the change at once. She is packing her bag for her day's work when Anna bursts in. Anna can only manage, "The bus never came."

"I suppose you need a ride?" her mother asks. She is focused on her tools.

"I suppose I do," Anna says, and her mother must hear something in Anna's voice, because she looks up, her face a mix of suspicion and hope.

"Well, let's get going. We'll both be late," she says. She is pretending to be casual, but she is watching Anna closely.

They walk out to the car together. Across the street, a rare daylight glimpse of Jim Fulson, his strong ex-football-player's arms flexing as he carries the garbage to the curb. She strains to see his face, overshadowed by a baseball cap. Anna hasn't seen it in full light for more than six years.

Despite the dark morning, the clouds thickening, everything is still aglow for Anna. She watches Jim Fulson walk slowly back into the house, his broad shoulders relaxed, like someone with no plans, nothing to do. He is wearing a simple white T-shirt, jeans that fit him well.

Anna rejoices in lifting her feet off the ground, one after the other. Her sweatshirt hood is down, its zipper open.

"So you're back?" her mother asks. Anna can see she is holding her breath.

Anna nods. She feels as though she can't trust her voice.

"Well, thank fucking God."

"Yes," Anna says. "Thank Him."

10

ANNA'S MOTHER DRIVES HER TO school. On the way, they see Lars trudging along the sidewalk.

"It's two miles," says Anna's mother. "It'll take him forever." She stops and beckons for Lars to get into the backseat.

"Thank you, ma'am," says Lars.

"You're welcome, but drop the 'ma'am.'"

"Yes, ma'am," says Lars, then apologizes, but it seems rote rather than sincere. He is looking at Anna and smiling as he speaks.

"I see you've been brought up a certain way," says Anna's mother. She doesn't say what she thinks of that method of child-rearing.

"Yes, I certainly have," Lars says with an uplifted chin.

"How are you liking our town?" Anna's mother would of course have noticed the bruises on Lars's neck, the ones his T-shirt can't quite hide. She is the noticing kind.

"Not particularly friendly, is it?" Lars asks.

"No. That we aren't." Her voice is softer, kinder. "Where did you live before?"

"Across the bay," says Lars. "Fremont." He shuts his mouth in a way that signals the topic is off limits.

After that, silence until they reach the school. Anna is acutely aware of Lars's presence, but then she is acutely aware of everything at this moment. She thinks of all the reading with her mother, how the words have been transformed from metaphors into truths. Daniel in the lion's den. Jonah and the whale. More than just tales. Vivid truths to learn from. She finds herself trembling at her awareness of His power. She realizes His strength, His benevolence. She is breathing deeply, there is richness in the air, she feels as though she could extract nutrients from it. She feels reborn.

"I want to get baptized," Anna says just as her mother pulls up to the school.

Her mother nearly drives onto the pavement. "What?" she asks. She regains control of the car.

"Yes," says Anna. "Baptized."

"We can arrange that," says Lars, from the backseat. Anna's mother looks at him in her rearview mirror.

"You stay out of this," she tells him. To Anna she says, "We'll talk about it later." She doesn't speak another word, not even to Anna's "goodbye."

"Don't worry," Lars tells Anna as they walk into the building. "She'll come around. She'll eventually see the light." Anna seriously doubts this but is struck by Lars's confidence. They part to go to their respective classes, only to Anna they are more like animated tapestries, so lush are the colors and textures of the day. She can almost see the words coming out of her teachers' mouths; they hang in the air, solid as the clothing the teachers are wearing, or the chalk they hold in their hands. They drip wisdom, Anna understands now that school, too, is a sacred place. The bang of lockers like the sound of trumpets, the bell signaling the end of class a call to prayer. How could she have missed what was under her eyes the whole time?

Anna can remember whole passages of her biblical reading with her mother. Psalm 96 rings through her head:

> *Let the heavens rejoice, and let the earth be glad; let the sea roar, and the fullness thereof. Let the field be joyful, and all that is herein: then shall all the trees of the wood rejoice Before the LORD: for he cometh, for he cometh to judge the earth . . .*

To judge, Anna thinks. Yes, that will be exciting.

11

WITH ONE HAND HE GIVES, and with the other hand He gives too much.

Several days after the morning at the bus stop, at first, an aura. A strange rosy light emanating from objects. A musty smell, like from the college trunk Anna's father keeps in the attic. The faint trace of something sweet. Violets or jasmine. Not unpleasant. Not right away. Then the light intensifies, the soft glow turning harsh, darkening. Then the colors. Starting with slices of deep blue and purple that merge and bleed into a river of vermillion that cracks the periphery of Anna's vision.

The first time this happens, Anna keeps quiet. She is in her room, awake after midnight, against her parents' orders. Reading the Book of Daniel. The story of Bel. The story excites her. How furious the duped king! How petulant yet satisfying his slaying of the false priests, their wives and young babies!

Then she is hit hard. By the colors, the smells. The visions. Wild. Unspeakable. Transformational. When Anna comes to, she is sitting on the floor with her back rigid against the bedroom door. She is breathing deeply. She is deeply moved. That night, she dreams of a cow, a red cow. The cow is motionless in a field, alone. Lonely, Anna can tell. But she can't get to it. Fences, barbed wire, deep ditches all impede her path, keeping the red cow out of reach. What could this mean?

Two days later, Anna is in the bathroom at school. A milder episode this time, but it gives her a bump on her forehead from hitting her head against the stall. Ignoring the stares, she tells Lars about the episodes at lunch, becomes uncharacteristically annoyed that he doesn't understand the color of the aura, which is the same color as the cow itself. "No, not just red. Vermillion. Pay attention, it's important." She had looked it up after the initial incident, so deeply had the particular color impressed her. The deep crimson color named after *Kermes vermilio*, the insect from which red dye was made in ancient times.

Anna dreams of the red cow every night. Every week, she has more of what she calls "the episodes." No less frightening than the first. But the visions! The visions she lives for. She would even die for them.

12

ANNA IS SITTING WITH LARS in the back of the Goldschmidts' Civic. The seat belts are broken, but they're holding them across their laps in case they pass a cop. They're on their way to church. Today is not Sunday. It is not morning. It is none of the things Anna associates with churchgoing. Saturday 8 PM, the San Jose city sidewalks and avenues busy with weekend celebrations.

A balmy evening for early May. The car passes men and women in evening dress, the women's bare shoulders gleaming in the streetlights, thronging around the entrance to the old vaudeville theater that is now the opera house. Anna sees single men and women tapping at laptops through the large windows of coffeehouses. Nail salon after nail salon. Empty storefronts that haven't been renovated since the 1950s next to gleaming glass skyscrapers, also empty, forty thousand square feet, fifty thousand, and more, available for lease. And on every corner a beggar, inevitably male, holding up a hand-printed sign. *Homeless veteran* and *God bless you* and *Will work for food* and, more originally, *Will eat to work*. Anna says out loud what she's always wondered. "Why don't homeless women ever have signs?" The

Goldschmidts continue gazing ahead. Lars simply shrugs. Anna keeps quiet after that.

They're almost past San Jose's tiny downtown. Anna thrills at everything she sees, although she knows all that is considered elegant, edgy, or hip lies fifty miles north. Even the homeless would rather be there than here. *San Francisco or bust* reads the sign held by a man at the corner of First and Santa Clara.

The car enters a more dubious neighborhood, full of bars and churches. Over the past year, the places of worship in Silicon Valley have multiplied. Churches, everywhere: in defunct movie houses, in abandoned drugstores of ghost strip malls. They even see a night service being held in a bankrupt Ford auto dealership, the backs of the worshippers visible from the street.

Anna's mother has expressed her impatience with this explosion of churches. Anna's father calls her a fundamentalist secularist on jihad. She still has her Noam Chomsky poster tacked on her office wall. He says she'll end up on the terrorist watch list.

"Are you crazy?" her mother had asked when Anna told her she wanted to accompany the Goldschmidts this evening. Then, after a look from Anna's father, "Okay. Okay. I guess it's good you want to get out." Both of Anna's parents have been walking on eggshells since that Tuesday morning. Exchanging looks. Giving Anna more hugs than usual. Clearly relieved but also puzzled, unsure of what to expect next.

The streets are growing wilder, more chaotic. Fewer viable businesses, more graffiti, more unsupervised children running into traffic without looking. And more churches. Anna counts the churches on one block, two, six, eight, no nine. Most church signs are hand-painted. Few are in English. Anna recognizes Chinese and Japanese, but many scripts are unfamiliar. The streets are packed with cars, some double-parked. No one has called the police. No one is getting ticketed. This evening is full of celebration and song, for singing can be heard everywhere they go. Anna keeps her window rolled down despite the growing chill.

"We don't sing," said Lars.

They drive into a residential neighborhood. The Goldschmidts' church is in what looks like a private home, the yard has been paved over for a parking lot, but the house gives no indication that it is a place of worship. No sign. No crosses. They park next to the chain-link fence that separates the parking lot from the neighbor's rosebushes, and enter through the front door without knocking. No altar, no statues, no paintings, no banners proclaiming His love. No furniture except for two large trestle tables groaning under the weight of casseroles, meat loaves, platters of pasta, and salads of all colors. The rooms are so full of people that they can barely squeeze their way in. Mr. and Mrs. Goldschmidt are greeted with hugs and quick kisses to the cheeks. Lars's hair is rumpled more than once. Anna reaches out and clutches the back of his shirt so as not to lose him as he weaves his way through the crowd. She is being led somewhere, through what must have been the original living room to the dining room, into the kitchen. She is brought to an older man, maybe sixty. He takes up a lot of space with his bulk, yet is otherwise undistinguished, his voice thin and weedy.

"Hello," he says to the Goldschmidts, then he turns to Anna. "I'm so glad you're here." He possesses none of the smarmy charm Anna associates with religious leaders. This man holds her attention with his stillness, his ability to tolerate silence. Anna hasn't dressed for this occasion, is wearing her standard uniform: jeans, Stanford sweatshirt, and sneakers.

The man extends his hand. "Reverend Michael," he says. Anna is surprised by the coldness and sweatiness of his grip. A tight one.

"So you've joined us," he says.

"Not necessarily," she says. She wants to make this clear. Whatever has happened to her, whatever was triggered at the bus stop that morning, she's unsure whether that entails *joining* anything. She is her mother's daughter, after all.

"Why so cautious? Lars says you've seen the Way." He says Lars's name with slight distaste.

Anna shakes her head. "I don't know enough about your ... group," she says. Her voice is less hostile than she'd have liked. She doesn't want him, or anyone else, to take her acquiescence for granted.

"We're not a *group*. We're a congregation," Reverend Michael corrects her. "We are the true faithful. Some of us will be martyrs. All of us will be saints and reside in His house upon the Second Coming. But you must know all this. More importantly, Lars says you are a believer. And Lars says you are gifted. You have visions, I understand?"

Anna sees that she has been discussed. Presented and judged, without her knowledge or permission. "I have no idea what he, or you, could possibly mean by that." This time Anna succeeds at making her voice as rough and uncooperative as intended.

He doesn't answer at first. Then, "You've borne witness to the Red Heifer?" he asks. "You are having the visions?"

54

"Yes," says Anna, after a pause. Lars has been indiscreet, she thinks. Then she asks, as if casually. "You know what the dreams mean?" For although Lars has been strangely excited about them, he has declined to explain why.

"Of course," says Reverend Michael. "When the Red Heifer appears, that is the beginning of the End. This is extraordinarily exciting news." And indeed he looks thrilled, so much so that Anna feels it herself. She notices Lars's face. He is intent upon her. He nods, and smiles. It is a complicated smile: it communicates apology, sympathy, and encouragement all at once.

"The Red Heifer," pursues Reverend Michael. "Don't you know how important your visions are?"

Anna shakes her head. She resents being put in this position, to be forced to acknowledge ignorance of something that is apparently of such importance.

"No matter," he says. "I have some materials I can give you. And you can find it online. You will soon know." He turns to Lars. "Keep bringing her." With one last smile for Anna, Reverend Michael greets some new arrivals.

Anna wanders out of the kitchen through a different door than the one she came in. This room was probably the former den of the original home. Thick red shag carpeting, not in the cleanest state. Wall paneling. Filled with people, none of whom look like the fanatics Anna had been half expecting. A gas fireplace. She feels a touch on her arm. It's Lars. "Let me introduce you," he says, and pulls her into the throng. His first stop is by the side of a middle-aged couple, each holding a glass of what looks like ginger ale.

"Tom and Marci, I'd like you to meet Anna. Tom and Marci are both deacons for our community."

Tom is tall and fleshy, Marci about Anna's height and weight, wearing thick glasses, her hair in a neat pixie cut. They are dressed in what Anna's father calls the Silicon Valley uniform: khaki pants and blue button-down shirts. Marci also wears a blue-and-gold scarf, but otherwise their attire is identical. Anna wonders if this causes problems on laundry day.

She shakes hands with both Marci and Tom. "This is Anna's first visit," Lars tells them. "She'd be interested in hearing about your preparations, either physical or spiritual."

"We're making good progress on our crisis garden," Tom says immediately.

Taking the cue, Marci adds, "We had a great harvest of winter vegetables: peas, spinach, cauliflower, and cabbage. Broccoli, too. Now we're planning our summer crops." She fiddles with her scarf as she talks. Anna sees dirt under her fingernails, at odds with her otherwise well-groomed appearance.

Another silence. All three of them look at Anna.

"What's a crisis garden?" She begrudges having to accept her role in the conversation as the uninformed newbie. She has a lot of research to do, she realizes.

"It's one of the ways we'll survive the coming Tribulation," says Tom. He takes a sip of his ginger ale and then pats his hip. Anna is shocked to see he is wearing a gun. She's not sure she's ever seen an ordinary person with a gun before, and she involuntarily takes a step back. "After all," he says, almost jovially, "we won't be able to depend on supermarkets being open during the End Days. Self-sufficiency will be the name of the game."

Anna thinks of the hundreds of cans and dozens of gallon bottles of water her father has stored in the garage in preparation for the Big One. "But you can't grow enough to satisfy all your needs," she says, remembering the careful nutritional calculations that went into her father's choice of foodstuffs to buy.

"Of course not," says Marci. She continues to fiddle with her scarf. Anna sees now that she, too, is wearing a gun on her hip. "We also have the usual stores put away. Lots of water. And gasoline. We also have our own generator. Tom has thought of everything."

"What's the deal with the guns?" Anna asks. Her father laughs at the crazier ideas some people have about disaster preparedness.

"We must be ready," Tom repeats. Still holding his ginger ale, he makes a gesture with his free hand as if pulling his gun from its holster and shooting it. "And we have plenty of ammunition of course." He doesn't look like a vigilante or nut job. Neither does he look like he could survive a week without the comforts of civilization. He has no muscle tone whatsoever, but instead the kind of gut spilling over the waistband that plagues people with desk jobs.

"What exactly do you expect?" Anna asks.

"We know that we'll face years of war and chaos and suffering," says Marci, cheerfully, as if announcing what she would be serving for dinner.

"And when the Godless armies rise up against the faithful, it is our duty to fight back," says another man who has come up next to Lars. He is wearing a jacket over blue jeans, boots, and a wide floral tie. All that's missing to achieve an urban cowboy look is a western hat. He must see something reflected in Anna's face, for he continues talking, in a voice that indicates he is quoting a script. *"You cannot trust your neighbors, for they will deliver you up and shall kill you: and ye shall be hated of all nations for my name's sake.*"

Anna likes this. She smiles.

Because the man spoke so loudly, people turned to look. Several more join their widening circle, Reverend Michael among them.

"You will be tested," Reverend Michael says, looking at Anna. "If you join us, you must be prepared to fight."

Anna finds that she likes this too, but looking around she can't imagine a more unlikely group to be speaking in such bloodthirsty terms. Lars puts a hand on Anna's arm, seems to read her mind. "We have preparedness sessions," he says. "A member of our congregation owns a ranch in Gold Country. We schedule regular weekends there. Target practice. Lectures on survival techniques. All the skills we'll need when the Tribulation begins."

"You'd train me to fight?" Anna asks. Despite her skepticism, her chest feels hot, under pressure.

"If you pass His tests." Reverend Michael says. "If you keep the faith."

"I will," Anna says fervently. And then says the words foremost in her mind. "I burn to serve."

"That's exactly what we want to hear," Lars says in his thrilling voice. He bestows one of his rare smiles on both Anna and Reverend Michael, and takes Anna's free hand into both of his. "Now it begins," he says.

13

THE END DAYS. THE RAPTURE. What rational person hears of these things and doesn't scoff? The previous year, a made-for-TV movie had dramatized it without irony. Anna watched it with her mother and her mother's best friend Martha, they having insisted that Anna leave her bedroom and join them in front of the television. The movie showed buses and airplanes suddenly half-empty as the godly were taken up to heaven. The righteous also disappeared from offices, streets, and schools, simply shedding their clothes and shoes, leaving little puddles of possessions where they had been sitting, standing, or sleeping. Some of those left behind repented, attempted to change their ways, to earn themselves a place with the saints. Others celebrated the Tribulation with carnage and debauchery. Both churches and brothels filled to capacity as the earth descended into chaos.

Anna's mother and Martha drank too much wine and laughed uproariously throughout the film. "The post-rapture world will be very testosterone-heavy if simply having the sulks damns you to hell," Martha had said when the film's protagonist realized he'd been left behind along with a belligerent teenaged son he hardly knew, his wife and three beautiful daughters having been taken directly to God. Men with pitchforks roamed the streets, setting fire to cars, drinking from bottles, kicking dogs. The depiction of a truly evil world resembled nothing worse than a bad Western B movie. Anna had been indifferent. Her mother would have preferred more scorn, but Anna was incapable at that point of any emotion that required so much psychic energy.

Now all is different. In the two weeks following her first visit to the Goldschmidts' church, Anna attends four services. She has spent time scouring the Web, and understands more, and better. Reverend Michael's congregation doesn't believe in the Rapture—the taking of the righteous immediately up to heaven—as it had been depicted on television. That movie was heresy. The members of the true church will endure half the Tribulation—three and a half years under the savagery of the Antichrist, the false prophet—before they are taken up to Him. Three and a half years of glory. Of fighting, good against evil.

Much of Reverend Michael's sermons go over what the faithful can expect in the months and years leading to the End Days. Harassment. Exclusion. Banishment. Blacklisting. "And, finally, extermination—that is, if we aren't prepared to fight back," Reverend Michael said.

Anna tries to explain this to her father. But she knows he won't understand. Still, she wants to try. She knows better than to approach her mother on this subject.

Anna catches her father alone one evening, he has changed from his suit and tie into jeans and a T-shirt; he is throwing off his lawyer persona and becoming the amateur scientist.

"So you believe the end of the world is near," he says. He is only half paying attention. He is hungrily downloading the latest USGS data.

Anna almost doesn't continue. She dreads his scorn. "You make it sound so silly," she says.

"Well? What do you believe, then?" Anna hesitates, then says firmly, "I believe that we will all soon be punished for our sins."

"Oh, really? By whom and for what sins exactly?" he asks, sarcastically as Anna's mother would have.

Anna pauses again. She is herself still unclear about some things. But she wants him to understand. So she tries again.

"By God"—she has trouble saying His name out loud to her father—"and for our refusal to listen to Him."

"And what exactly is He trying to communicate?"

This is one of the points that Anna is unclear about. She has her own dreams. The Red Heifer. But the story attached to that is such a strange one. She decides to challenge him.

"You yourself say we don't have much longer on this planet."

"That's right," her father says. "But not because some abstract or outdated moralistic code has been violated. And not because some God figure is going to destroy us. We're destroying ourselves. Humans are simply too stupid to take care of the world."

"Might not we be talking about the same things in different ways?" asks Anna. "I believe in prophecies about the approaching plagues and storms and earthquakes coming from a higher power, and you believe those things will happen because of man-made actions. After all, what is the boiling of the oceans predicted in Revelation if not the global warming you're always going on about?"

This gets his attention. Her father doesn't look directly at her, but she sees one eyebrow rise and prepares herself.

"But—if I understand how these doomsday cults think—you believe these things are happening because the world is falling into morally evil ways?"

"Reverend Michael's church is not a cult. And evil is already loose upon the world," says Anna. Then, articulating what she is most sure of: "When the time comes, our job is to fight that evil by whatever means we have at our disposal."

"Wow," says her father. "That's pretty heavy stuff. You mean, it'll be worse than when the Big One hits?" He makes a face of mock horror.

"Don't patronize me." Anna has inherited her share of his temper.

"No, really," he says, moving away from his PC. She sees that he is attempting to control himself, to really talk to her. "Do you see yourself as a sort of Joan of Arc, leading the faithful into battle?" he asks.

Anna is a little chagrined to discover that her fantasies could be so transparent.

"No," she lies. "But I am eager to be led."

"So this . . . church . . . you've been attending, it has plausible leaders?" Her father's voice again mocking.

Here Anna falters. She thinks of Marci and Tom, of the others she's met from the congregation, of their postage-sized suburban survival gardens, of their grandiose talk. She thinks of Reverend Michael, his high voice and unconvincing laugh. She has not found His leaders on earth to be all that they should.

"No," she admits. Then, "But the cause is real. And the Goldschmidts are the real thing. Lars is the real thing." Of this she is sure.

"And you think there will be actual fighting?" her father asks. "You really think you're up for that? For hurting, even killing, other human beings?"

About this Anna is certain. "I'm hungry for it," Anna tells him. For she is. She is eager to find out what she is capable of. In His name, of course. True believers will then be saved before the true Wrath of God, the Great Tribulation. "Much blood will be spilled," she says. "For the battle will not be metaphorical, but actual."

This stops her father for a moment.

"And where do people like myself and your mother fit in?" he asks. "Can we expect to be slaughtered in our beds one night?"

"Dad, I'm serious," Anna says. For she is. And her heart is breaking, for her parents will not be among the faithful. They will be, are, damned.

"So I must accept Jesus Christ as my personal savior?"

"No," says Anna in despair. "Yes." She has no words to describe what she wants of him, of them. She has no words to describe what has happened to her. *If you believe in fairies clap your hands.* Her parents would just as soon respond to that as to her entreaties on this point.

Anna's father continues with his mappings and his calculations, with his earthquake preparedness lists and survival plans. Like Anna and Lars, he's getting ready. Dreaming and planning. Statistically, he has a shot of witnessing it in his lifetime. The Big One. Probably not on the San Andreas Fault.

More likely the Hayward Fault. He lives for it. Nothing gives him greater joy than to see dogs and cats agitated, birds taking flight over the telephone wires. *Great earthquake weather* is his most cheerful greeting at breakfast. Like Anna, he lives for it. Lives for the End.

14

ANNA'S MOTHER AND MARTHA ARE sitting at the kitchen table, Anna's father long ago having gone to bed. Anna is in her room, awake, at her usual listening post by the door. Martha and her mother are both worked up, but her mother in particular. These evenings after choir rehearsals at Stanford Memorial Church are always like this. Music put her mother in a place beyond reach. Tonight, too much Thomas Tallis, an excess of euphoria. Anna's mother can't sit still. She tries for a moment, then stands again. Then sits. Then stands. And paces. Up and down the kitchen, into the living room, through the dining room, back again to the kitchen. She puts the teakettle on, and, when it whistles, makes a pot of tea that Martha has already refused. While pouring, Anna's mother knocks over the cup, spills hot tea over the counter and floor. Anna hears Martha groan. This is their routine. They are practiced. It has been nearly thirty-five years since Anna's mother, laden with luggage, knocked on the door of the San Francisco apartment she'd found in the "Roommates Wanted" section of the *Chronicle* and found Martha waiting. Anna hears Martha getting down on her knees to wipe the floor. After a few moments, Martha sits heavily again on her chair. "No one tells you how much being fifty-five sucks," she says.

Martha being Martha, she then begins singing. She has an indifferent soprano, but nevertheless her a capella voice comes out lilting, the melody haunting.

Spem in alium nunquam habui praeter in te
Deus Israel

Anna's mother joins in with her rich contralto.

qui irasceris
et propitius eris
et omnia peccata hominum in tribulatione dimittis

Together they finish.

Domine Deus
Creator coeli et terrae
respice humilitatem nostram

The duet ends on a disquietingly dissonant chord. Silence. Anna wills them to begin again, but the silence persists.

Anna has always wanted a Martha. A confidante and co-conspirator. Neither Anna's mother nor Martha makes a move without the other's counsel. Five years ago, Martha appeared at the house unannounced at dinnertime. As Anna's mother automatically set another place at the table, Martha casually announced her breast cancer diagnosis. Anna's mother nodded. She sat down. Still holding a steak knife, she drove it a quarter inch into the oak table. Her voice when she finally spoke was low and calm. "Damn you," my mother said. "God fucking damn you. How exactly am I supposed to process this?" Martha has now been in remission for eighteen months.

Anna's mother continues with her agitating, up and down, from this room to that. Anna hears the rattle of silverware, the crackle of newspapers. Music is not soothing, not to Anna's mother. It is a stimulant, a hallucinogenic, even. Lately her mother has been playing Mahler no. 5 repeatedly on the old boom box she keeps in the living room, next to her piano. The second movement: *Kraeftig nicht zu schnell*. Anna hears her start the CD now, playing it too loudly, so even in Anna's room it overwhelms the ears. But Anna likes it, the power, the urgency, the message that the abyss is near. It is true. It is real. Her father, to tease or please, Anna was never sure, programmed the horn solo into their doorbell at volume, so that anyone who comes to the house is greeted by the full force of its mournful wail. *Abandon all hope,* Anna's father is fond of saying when he opens the door after the lone horn has brayed.

Martha is talking freely. She has had too much wine. Because Martha talks too much at such times Anna finds out things about this mysterious creature, her mother, that otherwise would stay hidden. Because of Martha, Anna has learned many secrets.

"Ah, Mahler. Horn solo. Still mourning the One That Got Away. Will you ever get over that?"

"Don't be silly."

"But *he* knows."

"Oh yes he knows. But no need to rub it in his face."

"Isn't playing Mahler over and over quite an extreme form of rubbing?"

"No. Not anymore. More of an inside joke."

"Except for what he doesn't know."

"Except for that," Anna's mother says.

Silence. Anna strains to hear what's happening. Then, "You've got a more understanding husband than you deserve," says Martha.

"Yes," Anna's mother says. And then the important phrase, the one that makes Anna relive the moment again and again, to tear it apart, to parse and re-parse its meaning. "But I'm not ashamed of getting more than I deserve," says her mother. "For how else would I learn what I *do* deserve?"

15

THEY ARE IN THE GOLDSCHMIDTS' living room: Lars, his parents, and Anna. It's Sunday, noon, and they've just gotten back from church. There aren't enough chairs so Lars and Anna are sitting on the floor. Lars is worried about his parents, about their seeming helplessness in the world. He had been dismayed by Reverend Michael's sermon:

> So do not worry, saying, "What shall we eat?" or "What shall we drink?" or "What shall we wear?" For the pagans run after all these things, and your heavenly Father knows that you need them. But seek first His kingdom and His righteousness, and all these things will be given to you as well.

Upon hearing those words, Lars's father had given a slight nod, and reached out and taken his wife's hand. His parents were all too likely to take such words literally. They were wearing the same clothes they wore to work. Anna had wondered, not for the first time, how they behaved in their professional guises. For they deliberately deceived others. You could call their behavior deceitful. They hide their faith at work, he as an engineer for Lockheed, she as an accountant at a big tech firm in the valley.

"But how can that be right?" Anna asks them now. "Shouldn't you be bearing witness? Trying to save others, as Lars did me?"

Lars's father, as always, looks at his wife to take charge. Lars's mother thinks before she responds. She has perfect skin and dark hair, just beginning to gray at the temples. A gracefully aging Sleeping Beauty. Anna sees her leave for work in the morning, always impeccably groomed, not a hair out of place, carefully made up, wearing that black blazer and a crisp white shirt, and either a black, gray, or dark green skirt. Mrs. Goldschmidt knows how to blend in.

"There was a time when we thought as you did," Mrs. Goldschmidt says. "Did what you and Lars are brave enough to do at school." She smiled her smile, slightly crooked, a small scar at one corner, one of his mother's few mysteries, according to Lars. "But we each kept getting into trouble, kept getting fired, and having to find new jobs. We had to decide. Did we want to withdraw from the world entirely? Or compartmentalize? At the time we found Him Lars was ten years old. We were conflicted. How much did we want Lars to be in that world? How far should we retreat? We took counsel from Reverend Michael, who as you know believes that our kind should remain inconspicuous. That it is not compromising our faith to camouflage ourselves against the persecution that is coming. He showed us the answer in the Psalms: *If a foe were rising against me, I could hide.* We decided to live what would appear like a normal life to other people."

But their idea of a normal life was patently absurd. Lars had no chance of fitting in, not in Anna's insular suburb. As it turned out, Sunnyvale High was Lars's third high school in two years. That he would have to endure verbal or emotional abuse because of his faith was one thing. They would have suffered with him, but they would not have moved him. It is written, after all, that the faithful will be so persecuted. The beginning of the trials. But even they couldn't ignore the brutality of his tormentors, or fail to understand that something other than his faith was being punished. The black eyes. The bruises. His nose broken, twice. His locker repeatedly broken into, his books even shat upon. Eventually, the dislocated shoulder and fractured arm. So they moved again. And then again. And then finally to Anna's neighborhood.

"Why do your parents work in the real world?" Anna had asked Lars. "If money matters so little, why bother? Why not do odd jobs, forge independent lives like others in the church?"

He'd shrugged. "They wouldn't know what else to do. They're competent, intelligent. They found the Way late in life. They were entrenched. It was easy to keep the external structure of their lives intact."

"But knowing what's ahead, shouldn't they prepare?" Anna had persisted. "It's going to take more than spiritual resolve to make it through the trials that lie ahead."

"That's not their way even if it is ours," says Lars, who doesn't shy away from proclaiming his faith. Anna has been drawn into his acts of God, as he calls them. Even after twice being called into the principal's office, they distribute flyers in the halls at school, corner people in the cafeteria, try to get them to understand what is at stake. *For he punishes the children and their children for the sin of the parents to the third and fourth generation.*

They also know they must prepare for what is to come in practical ways. The Goldschmidts dimly comprehend this. Anna and Lars, however, know they must take care of their worldly needs as the time approaches. Anna has begun running ten miles a day, doing push-ups, sit-ups, and kickboxing. They will have to endure three and a half years of violence before Jesus descends again. It is necessary to plan, to be ready, to hone their survival abilities.

Sitting in the Goldschmidts' living room, Anna knows Lars is waiting for a chance to slip away, but his parents seem to be enjoying their company.

"Let us pray, together," Lars's mother says, and reaches out to hold Anna's hand. Anna reluctantly takes Lars's. As devoted as she is to him, touching him makes her uncomfortable, and yet he is always patting her arm or stroking her shoulder. It doesn't seem natural, but like something he thinks is expected of him. Everyone bows their heads except Anna. She still isn't used to this. Whatever has happened to her isn't compatible with quiet meditation. On the contrary, she is most content when hearing about the Tribulation. The earthquakes—Anna's father jokes that he is happy about that, at least—the floods and the plagues and the wars. About how the Antichrist will be revealed. The man so evil, so corrupt, so malevolent that he is worthy of leading the armies of the wicked against the virtuous. All this is terribly exciting.

"Amen," says Lars's father and smiles at Anna. She squirms a little, feels like a fraud. If she is being schooled by Lars in the

ways of the spiritual world, she is trying to help him cope with
the reality of the worldly one that they must live in for now.
And that means dealing with Lars's parents in ways that aren't
strictly on the up and up.

Anna appreciates that they are not quite of this earth. But
as parents, they should be more practical. Until recently, rarely
was there enough food in the house. Toilet paper and soap were
scarce. Lars routinely found his parents' paychecks lying loose
around the house, uncashed.

Anna encouraged Lars to appropriate a checkbook he
found in a drawer, and to call the bank and request a new ATM
card in his father's name. His deep voice convincingly mature.
Making sure he got to the mail before his parents did, Lars then
gathered up the uncashed paychecks from around the house,
forged signatures, and deposited them safely.

With Anna's help, Lars takes over the grocery shopping.
Anna borrows her mother's car and drives him to the Safeway
on Matilda Street, they bring back canned goods, fresh milk
and cheese and bread, vegetables. She helps him prepare meals
for his family before slipping next door to have her own dinner
with hers. Now Lars can withdraw cash whenever his family needs it, and he and Anna will have enough left over for
their own needs. For they are formulating plans. Like the other
members of the congregation of Reverend Michael's church,
they are stockpiling goods, saving money, getting ready—all the
things that Lars's parents are too unworldly to do by themselves.
Anna consoles herself with this thought when she feels a guilty
twinge about what she and Lars are up to.

One day she enters the living room to find her mother
playing the piano. Anna walks over and stands behind her. There

is no music on the stand. Her mother is playing the heartbreaking melody from memory.

"What is this?" Anna asks.

"Szymanowski. Étude, op. 4, no. 3."

"It's lovely," Anna says.

Suddenly her mother turns around and puts her arms around Anna's waist, buries her head on Anna's chest. "Oh, Annie," she says. "What did we do wrong? First your . . . blues, and now this."

Anna places one hand on the top of her mother's head, the other on her cheek. Mother and child. This is the hardest part.

"Tell me everything will be all right," her mother says. Anna does what Reverend Michael advises in such cases. She lies.

"Yes," she says. "Everything will be all right." Her mother looks at her, then turns back to the keyboard without speaking.

16

FRED WILSON GIVES A TALK at Reverend Michael's church. Not the burly, red-faced man you'd expect of a Midwest dairy farmer. Tall, well-made, with a stiff-legged walk due to early arthritis in his knees. Perhaps the same age as Anna's parents. Something quick in his glance makes Anna feel as though he sees her despite the crowd. He apologizes for needing to sit down during his talk. "Most of the hard work falls on others' shoulders these days," he says in the flat tones of his native Valentine, Nebraska, where he works the cattle ranch passed to him by his great-grandfather. "I'm now devoting all of my resources to the Red Heifer project," he says.

A pioneer in cattle embryo transplants, Fred Wilson explains how he is breeding a pure Red Heifer. "A cause that is worthy of our financial and spiritual support," Reverend Michael had said when introducing him to a full house. "You are our most direct link to Christ, Brother Fred."

At the words *Red Heifer* Anna sits up. Although she has asked, no one has yet explained the meaning of her dreams. She has been told to be patient. Lars, sitting next to Anna, sees her excitement and smiles, pats her knee.

Despite Wilson's manner, he is not shy. But he is profoundly dull. He speaks of complex progesterone compounds, of suppressing the pituitary release of FSH, and inducing bovine estrus. His voice a monotone. His eyes downcast. Dressed in a suit that makes him look as though he's never seen a farmyard. The furthest from a humble man of the earth Anna can imagine.

When he finishes his technical talk, silence. Then a scattering of polite applause. Reverend Michael lifts his hands to command silence.

"I know the scientific talk is a little difficult to understand. But this man is pursuing a terrible and wonderful vision," he says, and gestures back to Fred Wilson. Anna sits up straighter.

"We've had our share of failures, true, but we are close now," Wilson says. "So close." He looks at Lars and Anna seated in the front row, then focuses on Anna, and grasping the edge of his folding chair, stands up. Emotion stirs for the first time in his face. "We are living on the precipice of human history," he says. "Prophecies made two thousand years ago by Jeremiah, Ezekiel, Isaiah, and John will be fulfilled in our lifetime." Anna shivers with anticipation.

Fred Wilson coughs into his sleeve. Reverend Michael hands him a glass of water, which he drinks. When Wilson starts speaking again, his voice is stronger, even passionate.

"Certain ignorant people believe they can predict the date of the Rapture, or the year that the Tribulation will begin," he says. "Read your Bible. This is clearly untrue." A ripple goes through the room, this has always been a point of contention among the congregation, some believing in approaching dates, others arguing the End Days have already begun, the Antichrist already present and fully engaged in his evil work.

Fred Wilson stops to drink more water. "Three great events must take place before the Messiah can return," he says, his voice full of power. No one is bored now. "First, the nation of Israel must be restored. Second, Jerusalem must be a Jewish city. And, finally, the Temple must be rebuilt." Anna nods. She sees where he is going. "We have witnessed the first two events. Now we must join together to bring about the completion of the third." His last words thunder into the silent room.

"Tell us what you have accomplished," says Reverend Michael.

"We are working with our Jewish brethren at the Third Temple Commission, in Jerusalem," Fred Wilson says. "Our spirits have merged. We are resolute. His will be done."

"And what is the Third Temple Commission?" prompts Reverend Michael.

"The Jewish organization committed to rebuilding the Temple on the sacred Temple Mount," says Wilson. "I'm breeding Red Heifers to be used in the Jewish sacrifice for the ritual cleansing. Such a cleansing is required before anyone of that faith can set foot on the Temple Mount."

A Red Heifer. Anna shivers. She feels she must ask, and raises her hand. Fred Wilson acknowledges her.

"What is this Red Heifer, exactly?" Anna asks.

"Good question," Fred Wilson says. "Many people are unaware of this particular aspect of the prophecies." He is now addressing Anna directly. "A Red Heifer is a red cow, unsullied by work, that must be burned as sacrifice to purify anyone who steps foot on hallowed ground like the Temple Mount."

"But aren't there a lot of red cows to choose from?" Anna persists. "Why do you need to breed them specially?" She is finding it hard to breathe. Her visions.

"Because pure red heifers do *not* exist," says Fred Wilson. "Some imperfection always manifests itself."

Anna thinks of her red cow, the one of her dreams. It is perfect.

"And that would ruin the sacrifice," Fred Wilson explains. "The Third Temple Commission would not sanction it. I'm on my seventh generation of breeding, and we are getting close. I think that with my next gestation I will have achieved our goal of a pure Red Heifer. I plan to begin sending the embryos to Israel to be implanted in the wombs of Israeli cows within the next nine months. The first implantation will be at the New Year. The first birth nine months after. And only when we have purified our warriors with the sacrifice of a pure Red Heifer can we even contemplate entering the sacred space of the Temple Mount."

"What's in it for the Jewish people? Why are they helping us?" asks another member of the congregation.

"We're helping them just as they are helping us. They get the Red Heifers they need for the cleansing sacrifice. Thus cleansed, they can take back the Temple Mount from the Muslims and build the Third Temple where the Dome of the Rock now stands. Then, according to the Jews' own beliefs, their Messiah will come."

Someone in the congregation makes a derisive hoot.

"We of course know this to be untrue," Fred Wilson says, holding up a hand. Murmurs of agreement from the audience. "We know this event will trigger the beginning of the Tribulation. Which is, of course, our goal, and our end of the arrangement."

The End Days are that close! Anna feels as though she is electric, that anything she touches will light up.

"Why don't they just go to the Temple Mount now and begin building?" asks a young man. "I mean, if that will bring their Messiah."

"Two reasons. As I've already explained, the Temple Mount is sacred," Fred Wilson says impatiently. "As Jews they cannot even step foot on that hallowed ground until they have been purified with the sacrifice of the Red Heifer."

He seems to have finished, so someone prompts him. "And the second reason?"

"The Temple Mount is sacred to Muslims as well, their third holiest site," he says. "They call it the Noble Sanctuary. It's where they believe their prophet Mohammed ascended to heaven. They happen to control it now. The Jews will not be able to take the Temple Mount easily. Even after they are purified."

"You're talking about war," Lars says.

Fred Wilson is silent for a moment. Then he nods. "Yes," he says. "It will be difficult. The Third Temple Commission faces opposition from the Israeli secular government as well as the Muslims. The Red Heifer is such an incendiary thing even among the Jewish people that the Israeli Army was called out more than fifteen years ago when the Commission claimed to have found one. They shot it immediately. Destroyed every molecule of it."

Anna can hardly breathe. This is what her visions portend. Anna tunes out the rest of Fred Wilson's talk. At the reception, she asks to be introduced to him. He is clearly interested. "Reverend Michael mentioned you," he says, holding on to her hand for too long. "He says you are special." When Anna glances at him askance, he adds, "He says you have visions."

"I dream about the Red Heifer," Anna says.

Fred Wilson looks Anna over carefully. "We should stay in touch," he tells her. "I send out bulletins about our progress to a select group of people. I'd like you to be one of them. You can get my email address from Reverend Michael."

True believers have Fred Wilson. And now, thinks Anna, they have me. As she considers this her fate, she forgets about being rude. She quizzes Fred Wilson, pestering him with questions until he's led away by the Reverend Michael. She goes home to bed and contemplates what she's learned.

Chok. A divine commandment from God. A decree that defies understanding. It has no known origin, and it possesses no logic. But it must be obeyed. Its wisdom cannot be questioned, its mystery cannot be solved. *If you walk in my decrees and observe my commandments and do them.*

Anna is accustomed to *chok*s because of her mother: *Do this.* Why? *Because I said so.*

So when Fred Wilson explained about the *chok* of the Red Heifer, Anna was receptive. Like all *chok*s, it was beautiful because of the lack of logic.

It's a recipe for making yourself worthy of God, of entering a sacred space. A filthy recipe: You cover yourself with filth. Burn a Red Heifer. Take its ashes and mix with water. Rub into your skin. Only then, your arms and legs and face soiled with dead cow, will you be purified and worthy of entering the Temple. Worthy of Him.

To qualify for the sacrifice, the heifer must be wholly red. No impure tufts of white or black. She can't be disfigured in any way. The heifer must never have been harnessed for practical purposes. She must never have been impregnated. No milking. No pulling of wagons or machinery. To ensure she has never been yoked, the hair on her neck, back, and stomach must be perfectly straight. And, naturally, she must be born in Israel.

A true Red Heifer is very rare, Fred Wilson had told Anna. There have been only nine since Moses's day, and none since the destruction of the Second Temple in Jerusalem. So this ritual has not been performed for more than two thousand years. And until it is performed, He cannot come again. "It has been so prophesied," Fred Wilson said.

Anna longs to perform this *chok*. She longs to see the Red Heifer, to slather herself with sodden ash. To be ready. *For I am passionately in love with death.* The words that won't leave her.

17

ANNA'S SEVENTEENTH BIRTHDAY. MAY 30. Her parents still hope at this point, are still trying to lure Anna back. She comes home from school to find both her parents there despite the fact that it is a workday. They lead her to her room and open the door with great fanfare. In the corner is a white vanity table. On top of the vanity, a movie star mirror surrounded by bright lights. And piles of the most beautiful stuffs imaginable. Stacks of small round pots holding green and blue and purple powders, tubes of magenta and russet and bronze. Bottles of creamy lotions. Long-handled soft brushes to gently apply the ungodly materials. Tears spring into Anna's eyes. And then she looks at her parents and shakes her head. No. No. And sees the tears in theirs. Even her father. They are her trial, Anna's parents. Both God and Satan use them, the one to test so as to purify, the other to lead her into temptation. *No!* she nearly cries. But she stays quiet, hugs her mother and father and leaves the room. No one touches the gifts. They remain there, arranged so prettily that Anna knows her mother spent hours placing them just so, to best advantage, to surprise her. Gradually dust covers them. They are Anna's penance. They remind her that she could fall at any moment.

During the dark period Anna's vanity had been repressed. But it has, oddly enough, awakened with her faith. She finds she is proud again of her long blonde hair. Of her figure, even. Tall, and willowy, a bit wide in the hips, but still slender enough to be acceptable even by the brutal standards of her peers at school. She is now beginning to be complimented again, not by boys her own age, but by older ones, or friends of her parents.

Anna is concerned. She knows it is a weakness, that it is wrong to lap up such words as evidence of her worth rather than as something unearned, something that He has bestowed upon her. She reminds herself that any beauty she has is by the grace of God.

Anna decides to take action. She rummages in drawers until she finds a pair of kitchen shears. She locks herself in the bathroom. The mirror. Now she can look into it without shame, without fear. Since she found Him there is nothing to fear, after all. Anna pulls her hair back from her face with her left hand. Her right hand holds the scissors. She begins cutting. The long blonde strands fall into the sink, onto the floor. She keeps going. With each slice of the scissors she feels heavier, more weighty, more serious. Her face emerges from the cloud of hair, tufts sticking up at her forehead, around her ears. She is almost completely shorn. She can see her skull. A new person. A bubble of joy in her heart, a smile on her lips. Truly, she is now ready.

Her mother shrieks when she emerges from the bathroom. "What have you done! My beautiful, beautiful girl!"

"Don't cry, Mom," Anna says, but the tears still pour down her mother's cheeks. "It's for Him," putting her hand on her mother's arm. "I need to be fully committed."

"Oh, Anna!" her mother asks. "Don't talk about commitment. We were happy that you weren't depressed anymore, but we were hoping..."

"What were you hoping?" Anna asks. She takes her hand off her mother's arm.

"That this was just a phase," her mother says.

"Please, Mom. I deserve more respect than that," Anna says.

Inwardly, though, Anna is pleased by the reaction. She goes back to look in the mirror. Her exposed face and neck, making her cheekbones more prominent, her eyes unnaturally large. "What big eyes you have, my dear," she says into the mirror and laughs. She is happy with what she's done.

But outside her home her act doesn't have the effect Anna had hoped for. To Lars, none of this matters. She is disappointed, wanting her gesture to be appreciated. Anna doesn't think he even notices her shorn head despite the amused and aghast reactions of others.

Students stare in the school halls, but in math class, John Martin reaches over and strokes her bare head. "Like Nefertiti," he says, almost in awe. Despite herself, Anna is pleased. The flesh still so weak.

18

LARS AND ANNA ARE IN the science hallway at school, outside the boys' bathroom, their usual place to touch base between classes. They clasp hands briefly, their secret handshake. Then enemies appear. They are younger, but larger. They don't yet have mastery of their hands or feet. Like puppies, their limbs in a state of uncontrol.

"Look who's here. The homo and the Jesus freak."

"How weird can you get? Aren't you supposed to hate each other?"

"Who converted who? Did he teach you to love Jesus? Did you teach him to love boys?"

Here they can say such things and get away with it. What a difference fifty miles makes. In San Francisco they'd be toast. But Sunnyvale—Sunnyvale is not San Francisco. Still, Lars warns Anna not to fool herself. Their kind—by which he means End-of-Dayers—would be shunned up there, too. *Their kind.*

Naturally, the boys are largely focused on Lars. People are still tentative about Anna. Her shorn head, black clothes, scrubbed face—is this social suicide? Or does it mask some new height of coolness? But Lars is an easy target. He is pinned to the lockers, his backpack torn from his thin shoulders and flung down the hall. Anna is left outside a wall of burly backs. She pushes her way through. A hand gropes her right breast, moves lower to her belly, tries to go farther, but she gives a sharp twist to her hips and loses it. Then she finds herself being forced, face-first, toward Lars. Her body pressed against his, but because Anna is so much taller, she can feel his eyelids fluttering against her lips.

"Give the homo a kiss," says one of the boys. "You know he wants it."

"Yeah, and then he can do something for you. Given that he only reaches your crotch anyway."

They're still laughing at their wit when Anna kicks backwards, hard, with her right foot. She makes contact and hears a surprised yelp. Then she manages to turn around. She's facing four, no five, of them, all taller than Anna, their arms a tangle reaching out to grab, restrain, but it's her left knee this time that shoots up and catches someone in the thigh. A nice, bruising blow. Another yelp. She swings her leg and tries again, hitting softer matter this time. A screech of real pain and an expletive. "Bitch," and a hand is around her face, the fingers going too near her mouth so she bites down, hard. A crowd has gathered, but no one is helping. Lars is now free, everyone is concentrating on Anna, hands everywhere, grabbing her breasts, neck, buttocks. With enormous effort Anna wrenches herself away and breaks through the circle of onlookers, pulling Lars along with her.

Anna hurries him to the classroom she'd left five minutes earlier. The chemistry lab. Turns the handle. Pushes the door. Makes sure Lars makes it in behind her. Slams the door hard after him. If something fleshy got caught between the door and doorframe, if Anna hears, as she thinks she does, a cry of surprised pain, so much the better.

Lars and Anna lean their backs against the door. The door handle moves; they feel the strength of those on the other side. Both of them breathing hard, Lars even panting.

Then an emphatic "Well?" Anna looks up. At the front of the room sits Ms. Thadeous, the chemistry teacher, at her desk, her pen poised above a stack of papers.

Ms. Thadeous says nothing as she walks over to Lars and Anna. She gestures them aside, opens the door, and faces the boys there. One look at her face and they melt away. Ms. Thadeous closes the door. Then walks back to her desk and sits down once more, picks up her pen. But she keeps her eyes on Lars and Anna.

"Again?" she asks. Her voice is not sympathetic, but neither is it hostile.

Lars nods, his usual guarded self in public, revealing nothing.

"What do you mean *again*?" Anna asks. She still feels the hands on her breasts, buttocks. Violated.

"Don't be an imbecile. It doesn't suit you," Ms. Thadeous says. She doesn't sound like the boring and obviously bored teacher who just finished lecturing Anna's class on absolute zero less than ten minutes ago. Her voice is sharp, her face alert.

"You two have had quite a month," she says. "Not that you haven't asked for it. You and your Children's Crusade." Ms. Thadeous is dressed simply, in a plain white blouse and black trousers. No jewelry, not even a wedding ring. Carefully applied makeup. Anna estimates her age to be early thirties. A little heavy around the waist but not unattractive. Petite frame. Perfect, ramrod posture.

Anna dismisses her and turns to Lars. A raised bruise is starting to appear on his right arm, below his short shirtsleeve.

Ms. Thadeous sees it, too. "Hold on," she says, and goes to the large red-and-white first-aid kit hanging on the wall behind her desk. She brings over an ice pack, cracks it, and places it on Lars's arm. She is not particularly gentle. Lars winces.

"You two up to your usual tricks?" she asks as she returns to her desk.

Anna has never heard Ms. Thadeous talk like this before. Everyone calls her Ms. Tedious. Today she seems different. Meaner. More interesting.

"You have no one but yourselves to blame," she says. "People like you need to keep low profiles. Wait out the high school years. Don't expose yourself until after graduation. Then move to Colorado Springs. Grant's Pass. Find yourself a nice, isolated tract of land, and haul in the double-wide trailers. Call it a religious community. Break bread with your own kind. Make sure to identify and kick out the sexual predators before the Feds move in."

Lars takes the ice pack off his arm. He is clearly searching for the right thing to say. "We're not weirdos," is all he can come up with. Anna is surprised at how vulnerable he sounds. "And we have no intention of hiding the light of our faith in Grant's Pass."

"The light of your faith," Ms. Thadeous repeats. She is almost jeering.

"Why didn't you help?" Anna asks Ms. Thadeous. "You must have heard us being attacked."

"I don't believe in helping those who ask to be victimized," Ms. Thadeous says. She picks up her pen, draws a hard line across an equation on the paper in front of her, then puts it down again. "If you and Lars would cooperate when the police come, that would be one thing. We can get the boys who are doing these things under the hate crime law. Penal Code 422.6. God, I've signed enough police reports with that number on it! You've got double cause: your religious beliefs, and Lars's sexual orientation." Lars looks up, startled, but Ms. Thadeous continues. "But no. You have to turn the other cheek. And you've muddied the moral waters considerably. By continuing to engage in inappropriate activities on school property, despite numerous warnings."

She pauses for breath. "If you would just make a statement to the police . . . ?"

Lars shakes his head vehemently. "No. Out of the question." Anna is relieved to see that the bruise on his arm is the only sign of injury. They've had days she needed three, four ice packs, half a tube of antibiotic cream, and the largest adhesive bandages Anna could find.

Ms. Thadeous sighs. She randomly starts shuffling the papers on her desk. Anna recognizes her handwriting on one of them. Ms. Thadeous has already graded it. Even upside down Anna can see the big red D, and the scribbled question mark followed by an exclamation point. All her teachers are having the same reaction. Let them. *His will be done.*

"It's probably safe now," she says. "Go to your next class, both of you. I'll write you late passes."

"I have algebra," says Lars. "And Anna has gym." He stops, and looks at her. Anna knows that look. It's his let's-use-our-moral-high-ground-to-get-something-we-want look. It's a more calculated version of what Lars's parents do when they put on their professional clothes and enter the working world. It's his us-against-them-and-all's-fair attitude. Not his most admirable quality. But one of his more useful ones. "But," he continues, seemingly addressing Anna. "It's not a big deal if we're a little late. Nor would it be a disaster if we missed the whole period." He doesn't look at Ms. Thadeous when he says this.

Neither does she look at him or speak, but just buries herself in the papers again. Yet some communication passes in the silence and Lars smiles for the first time since the fight. "Thank you," he says, and he's smart enough to say it with humility and gratitude that Anna knows he doesn't feel. Lars is neither a particularly humble nor grateful person, Anna has learned. He is accepting Ms. Thadeous's gift as something he's owed. "We'll sit over here in the corner," he says. "We won't bother you."

Previously, in Anna's now-vanished life, the chemistry lab was one of her favorite places in the world. Anna loved the long countertops, the shiny mysterious bottles filled with multicolored liquids, the careful measuring and pouring of substances from one container to another. The possibilities of creation.

"Anna," Ms. Thadeous says, startling her.

"Yes?"

"What exactly do your parents think of all this?"

"All what?" Anna asks, cautiously.

Ms. Thadeous gives her a look.

"They let me be," Anna says, with a touch of belligerence. Lars smiles at the floor.

"Fools," Ms. Thadeous says. "I just don't get it. An intelligent girl like you."

Anna quotes Proverbs 14:10. "The heart knoweth his own bitterness; and a stranger doth not intermeddle with his joy." She smiles at Ms. Thadeous.

Surprisingly, Ms. Thadeous has a reply. "*And the simple believeth every word: but the prudent man looketh well to his going,*" she says. "Proverbs 14:15."

"Idiots, both of you," Ms. Thadeous says, and gets up and leaves the room.

19

ANNA'S FATHER IS FLIPPING PANCAKES at the stove. It's one of the few times they've been alone together since what her mother refers to as Anna's road-to-Damascus moment. Her mother tries, but can't quite keep the scorn out of her voice when she says these things. This might have hurt Anna deeply once. Before.

"Religion is the one point on which your mother is not quite rational," Anna's father says now. He puts a plate in front of Anna, and she quickly devours it—she has gotten her appetite back and is starting to regain the weight she lost.

"Like you and your earthquakes?"

"Like me and my earthquakes," Anna's father agrees. She loves him like this, jovial and reasonable and able to joke with her. She knows however that his mood can change at any moment.

"Dad?"

"Yes, Little Man?" His pet name for Anna ever since she was seven, when she refused to mother her dolls, only to father them. To throw them up in the air, to roughhouse, discipline them. Her bewildered parents let this go, as they did most things. Laissez-faire parenting.

"What do you think about my ... road-to-Damascus moment?"

Her father answers promptly. He has evidently been thinking about it. "As a stage you're going through. Not as bad as drugs or sex or any of the other things teenagers can get into, thank goodness. But not particularly productive, either. Your mother and I will be glad when this, too, passes."

"What if I said that about your earthquake fixation?" Anna asks. Her father makes frequent trips to Parkfield, one hundred and eighty miles away in the Central Valley. The Earthquake Capital of the World. Hundreds of quakes rattle the windows of the small town every year. Experts predict that the Big One, long anticipated, will have its epicenter near Parkfield. The city's motto: Be here when it happens.

Anna's dad chooses not to answer, pours himself another cup of coffee and opens the newspaper. They would live in Parkfield if Anna's father had his way. His retirement dream is to live in a house made of redwood and steel, steel that would bend and flex with the seismic shocks, with bulletproof windows and enough land for him to place sensors in the earth for his own experiments. He wants to be the third little pig. Safe in the midst of danger that no one else has been wise enough to prepare for.

In one of Anna's earliest memories, she is sitting on her father's shoulders on a hill overlooking the dry fields of a California midsummer. She smells dead grass and hears the buzzing of cicadas. Then the trees begin to quiver and her father is trembling and holding out his arms straight to balance on the rolling earth as if on a surfboard. Anna clings tightly to him as they sway in the hot sun, and she can, if she tries, still feel her knees gripping his shoulders, his heart beating so hard and fast she swears she can feel it reverberate in her own body. Even as her father struggles for balance, he opens his mouth, lets out a wail that echoes against the rolling hills of the empty countryside. A primal call.

For as long as Anna can remember, her father went to Parkfield at least once a month, a three-hour drive that her mother refused to make, preferring to stay home and practice. Anna accompanied her father when she was young and on the way to Parkfield he would talk to her of fracture propagation and asperities and elastic rebound theory. His idea of good parenting, teaching Anna to fear the earth she stands on.

Anna tries again. "Dad?"

He doesn't look up. "Yes?"

"I'm bringing this up again because it would be remiss of me not to." Despite herself, Anna's voice rises.

Her father puts down the paper and takes another gulp of coffee. "You really shouldn't get yourself so agitated," he says. His voice is kind. He can be a kind man, and generous, if you catch him at the right time. "We don't want you to relapse."

"A relapse is incidental compared to what I'm talking about," Anna says. She had told herself that she would remain calm. But so much is at stake.

"Yes, I know," her father sounds slightly irritated now. "Your mother and I will be damned to eternal hell for not believing. Well, so be it." He picks up his newspaper.

"You don't understand," says Anna. "When the Tribulation comes, I will be forced to take arms. Against you and the other ungodly people." She is close to tears.

"Ungodly, eh?" her father says.

"Dad, please," Anna says, and her father must hear the urgency in her voice, so he looks at her over the paper, reaches out, and takes Anna's hand.

"Little Man, you couldn't convince me of this any more than I can convince you about the importance of being prepared for the Big One," he begins.

Anna interrupts him. "I do believe in the Big One," she says. "But statistically, it could be three hundred years from now. You've said that yourself, many times. But the End Days are nearly upon us." She has finished her pancakes, and takes the sticky plate and silverware to the sink, rinses them off, and puts them in the dishwater. Her father's plate sits on the table beside him with the remains of a pancake soaking in syrup. Anna knows that he will leave it there, and that no amount of threatening or cajoling of her mother will induce him to take dirty dishes to the sink. Her mother says it isn't in his DNA to obey orders.

"Dad, don't you believe at all in an afterlife? A place we go after we die?"

Rattling his paper, Anna's father says, "What I believe is that this conversation should come to an end."

But Anna isn't ready to give up. "Okay," she says, "for now."

20

"HEY. HEY!"

Jim Fulson has come out of his house. He has actually spoken to Anna. She is waiting for the bus, alone, Lars being sick with the flu. Jim Fulson joins Anna on the sidewalk; he stands on the *c* in *C-A-R-O-L-I-N-E*, Anna is on the *r.* It feels too close. She retreats to the *l.* A moment of awkward silence.

"I've been watching you," Jim Fulson finally says. Even now, Anna doesn't know how to think of him except by his full name. *Jim* sounds too familiar, Mr. Fulson pompous and ridiculous. But *Jim Fulson has been watching me?* For the first time Anna regrets her shorn head.

"You've been really pushing your workouts," he says. "Training for anything special?"

"No," Anna manages to say. "Just trying to get in shape."

Jim Fulson laughs. "You must certainly be that," he says. "What's your name again? Ann? Annie?" He smiles, and it is a genuine one, but with a good deal of pain in it, too. When Anna nods, he smiles again. "You were a cute kid," he says, then backtracks. "Not that you aren't cute now. I was just remembering. Do you recall the day I caught you hiding under my car? Right behind

96

my back wheel. I was about ready to reverse when I saw your foot from my side mirror. You gave me a scare!" And he presses his right hand to his left breast. "You must have been seven or eight."

"We were playing hide and seek," Anna says. She remembers that day well. "I didn't want to be found."

Silence.

"So," Jim Fulson says, gesturing at Anna's head. "What's up with that?"

Anna doesn't feel like going into it. "New fashion," she says.

"Well, if anyone can carry it off, you can." His words are flirtatious but there's nothing in his manner except a sober sort of propriety, as if he has aged at double Anna's rate. If his manners are mature, everything else about him rejoices with health and youth. He must be twenty-five by now.

"So what's the deal? Why are you back?" Anna asks, feeling courageous. Jim Fulson kneels down, adjusts the laces on his sneakers, then says, "I'll tell you if you tell me what you and that new kid are up to."

"How much time do you have?" Anna asks, acting as though she thinks it's a joke. She does want to hear his story, badly, but not necessarily by telling her own. To be scorned by the boys at school is one thing. To look ridiculous in the eyes of Jim Fulson is something else. She stops short when she realizes it. Is her faith so shallow? A stab of anger takes her by surprise.

He somehow senses this, because he takes a step back, and his eyes look off in the distance. He points to the bus stop sign. "This has been here since I was your age," he says. "Only I rarely took the bus. Had to get to school early for practice, and stayed late for the same reason. I still drive by the school sometimes. Everything looks the same."

"Nothing ever changes," Anna says, repeating a phrase she hears the teachers at school use. "I probably even have the same teachers you did."

"Who's that?"

"Mr. Roberts. Ms. Evans. Señora Sharp. Ms. Tedious."

"Ms. Tedious?"

"I mean Ms. Thadeous. She's boring."

"I remember Clara Thadeous. She was a student teacher my senior year. In science. So they hired her."

Anna shrugs.

"She was anything but tedious," he says, and there is something in his expression that puts Anna on alert. He notices her watching him and gives a little laugh. "Teacher crush," he says. "Funny to remember. She was only a few years older than we were. So we gave her hell. She gave us hell back. She was pretty cool."

Jim Fulson lowers himself down and arranges himself cross-legged on the grass. Anna remains standing. He picks a small white pebble off his parents' flowerbed and throws it at the nearest tree, the same one he'd used to teach Anna a lesson all those years ago.

"I hate these trees," he says. "Reminders of my wasted youth." Although the subdivision is more than fifty years old, none of the trees look mature. No matter how much individual homeowners nurture or neglect them, all the trees turn out the same: scrawny and crooked with fly-specked leaves that turn brown and fall off in the middle of summer. The temperature in their neighborhood is always ten degrees hotter than the other subdivisions lining El Camino because of the lack of a tree canopy.

"What's been wasted?" Anna asks.

"You go first," he says. "What's up? Not just the things you're hauling, but your hair, and the fact that none of your old girlfriends come over anymore."

"How do you know that?" Anna asks, startled.

"You're pretty much the only show in town," Jim Fulson says. "Not much else to do around here but watch it."

"There's not much to tell," Anna says, shrugging. She tries to look like she's telling the truth, that there are no mysteries here, that the only thing different about her is that she's more mature than other seventeen-year-olds.

"Okay, but I'm not letting you off the hook," Jim Fulson says. "I'll get your story, sooner or later." He picks up another stone, idly tosses it into the air, and they both watch it bounce off the sidewalk into the grass.

"I did everything right," he says, finally. "Went away to UCLA. Got the degree in management. Got a job at one of those consulting sweatshops, where you spend sixty, seventy hours a week on the road getting paid a ton of money to pull business advice out of your ass. I worked hard. You could say I was clawing my way upward."

"And you decided you couldn't take it?" Anna asks. She is trying not to appear too eager. How he ended up in his parents' rec room. She wants to hear something that will reveal her own future to her.

"No, all that was okay. I found an apartment with two college buddies in LA, and within a year had racked up more than a quarter of a million frequent flyer miles. The lifestyle was brutal, but I didn't care."

"Did you have a girlfriend?"

"I was just getting to that," he says. "I didn't, but one of my roommates did. Maxine."

"Ah," Anna says.

"Yeah."

"And . . .?"

"The girl was just incidental," he says. "It was even working out okay. We decided we liked each other, my roommate decided he didn't like her so much, and everything looked as if it was easy going for me just the way it always was. If not an A+ then not a C either. Right down the middle of the fucking—I mean frigging—road."

"Don't worry," Anna says. "I've heard it all."

Jim Fulson laughs and reaches out, rubs her shorn head, she can hear the rough bristles buzz his palm. "You look so young like that," he says. "How old are you, anyway?"

"Seventeen," Anna says. She doesn't like being patted on the head. Not by Jim Fulson. "But what happened?"

"I just lost it," he said. "I woke up one morning and couldn't get up. Couldn't get my head off my pillow. I thought it was physical. Went to my doctor, and she was concerned enough to run a battery of tests. Nothing. Eventually, they gave up. Said I was depressed. But that's not what it felt like to me. Something more shameful."

"Yes," Anna says, careful to look away. "But they can treat that now. I know lots of Zoloft zombies at school. They're even proud of it."

"But they said my particular depression was resistant to treatment," Jim Fulson says. "They tried all sorts of drugs, concocted all sorts of cocktails, as they called them. No luck."

He stretches his arms above his head, and the loose sleeves of his shirt fall back. Anna sees. Did he want her to? On his arms. The marks. The raised white lines that extend in long graceful vertical strokes from his wrists up to the bends of his elbows. On both arms. Anna counts four, no six, long scars before he pulls down his sleeves. Anna knows what she has seen. Jim Fulson, braver than she will ever be.

He sees that she understands.

"I am tenacious, if not particularly effective," Jim Fulson says, and they both sit for a moment. Anna looks out at the trees.

"So I ended up twice at Aurora Las Encinas. The hospital for the crazies in LA, at least the ones with a death wish and good insurance. I was thinking of trying for a third time when my parents brought me home." He pauses. "Now," he says, "your turn. My sources tell me you've found the Lord."

Anna can't tell if he's making fun of her.

"Yes," she says. "But not in the Lord-Jesus-Christ-is-my-savior way. I'm more of a Book of Revelation kind of girl." She is trying to keep her tone light.

Then Jim Fulson puts a question to her that no one else has bothered to ask, not even Lars. Certainly not her parents.

"How's that working out for you?"

Anna is taken aback. She has to think about this. "It's not exactly a choice," Anna says, finally.

Anna feels Jim Fulson is about to speak again when the bus rounds the corner. He's immediately on his feet. "Talk to you later," he says and he's walking away, disappearing inside his parents' house before the crowded bus even pulls up at the stop.

21

SCHOOL ENDS. A DRY HOT summer ensues, the hottest of the past decade. Then, late one July night when Anna can't sleep she runs up against Jim Fulson again.

At midnight she escapes her stifling house and is walking aimlessly around the subdivision, pacing along the familiar streets. She is wearing a T-shirt and gym shorts. On one of her trips past C-A-R-O-L-I-N-E, suddenly Jim Fulson is there, sitting on the stoop of his parents' house. He is more formally dressed than Anna, in jeans and a button-down shirt, but his shirttails hang out and some of his buttons are undone. It is nearly 2 AM.

"Clara Thadeous," he calls out to Anna as she approaches. "An interesting woman."

"She's not a woman," Anna says, standing awkwardly by the stoop, looking down at him. "She's a teacher." Then, curiously, "Why do you say that?"

"I just had the pleasure of spending an hour in her company. One of the few pleasurable hours I've had in the last two years, I might add." Anna can't see his face in the shadows, only his hands and legs are lit by the streetlight.

"And where did you meet her? A PTA meeting?"

"No. A place sixteen-year-old girls don't go."

"I'm seventeen. And what's that mean? A brothel?" Anna asks. She is hurt by his flippant tone, but tries not to show it. To prove that she is neither timid nor intimidated, she sits down next to him.

"Of course not. And what do you know about brothels?" He has to turn to the right to see her. She can smell the alcohol on his breath.

"I read the Bible," says Anna. "And I'm not an imbecile."

"Ah yes, I forgot. You read the Bible. You know every vice on the planet and then some." Jim Fulson lapses into silence, begins to examine his hands.

Anna considers Ms. Thadeous. The last time she'd seen her was the day school ended, monitoring the final assembly. Although early June, the heat had already settled in, and Ms. Thadeous's face was red and shiny with perspiration. Anna envisions her in a dark bar, her thick waist pushed against a table, leaning over it, looking into Jim Fulson's blue eyes. They would make a nice couple, Anna thinks spitefully. A Godless pair. She stoops and picks up a pebble next to the stairs and viciously throws it. It hits nothing.

"I don't feel depressed," Jim Fulson says, following his own thoughts. "Just diseased." And he traces one of the scars up his right arm with his left index finger. When he reaches the end, near the crook of his elbow, he pinches, hard.

Anna has not, until this moment, fully understood the meaning of *self-hatred*.

"I was ... melancholy ... once," she says. "That was before."

Jim Fulson half smiles. "I hate the 'D word' too," he says. "Melancholy. That's a good one."

"No, listen," Anna says. "I got better." She is desperate to communicate this, feels that the moment is urgent.

"But at what cost?" he asks.

"What do you mean?"

Jim Fulson hesitates. Then he says, almost tenderly, "You've become a bit of a nutcase, haven't you?"

Anna isn't offended. It must seem this way to people, she knows. Still she reaches up and strokes her head self-consciously. She has found that it is easier and more effective to use her father's razor rather than the kitchen shears. The stubble feels rough under her fingers.

"It's not a route I'm inclined to take," says Jim Fulson. "But," he continues. "Back to Clara Thadeous . . ."

"Ms. Tedious."

"That I will never allow to be true," Jim Fulson says and suddenly stands. He wavers a little before he can get completely upright, but when he has control of his balance he looks severely down at Anna. She finds she can't meet his eyes.

"I hereby declare Clara Thadeous off limits for you to denigrate," he says.

"What are you, her knight in shining armor?" asks Anna, but she finds she is ashamed of herself for her uncharitable words. He would not approve.

"I'm sorry," she tells Jim Fulson, and he must have heard the sincerity in her voice because his face softens and he sits down again.

A momentary silence, then Anna says shyly, "So you like her?"

"A lot," he says after a pause. "Even more so meeting her as a person rather than as a teacher."

"So the teacher crush turned into a real crush?"

Anna isn't sure due to the dim light, but she thinks Jim Fulson is blushing.

"Perhaps," he says. Then he turns to her. "And would that be against your newfound religion? Two people coming together?"

"I don't know," she admits. "To me it seems like it might be frivolous to be thinking of such things when the crisis is near at hand."

"By 'crisis' you mean the end of the world?"

Anna nods.

"Well, if the world ended tomorrow I would die happily knowing I spent my last evening with Clara Thadeous," he says. His voice is solemn.

To this Anna has no answer. But something within her quivers.

22

SUMMER PASSES WITHOUT MUCH OF note happening.

Anna is nothing if not ambitious. Her ambitions fuel her ten-mile runs every morning, and her kickboxing in her parents' rec room, where there is a television and DVD player and an aging cache of fitness videos. Anna spends hours down there, mimicking the moves of the beautifully muscled instructor on the video screen. *Kick right! Kick behind! Twist and extend both arms and kick up!* She is dripping with sweat by the end of the workout. Anna is waiting for her instructions. She will do anything, is ready to lead armies, to smite the ungodly in battle. To burn. She is burning already. She most longs to be Fred Wilson's handmaiden—to help make the Red Heifer prophecy come true. She feels chosen. She wants to get on with it.

Anna emails Fred Wilson regularly. She is determined to know more; she feels that she has been called to help in some way.

The first email from Fred Wilson is a form letter, with Anna's name printed in slightly larger type than the rest of the words.

Dear Anna,

Thank you for your interest in the Wilson Ranch and the work we are doing with the Third Temple Commission in Israel. As you can imagine, our work is very labor and capital-intensive, and thus we are grateful for any donation you can make. Our seventh generation of cows is now gestating. We expect to have great news to announce before Christmas! We accept payments by personal check, PayPal, and all major credit cards.

Yours in Christ,
Fred Wilson

Anna answers it promptly.

Dear Mr. Wilson,

I don't know if you remember me from Reverend Michael's parish in San Jose, California, but I am very interested in helping you any way I can. I will be both eighteen and personally independent this coming spring. I am hoping to have a place in your operations. You could think of me as an intern. I am willing to do anything. Or, if you need couriers as you mentioned in your talk here, I would be happy to act in that capacity. I have a valid passport and would feel honored to be associated with your work.

Sincerely,
Anna Franklin

Fred Wilson emailed back almost immediately, a personal note.

Anna,

Of course I remember you. Despite the crowd, your beauty of person and spirit shone through. I would welcome you as an intern on the Wilson Ranch. As far as becoming a courier, that depends on the circumstances. Certain complications have arisen with exporting the embryos as we have been doing. Please keep in touch and we will make plans as you near your date of emancipation.

Yours in Christ,
Fred Wilson

Anna draws a circle around May 30 on the calendar. Her eighteenth birthday. The day her real work on earth begins.

23

EARLY AUGUST. THE SUN HAS broken through the fog. For the first time in weeks Anna revels in a gorgeous day of the type she is used to taking for granted in the California summer: clear skies, mid-70s, a slight, fresh wind.

Anna's father is rolling up one of his geological maps. A series of mild temblors had shaken Central California this bright Sunday morning, and he is anxious to get to the epicenter, near Parkfield of course.

This morning he asks Anna if she would like to go. "Come on, Little Man, we'll have a ball," he says. He is on his third cup of coffee and because the jitters don't hit him until his fifth cup, there isn't any irritation in his voice yet.

Something makes Anna hesitate before giving her usual "no."

"Are you actually considering it?" her father asks. His eagerness makes her give in.

"All right," Anna says, and instantly regrets it once she sees how happy it makes him. She doesn't want that responsibility.

He's now packing sandwiches and bottles of water into the cooler with more enthusiasm. There's nothing in Parkfield except a tourist cafe, nowhere to eat real food, nowhere to buy gas, *nowhere to shit,* as Anna's mother used to say. Her mother's hatred for Parkfield was something Anna had always taken for granted but now she asks her father why her mother is so vehement.

Anna's father shrugs, and puts the cooler and his equipment into the trunk of the Toyota. He's brought a supersized paper cup of coffee with him as well. "One day she'd had enough. Said that this obsession wasn't healthy. That she preferred a different scenario for the future than the one I was fantasizing about."

Anna's father rubs his forehead as he starts the car, puts it in reverse, begins backing down the driveway. "I was disappointed by her decision. To me, it was our family time. Driving together. Playing your *Sesame Street* songs. Once it was so hot that the car began overheating and we couldn't use the air-conditioning. We stopped at a Motel 6 outside King City, paid the manager fifteen dollars and literally threw you into the pool, still dressed in your shorts and T-shirt. You were three, maybe four. Your mom and I also went in with our clothes on. We figured they would dry in the heat. You should have seen your mother then. So pretty—and so game. Nothing would stop her from doing the most outrageous things."

"But you're happy together, right?" Anna asks. She realizes how much she's missed talking to her father. They're flying past the wasteland south of San Jose and will soon start hitting the outlet malls at Gilroy. When Anna's father and mother were first married, all this was still farmland. They told Anna of the picnics they'd have up in the hills overlooking the valley, of the need to walk and talk loudly to scare away any mountain lions.

Her father takes another gulp of coffee. "What does a happy marriage look like?" he asks.

Then, after a moment, "We don't fight an awful lot. She makes direct confrontation impossible, yet always manages to get her way. Haven't you ever wondered why she doesn't wear a wedding ring?"

"She's always said it gets in the way when she plays," Anna says. "She doesn't wear any jewelry. You know that."

"Only partially true," her father said. "She used to love jewelry. Not rings or bracelets or anything that encumbered her hands, but necklaces and earrings, she was crazy about them. She used to wear these long chandelier earrings made of red crystals. They came with two matching bracelets that she wore around her ankles. They chimed when she walked. It was the most heavenly sound." He is talking more to himself than to Anna.

"But the wedding ring?"

"She refused to wear one. I was young and stupid and told her that it wasn't a proper marriage without exchanging rings. God knows where I got that idea from. My stubborn-ass father, probably. She gave in, or so I thought. We had the ceremony, I put the ring on her finger, all that good stuff. Then we went on our honeymoon to Hawaii. Kauai."

"I've seen the pictures," Anna says. Her parents, looking impossibly young. Her father posing in front of a waterfall. Her mother, knee-deep in the surf. Never any photos of them together, as someone always had to be holding the camera, and back then her parents would have been too shy to ask strangers to take pictures of them.

Her father takes another big gulp of coffee. His fingers begin to drum on the steering wheel. "On our first day, we went for a long walk at the beach. Sometimes we could walk on the sand, but other times we had to climb over rocks that blocked the way. We got to this one massive outcropping—it must have been thirty feet tall that extended about fifty yards into the sea. I wanted to turn around, but your mother insisted. So we climbed to the top of this rock pile. I have to admit, it was spectacular. The sun was just setting, and the tide was coming in, and hit the rocks with such force that the spray shot up like a fountain. We were soaked but we didn't care. I remember looking at your mother and thinking *we're married!* and believing it for the first time. That was exactly the moment that she took off her wedding ring and, pulling her right arm as far back as it would go, threw it into the water. She then turned to me and calmly said, 'I told you I didn't like rings.' I noticed from that point on she stopped wearing other jewelry as well. I never asked her, but I think she made some sort of pact with herself. That she'd give up all jewelry to make up for her refusal to wear the ring."

They are silent for a mile, then two. They have passed the outlet malls and are heavy into garlic country. The rich pungent scent invading the car, even though the windows are closed. Roadside stands advertising garlic sausage, garlic cheese, garlic ice cream.

"A happy marriage? Yes, I'd say it was," Anna's father says.

More silence for more miles. Then he says, too casually, "So what's going on in the born-again club these days?"

"Dad, I'm not born-again," says Anna. "That's something else altogether." She abruptly rolls down the window, sticks her face out into the balmy, heavily garlic-scented breeze. "Don't trivialize the path I'm taking."

"No one's trivializing anyone here." Anna's father takes huge gulps of his coffee, which must now be cold. He has abandoned his previous good humor, is predictably irritated by her words. This is the father Anna knows best. "I'm just curious," he continues in a voice that makes it clear he isn't curious at all, "is there some rite of initiation, like sprinkling water on your head. Any breaking of glasses? Any sign or symbol that you've crossed some threshold?" Anna's father was raised in an atheist household, and although not as militant about it as Anna's mother, is suspicious of faith of any kind, views religion as some sort of scam.

"No, I've done nothing of that sort," Anna says, trying not to sound irritated herself, and refuses to say more. She deeply regrets coming.

"What about your grades?" he asks. "When did your report card come?"

Anna braces herself. "It came last month," she says. "But you won't like it."

"Why?" They're passing the Monterey turnoff. Traffic falls away to nothing as the needle edges from 70 miles per hour to 75.

"Dad, not so fast," Anna says. She curses herself for getting drawn into this discussion. They've had it too many times, and the results are the same. Anger and misunderstanding. Or anger because of too much understanding. Perhaps she is too clear about what she thinks and is doing. She should take her mother's route, hide behind a smokescreen. But Anna and her father have always demanded honesty from each other and turn spitting mad when they get it. After the storm, usually a period of calm and mutual acceptance.

"What will your report card show?" Anna's father asks.

"I haven't been doing so great in school lately," Anna says. Tired of the wind in her face, she rolls up the window, slumps down in her seat as far away from her father as possible.

Her father continues accelerating. Soon he'll hit 100.

"Slow down, Dad, you'll get caught."

He ignores her. "Goddamn it, Annie, you've let this religion thing go too far. How are you doing on your college applications? They're due next semester, right?"

Anna has been dreading this moment. "I'm not applying anywhere," she says. "My path lies in another direction." The minute the words are out of her mouth, Anna regrets telling him. It would have been better to have led him and her mother on as long as possible, until it was too late for them to argue.

Anna's father's face is mottled, but he is speaking more quietly, a bad sign. "You're shutting yourself out of the real world. Soon you'll have nothing left. And that includes your family. Do you really think I'd stand for this? After all we've done to make sure you get into a good college?"

Anna can cry, or get angry. She decides on the latter.

"You should know," she says.

"What does that mean?"

"It means you know what it is to shut down and shut out others because you're pursuing your own . . . interests."

"You . . ." he says, then stops. He is not so out of control that he has stopped monitoring the highway for cops. He suddenly slams on the brakes so he's lagging behind the speed limit, only 50 miles per hour, a sign that he's spotted a policeman. Sure enough, Anna sees one in the right lane. He's in the middle of a cluster of cars, staying with them to appear innocuous.

"I mean that Mom told me about your drinking."

"What do you mean? *I've* told you about my drinking."

"No, *really* told. How bad you were."

Anna's father goes still. "It was a rough time for all of us. Except you. You were too young to have noticed."

But he's wrong. One of her earliest memories. She couldn't have been more than four or five. She'd heard a noise. Never thinking that the house could be anything but safe, she climbed down the stairs in her footed pajamas. The noise was coming from the kitchen, a kind of rhythmic shuffling. Anna stopped at the kitchen door. There she saw her father, alone. He was dancing. Eyes closed. Not seeing her, not seeing anything. Just dancing. And not in a silly way, as in the movies, where men use a broom, or place their hands on the imaginary waists of imaginary partners. No. He gracefully lifted one bare foot, placed it down again, and then did the same with the other foot. All while making lovely undulating waves with his arms. The music he was hearing must have been sublime. The drink was a part of it. The drink in the clear glass, no ice, just a pale colorless liquid, sitting on the table as he paid it homage, adored it with his body.

"So," Anna asks. "What exactly happened then, that I was too young to remember? I'm old enough to understand."

"Don't change the subject," her father says. The police car is now directly behind them, following close. Anna sees drops of perspiration on her father's face. He is, with great effort, keeping his voice level. With his eyes on the rearview mirror and only half paying attention to Anna he says, "I want to talk about your future. Do you want to take a year off after high school? A gap year? Your mother and I could probably live with that."

The police car puts on its signal, merges into the right lane, and passes them. Anna's father heaves a sigh of relief.

Anna knows she's lost him. She tries again.

"Dad, please. I need to know," she says.

"Know what?" He is starting to speed again already.

"Your drinking. Mom has told me about it. You mention it sometimes. Was it a big deal?"

Anna's father gives a short laugh. "A big deal? I'd say. A very big deal."

He is calmer now, his voice at its normal pitch and volume. "Your mother gave me an ultimatum. Quit, or she would leave. With you, of course."

"And you chose us," Anna says impatiently.

"No," he says, "I didn't." He is staring straight ahead. Highway 101 is utterly flat at this point, with the artichoke fields stretching out to infinity to the east and low, ugly brown hills of dirt to the west. "You could say that I chose to follow my bliss. And it wasn't you or your mother. Not then."

Anna hadn't been expecting this. Her hand grips the door handle.

"I chose the booze. And you and your mother left. For approximately seventy-two hours. She went to Martha's. And then came back, obviously."

"Because she loved you," Anna says, confident she knows the end of the story.

"No, more because she couldn't stand being stuck alone with you, couldn't think how she would raise you on her own."

Anna is unprepared for the pain. It hits in the abdomen, right below her breasts. Makes it hard to breathe.

"You were a difficult baby. You had colic, cried all day every day. Then, the terrible twos turned into the terrible threes turned into years of bad behavior. You fought us on everything. Then one day, in your fifth year, the Anna we know today emerged. A little quirky, but fairly docile. The wildness gone. The pediatrician thought it might have something to do with you being a late talker, finding it difficult to communicate. That you were frustrated. We didn't know. We thought we had a bad seed."

He pauses and concentrates on driving as a truck pulls onto the highway outside Salinas, causing the cars on the two-lane stretch to hit their brakes. Anna's father slams the horn.

"On the third day she came home, you trailing behind her," he continues. "You hadn't stopped crying since you'd left. You were crying for me, your mother said. She'd finally put you to bed in Martha's back bedroom and realized that she would do anything to ease the burden, even if that meant crawling back to me. Which she did. Knowing your mother, you can imagine how much that cost her."

Actually, Anna can't imagine. It hurts too much to try.

"I was still drinking. Drunk the morning she walked in," her father says. "But somehow things were okay between us. I was safe again. I sent her to bed, and tried to get you to quiet down, even momentarily. I hoped you'd eventually pass out from sheer exhaustion. No luck. Finally, desperate, I ground up a couple Valium, put them in a glass of warm milk, and coaxed you into drinking it. So on my last night of drunkenness, you got stoned right along with me. Rather sweet when you think of it. You pretty much passed out, I passed out, and when I woke, things were normal. Except all my bottles were gone, and you were gone and your mother was holding a knife to my neck. I'm not kidding. When I came to I was slumped on a chair in the kitchen, my head resting on the table, and a steak knife pressed against my Adam's apple. *Try that again, and you're a dead man,* your mother told me, and I believed her. I guess you could say she scared me straight."

"But," Anna says.

"But what?" he asks, not looking at her. She wants to ask. The dancing. Did she make it up? Was it a dream superimposed on the past? Or simply an early manifestation of what Dr. Cummings calls her *illness.*

"But I saw you," Anna says, finally. "Drinking." Does she want him to confirm or deny? Which would be worse? To have actually seen your father smile in a way that made all subsequent smiles false? Or to think your father incapable of joy?

He doesn't bother to ask what Anna is talking about. "No, you didn't," he replies. "You couldn't have."

"You were . . ." Anna almost says *happy* but stops herself. "Definitely a bit hammered," she finishes.

Anna wonders how her father views himself. Parent of a test-tube baby, not of his genetic making. Indifferent lawyer. Watcher of clocks. Wearer of hats. Chaser of disturbances. Desirer of cataclysms. His obsession with anything to do with matters of seismic, geothermic activity, elastic rebound theory. His measuring devices, many of them homemade. His charts and graphs. His maps of squares and diamonds and circles, all precisely color-coded based on USGS data. Every tremor on the San Andreas Fault marked in red. The Calaveras Fault, green. Concord-Green Valley Fault, yellow. Greenville, Hayward, Rodgers Creek, and San Gregorio faults: blue, purple, orange, and black. Other fathers get text messages from friends and family. Anna and her mother are forbidden to text him. That method of communication is sacred for earthquake alerts within one hundred miles of the Bay Area. He doesn't miss work. But at any other time, anything above a 5.0, he's gone.

Perhaps he could understand what Anna is yearning for. Perhaps he does understand. He is as enamored with the idea of widespread destruction as the bloodiest-minded members of Reverend Michael's church. And his response to the coming cataclysm just as selfish. He doesn't give seminars, donate time to earthquake preparedness committees. Instead, he delights in knowing he will be among the informed, among the prepared, among the surviving.

He is now silent. He finished his coffee long ago, but picks up the empty paper cup and makes as if to drink from it. A sure sign he is stressed. Anna has seen him lift an empty fork to his mouth when asked a question he didn't want to answer at the dinner table. During business calls he takes at home, he pretends to write things down with his finger on the tabletop while repeating words and numbers back into the phone.

As he drains the imaginary dregs from his cup, Anna sees his left leg start bouncing up and down.

"I'm not sure what you're doing . . ." he begins.

"Nothing," Anna says, as quickly as she can.

"This isn't about me. It's about you. This weird . . . phase."

"I've told you, it's not a phase," Anna says. "It is a new life."

"It's hard to keep up," he says. "One minute you're deeply depressed and the next you're running around with a wacko cult that wants to save the world."

"Not save," Anna says.

"What's that again?"

"We don't want to save the world," Anna explains. She is patient on this point, since this is what most people misunderstand about her faith, and therefore her calling. "We don't want to *prevent* the mayhem of the Tribulation. Any more than you want to prevent the Big One from happening. If you could throw some TNT into the San Andreas Fault, you'd do it in a heartbeat. Anything to speed up the process."

"And you?"

"Perhaps we have more in common than you think," Anna says.

"Isn't this where you tell me that nurture beats nature every time, given you're not really my daughter?"

"Isn't this when you say it doesn't matter one iota to you which man's sperm I came from?"

"We do know the script," he says.

"We do know our roles," Anna says.

"No, you're forgetting yours. You're forgetting that you're still a minor. My daughter. Under my control."

"Even He doesn't pretend to control us. Even He believes in free will," Anna says.

"You're not in His car. You're not living in His house. You're not eating His food, or wearing clothes He bought you," Anna's father says. "Those are mine. All mine. That's mine," and he tugs at the sleeve of her black sweatshirt. "Those are mine," he says, pointing at her sneakers. "And your blonde hair? Mine. Brown eyes? Mine. I picked them from a database."

"No, that was Mom. Mom's choice," Anna reminds him. She knows she is treading on dangerous ground. But worse things are coming. Wonderfully terrible things are coming.

"As for what's up here"—and with that he tapped Anna's head, hard, with his index finger—"I'd be ashamed to lay claim to that. *You* should be ashamed."

"Turn around," says Anna.

"What are you talking about?"

"Pull over. Stop. Then make a U-turn. Now. Take me home."

They're passing Soledad. Anna's father doesn't say anything, but puts on the brakes, Anna looks at the speedometer. He's dropped down to almost a standstill by his standards: just 35. She thinks he's considering her request, there's a place to turn around up ahead about two hundred yards. On the right, a cattle ranch, with large enclosures full of black cows. The car bounces as it slowly winds to a stop. Its shocks need replacing, but Anna's father always delays repairs. He puts on his blinker.

"No," he suddenly says, and his voice is lowering again, he is practically whispering, "Goddamn it, Annie, we're going to take this trip and we are going to talk during it and I am going to pound some sense into your head." He steps on the accelerator.

Anna opens the car door and jumps. She hits the gravel with such force her right kneecap cracks. After a wrenching half somersault her left shoulder slams the ground. Her face hits hard. Rocks grind into her flesh as she rolls. For a moment she's lost to the world. When she comes to, she's on her back gazing at telephone wires and a cloud shaped like a foot. She hears shouting. Her father. Faint but getting louder. "Anna! Little Man!" Despite her pain she recognizes the panic and shame in his voice. Her jaw aches and she is feeling around her mouth with her tongue to see if she cracked any teeth. Then she smiles. Her father, fanatic devotee of sudden shocks, has been vanquished.

24

IT'S 4 AM TWO NIGHTS after she jumped from her father's car, and Anna is out of pain meds. She sits on her bed and stares out the window. Anna's bedroom faces the street, and she can just see the Fulsons' house. The rec room windows stream light onto the grass, catching the early dew on the blades and causing them to sparkle, a sea of tiny spiky lanterns. Then, so gradually that she almost doesn't notice it, the front door of the house swings open and a form emerges, walking carefully, as if treading on glass. It's not until Anna sees the shoes being held in the right hand that she understands why the woman—for it is definitely a woman—is feeling each step with her foot before trusting it with her full weight. To see better, Anna kneels on her bed, grimacing from the pain. A dark figure, taller, appears behind the woman. Jim Fulson. The woman turns, is enveloped in a swift embrace. Despite her best efforts, Anna feels bitter. *When lust hath conceived, it bringeth forth sin: and sin, when it is finished, bringeth forth death.* She knows this, but it brings no comfort.

25

SCHOOL BEGINS AGAIN IN SEPTEMBER, and a long grim autumn descends. Unusually cold for Northern California. A baleful dark chill. Mist that blankets the streets every morning and refuses to clear until long after noon. The number of auto accidents shoot up, the number of fatalities quadruples from previous years. Babies are born early at local hospitals, at reduced weight. Retail sales plummet, more restaurants and boutique clothing stores close, more nail salons open. There is a swift but fleeting epidemic of cupcake shops. Bus schedules are cut due to budget shortfalls, hot lunches are cut, janitors are cut, teachers are cut.

Anna is annoyed at the sudden crowd in the high school library during lunch period as other students used to eating outside in the bright and warm Indian summers seek shelter from the fog and cold. They intrude upon Anna's precious time with Lars, upon their plotting and planning. Still, they see all these things as harbingers. The world is getting worse by the day, so much is clear, so much is good.

They step up what they call their *outreach* at school. They are taking a route that is against Anna's better judgment. Not because she doesn't agree with Lars's goals. Just the means. "This won't work," she tells him. "If anything, it'll gross kids out, push them away," Lars pays no attention. He has been busy on the Internet, searching for the most graphic images he can find of death, dismemberment, atrocities. At his insistence, Anna prints them out on her father's color printer. Today they are taping the most lurid photographs on the walls of the empty cafeteria before the first lunch bell rings. A bloody fetus, the head and eyes discernible. A beheaded corpse. A hand-printed sign: *What awaits you at the End of Days.*

The signs will get taken down almost immediately, as soon as the bell rings and the students begin lining up to get their sodas and an adult monitor enters the room. Anna and Lars will be sent to the principal's office for yet another lecture, and yet more phone calls to their parents. "What can we do?" Anna's mother and father have asked her, again and again. To which she just shrugs. Lars's parents never get the messages left on their voicemail, Lars simply erases them. Not that they'd check, anyway. Anna and Lars have been warned that unless these demonstrations stop, they will be suspended.

They are so busy hanging their grisly trophies that they don't notice Ms. Thadeous entering the cafeteria.

"Are you really so determined to get thrown out?" asks Ms. Thadeous. Once again, she is no longer the mediocre chemistry teacher. She is sparkling. Anna sees that she hasn't come into the cafeteria to accost them, but for reasons of her own. Ms. Thadeous goes directly to the large windows. She looks out. She is smiling. She raises her hand in a salute. There, among the cars, stands a solitary figure. A man. Bundled against the autumn chill, but still recognizable. Jim Fulson. Standing outside the school like a lovesick Romeo. Anna realizes he can't see into the cafeteria because of the glare of the windows. He believes he is unobserved. So he stands and worships unashamedly. This is his church, and Ms. Thadeous his high priestess. May God have mercy on them.

"Take these off," she orders, and walks over to the wall and begins pulling down the photos herself. "Don't be fools. If you're expelled, how will that advance your cause? Will you start going door to door in Sunnyvale, handing out pamphlets? Good luck with that."

Lars opens his mouth then shuts it again. Anna realizes that neither of them has thought this through sufficiently. Ms. Thadeous sees this and laughs. It is not a friendly laugh. "Finish this," she says, and Anna dutifully goes to remove the rest of the photos and posters.

"If you must preach this drivel, at least do so in a productive manner," Ms. Thadeous says.

Anna looks at Lars. She has been gradually losing confidence in him, and this incident does nothing to raise him in her eyes.

"So what do we do now?" she asks after Ms. Thadeous exits the room.

"We think," Lars says, but nothing in his voice gives Anna faith that he has answers.

26

DUSK. THE BUS HAS JUST pulled into the high school parking lot after a long field trip to the National Steinbeck Center in Salinas. Lars is still asleep, his dark head against Anna's shoulder. Everyone around them is stretching, then, after being given permission, they turn on their phones, begin to call and text their parents for rides home, a flurry of small *dings* erupting from nearly every seat. Anna powers up her phone to call her mother. She sees that she has missed twelve calls, caller ID blocked on all of them, no messages left. She dials her mother's cell, but gets voicemail. Same on her father's. She tries the house number, although no one ever answers that, and no one ever checks the voicemail box, a sore point for her mother who wants to disconnect it, but Anna's father, ever conservative, feels safer with a landline in case of emergencies. In the closet he even keeps an old-fashioned rotary phone that doesn't require electricity for when they lose power—as they invariably will when the Big One comes, he says.

No one picks up. Anna sighs and dials her mother's cell phone again. Still no answer.

Anna nudges Lars.

"You'll have to call your parents," Anna says.

He shakes his head. They both know that even if he can reach them, there will be a long delay before they come. They'll be in the middle of a prayer session, or reading, and his call will float out of their minds as soon as he hangs up. Still, he takes Anna's cell phone and dials. As they expect: no answer, and no way to leave a message. They start walking home. Two miles. An easy thirty-minute walk. Anna passes the school on her runs every day. But the temperature has dropped with the sun and neither of them is dressed for evening.

They turn left on Columbe and head south toward El Camino, that sea of car dealerships, strip malls, and fast food eateries named after the orchards they replaced. The Cherry Farm Center. Smith's Ranch Shops, Orange Farm Shopping Mall. Anna is filled with a sense of exhilaration triggered somehow by the steamed-up windows of the pho shops, the scent of jasmine and lavender wafting from the foot-massage parlors, the brake lights of the cars lined across all four lanes of traffic, the crisp wind against her face. Even the teenaged boys boisterously shoving each other as they exit the video arcade at the corner of Matilda and El Camino seem touched with grace. Anna finds herself filled with an aching love for everything around her—the last gasp of a doomed civilization. They pass a storefront megachurch, with a fluorescent sign out front. *Turn off your phone and say hello to Jesus!* A car stops too suddenly at the corner and another car bumps into its bumper, but even that event is a blessed one, for the two well-dressed people who emerge from the cars—one man, one woman—greet each other cordially, inspect the respective front and back of their vehicles, shake hands, and drive off. A sort of delight bubbles inside of Anna. Lars looks at her curiously. He can sense something. She can't keep the smile off her face. God has bestowed a gift on her, this magic evening. She used to try to be analytical, figure out what she had done, choices she had made, to get this feeling, anything that seemed to hint at cause and effect. But now she knows, this is unearned benevolence. Yet she is so grateful that she has to restrain herself from making promises to retroactively earn it: She will make her bed and straighten her room, she will be nicer to her parents. That would only cheapen His gift. He has bestowed this joy on her precisely because she doesn't deserve it. She takes Lars's arm, and laughs out loud. He is startled. She has not exactly been a lighthearted companion in the months they have known each other.

Anna's phone rings, She checks. *Blocked.* She ignores it.

Many of the stores already have their Christmas decorations up, although Halloween has barely passed. Anna will not be celebrating the holiday this year. Christmas will be a time of fasting and renunciation. Still, she is as excited by the lights as she was when she was a small child. Her father would buckle her into the car and drive around the South Bay, seeking the most garishly decorated houses, the ones blasting out the most colorful lighting. Inevitably, the most splendid Christmas decorations would be in the most implausible neighborhoods, run-down cottages in South San Jose with tiny postage-stamp yards but every twig, every corner of the house adorned and blazing with lights.

Anna and Lars reach the edge of their subdivision. Here also, jolly Santas and cardboard reindeer and trees dripping strings of lights are beginning to appear. Some religious icons, but not many. Perhaps this is a good sign, the dropping of the pretense that this is anything but a pagan season.

They walk slowly, Anna savoring her lingering euphoria.

They turn the corner to the Street of Children's Names and stop. Violent flashes of red and blue lights. Dozens of people in the street, forming a semicircle around four police cars parked in front of Anna's house. She recognizes the foul Hendersons, and the Greens, and the older Fulsons, although she doesn't see Jim Fulson. Walkie-talkies are spitting out undecipherable crackling sounds. Half a dozen police are lounging around the squad cars, two leaning against Anna's mother's Ford in the driveway. No sign of her father's Toyota. The house is lit up as if for a party.

Anna starts running, leaving Lars behind, for once not caring what he does. By the time she arrives at the circle of people and begins to push her way through, she is out of breath.

"What's going on?" Anna calls, addressing no one in particular. Her chest hurts. Faces are turning toward her, full of both pity and excitement.

A policewoman hurries over. "Anna?" she asks. "Anna Franklin?"

Anna nods.

The woman picks up a device and speaks into it. "We got her." Then she puts her arm around Anna's shoulders and begins to gently walk her past the other uniformed officers into the house.

Anna brought this on, whatever it is. She knows that. She does.

PART III

Goodbyes

27

FACT: ANNA'S FATHER WAS DRIVING too fast. But was the light already red? Witnesses disagree. That the truck barreled full speed down Page Mill Road and roared into the intersection at El Camino at more than 50 miles an hour is another fact. Did the truck driver have the green light? Or was he anticipating it? Whatever the truth, the driver of the truck died instantly, as did Anna's mother and father.

Anna's Aunt Ginny and Uncle Bob fly in from Columbus, but because the will is simple and clear—Anna's father was a lawyer, after all—they have little to do. It is impossible to display the ribbons of flesh and splintered bone. Cremation is the only option, and so Anna's aunt and uncle are able to take action without dithering.

None of Aunt Ginny and Uncle Bob's other decisions are wise ones. As Anna's parents lacked connection to any church, her relatives opt to hold a memorial at the house, catered by a delicatessen known locally as The Rat Trap. Her aunt can't even order provisions.

"We'll have ham," she says into the phone. "No, turkey. Four pounds. No, six pounds." She posts the wrong time for the gathering in the *Sunnyvale Times,* and when guests start showing up two hours earlier than expected she panics and simply points to the living room. She then escapes to the kitchen without introducing herself or offering food or drink. Anna's mother had been equally shy but possessed far more social bravado. She may have quaked inside, but Anna's mother would have pulled the situation off with aplomb. A magnificent deceiver.

Anna watches from the top of the stairs. The initial awkwardness of a hostessless gathering doesn't last long. Three neighborhood husbands disappear and twenty minutes later burst in through the front door carrying provisions: potato chips and pretzels, carrot sticks and sliced apples, and half a dozen extra-large pepperoni pizzas. Four cases of microbrewery beer appear on the dining room table. Those are quickly depleted and replaced by a keg of Coors, bottles of vodka and whiskey and tequila.

Anna is not crying. Anna is not sad. Anna is carefully tracking the number of hours since her parents left the earth. Thirty-six. Thirty-seven. Forty. She frets over the passing of each minute, believing that time matters, that the longer they are gone the less chance she has of getting them back. Insane thinking. Anna is insane. Acting as if her parents are trapped under water. As if there is only so much time to rescue them. Four to six minutes before brain damage. Ten minutes before they lose consciousness. Fifteen before they die. That first night she comforted herself with the thought that it had only been *five hours, just six hours, there was still hope.* As the night stretched on the idea came to her that if she just said the right thing, acted the right way, believed enough, He would permit them to return to her. Her responsibility is to have faith. Grieving is out of the question. She is too busy willing them back to life.

By 4 PM a surprisingly large, surprisingly affable crowd is milling through Anna's house. After finishing the food, everyone is apparently settling in for an afternoon and evening of hard drinking. No one appears to be thinking of leaving. Not out of a sense of guilt or neighborly duty, but because they are actually enjoying themselves. One of her father's Parkfield earthquake buddies is flirting with a baroque flutist friend of her mother's. The chair of the music department at the college where her mother was the on-call piano technician is laughing with her father's administrative assistant, a malnourished-looking young man Anna's father infected with earthquake mania.

Even the older neighbors are mingling, talking directly to each other. A strange sight. So pervasive is the joie de vivre that the old guard is actually speaking to the younger set.

Anna is under siege. Hands reach out to reverently touch her shoulders, arms, back, as she wanders through the rooms, as if her nearness to tragedy bestowed sacred powers. That her garments were holy relics. But she refuses all direct and indirect offers of solace. To every apology (*I'm sorry, I'm so very sorry*) she is silent. No one can make her speak a word. She watches the clock.

She has re-shaved her head. Eschewing color, she's wearing a pair of her mother's white capris and one of her father's white cotton work shirts. She has neither shoes nor socks on. She keeps her arms folded across her chest. She tries not to listen to the blasphemous chatter. *Your parents are in a better place.* They are not. *They were good parents, they loved you.* Yes, too good, and too much. But sinners, just the same.

To believe is essential. For, less than two days ago, Anna thought she still had enough time to wean her parents from their earthly concerns. To help them see truth, channel their energies more appropriately toward Him. The stakes were so very high. Now they have been cast naked into the abyss. Unprotected. And when the unholy dead are reanimated, when the foul ranks arise and take up weapons against believers, Anna's mother and father will be among them. When Anna battles the abomination to come she will be smiting her own flesh. Anna leans against her mother's piano. Her head aches. She hasn't seen Lars. Not since. Not since. Everything around her she taints.

"Anna!"

Martha is suddenly at Anna's side. Anna doesn't know which unlucky person told her about the accident. Did Martha receive a call? Or was she alarmed by the silence? She and Anna's mother spoke three or four times a day. All Anna knew was that Martha had appeared at the house yesterday morning, nearly assaulting the woman from Child Protective Services. She had strode across the living room, stopping in front of the couch where Anna sat. At first they had just looked at each other. They'd never been close. Too much jealousy, too many disputes over territorial rights to Anna's mother's time and attention. Martha had stared at Anna, then around the room as if expecting her mother to appear. Her eyes fell on the piano before she left the room without saying a word.

Today Martha exhibits no emotion. Like Anna, she does not appear to be grieving. She reaches her arms around Anna's shoulders, supporting Anna's full weight with no apparent effort. Without her help Anna would have fallen; she hadn't realized she was so weak. Anna reaches back and feels for the piano, finds it, and manages to pull herself free from Martha. She discovers she can stand on her own. Martha steps away.

"I like the look," she says, gesturing to Anna's white clothes. Anna is the recipient of one of Martha's rare smiles. She is radiant in her grief. Anna understands, not for the first time, why her mother loved her. They stand in silence, but Anna is not uncomfortable. People are giving them space, pretending to ignore them.

Martha appears to be searching for something to say.

"Tell me about your God," she says. It comes out clumsily. Several nearby neighbors stop talking to listen.

"Yours, too," Anna says. She motions around the room. "Theirs too."

"Perhaps. But let's take a pass on that particular discussion for now." Martha says.

Anna feels patronized, and a tremendous anger she's been holding at bay breaks through. "What do you want to know?" Anna manages to ask. Her voice is full of contempt. More people around them lean in.

"Is She a merciful God?" Something Anna's mother and Martha shared, this refusal to use a masculine pronoun when referring to Him.

"Why?" Anna asks. She's under no illusion that Martha is genuinely interested. Martha's heart, like Anna's parents', is utterly closed. She'll only attempt to manipulate Anna using words. This is so akin to what Anna's mother would do that Anna's heart is suddenly pierced. She looks at her watch and starts trembling again. More time has passed. Too much time. Outside, the sun is long gone. Anna can see a pale sliver of moon out the window. Her parents are slipping away.

Martha takes a step forward and places her hands on Anna's shoulders, but Anna pushes her off. She inhales deeply.

"Why?" Anna repeats. "What does merciful have to do with anything?"

"I was simply wondering. If you can't cut yourself any slack, perhaps She will?" Martha asks. A small circle has opened up in the crowd, with Martha and Anna in the middle.

Anna's anger makes it almost impossible to speak. Finally, she forces some words through her lips. "They are beyond mercy," she says. "They chose their path. Now they must reap the consequences." Someone behind Anna gives out a little whistle.

"They?" Martha asks. She is standing straight, her hand flat on Anna's mother's piano as if seeking sustenance from it. "Do you mean your parents?"

Anna repeats to Martha the words she'd written on her parents' mirror the previous night with permanent marker. "The LORD *is* slow to anger, and great in power, and will not at all acquit *the wicked*." Her voice is louder than she intends, but that is of no importance. More words are coming. Terrible words.

Martha takes a step back. She is among the crowd circling Anna. All conversation in the room falls away. "Anna," Martha says. "Annie, darling, you can't possibly mean this. We're talking about your parents! Not some abstract religious theory!"

"You're right," Anna says. "There is nothing abstract about this. His fury is poured out like fire, and the rocks are thrown down by him," she says, and she means to be heard by everyone in the room. *"And I will make your grave, for you are vile."*

Utter silence. Anna looks around. Some concern. Some disapproval. Some amusement. Mostly, people have their polite faces on, as if listening to the rant of an unhinged street preacher. Only one face comforts Anna. Mrs. Goldschmidt. She is sitting in the corner with her husband. They are not drinking, not even holding cups. Anna doubts they have spoken to anyone. Mrs. Goldschmidt's face, always pale, is almost white in the low light. Her expression, blissful. She keeps her eyes on Anna and nods. Her hands are folded quietly in her lap, but as Anna watches, she unclasps them. Slowly, she raises her right hand several inches in the air. She makes a sort of gesture—a circle? a half wave?—before lowering it again to her lap. She then nods once more. Anna finds she can breathe again.

People resume their conversations, but more quietly. Many continue to glance over at Anna and Martha. A dim-witted software engineer from Anna's father's company leans in and wiggles his fingers to get her attention.

"Your faith must be a great comfort to you," he says.

"Sometimes it is," Anna says. "Sometimes less so."

Martha raises a warning hand to the man. She manages another one of her smiles for Anna. "Little Man," she says, and there is great affection in her voice. "Call me when you need me." She moves away without attempting to touch Anna again. Hands reach out and pat Martha on the back as she passes.

"Anna." A voice behind her, this time a man's, and too close. Anna prepares for another attempted embrace, stiffens her shoulders and arms to make it as uncomfortable as possible for whoever it is. Then she sees that it's Jim Fulson, and next to him, Lars. Lars as Anna has never seen him. A frightened Lars. Lars at a loss. He looks even smaller than usual. He glances everywhere except at Anna.

Jim Fulson speaks again. He says the first sensible thing Anna has heard all day.

"You need to eat." He holds out a plate with a slice of pepperoni pizza on it, some carrot sticks. Anna realizes she is hungry, and takes the plate. Lars and Jim Fulson watch her wolf down the food. Then Jim Fulson says another sensible thing.

"Go get your running things on. I'll wait for you outside."

When Anna hesitates, he gives her a little push. "That's right, come on," says Jim Fulson.

In ten minutes Anna is out in front of the house in her sweats. Jim Fulson is already there, stretching. Anna follows his example, reaches down and extends her right leg, then her left. "Okay," he says, "let's do it," and they take off. Anna feels lighter the farther they get from the house, and by the time they reach Caribbean Drive she's fallen into her usual rhythm.

"How uncomfortable is that hair shirt under there?" he asks, reaching out and tugging on Anna's orange Sharks sweatshirt.

"What would you know about that?" Anna asks. She doesn't look at him, but concentrates on putting one foot in front of the other without stepping on any breaks in the cement. *Step on a crack, break your mother's back.* Then she remembers that's no longer a problem.

"I've been talking to Lars, trying to understand how your . . . faith . . . would affect how you deal with this," he says.

He pauses to give Anna a chance to respond, but she just keeps watching her feet as they pound the cement. Right. Left. Right. Left. So he continues.

"I'm not going to tell you what I believe in the hope that it may comfort you," he says. "I doubt it would comfort anybody. But I am going to tell you to stop being so goddamned arrogant."

Arrogant? Anna stumbles. She had expected gentleness, perhaps a clumsy attempt to provide solace, and had armed herself against it, was prepared to attack. She hadn't expected to be attacked herself.

"Yes," he says. "Thinking of yourself as some all-important being. As someone who is so special that God selected you to make an example of. I notice he didn't smite you personally, but instead chose to teach you a lesson by killing innocent bystanders."

"Not so innocent." Anna almost breaks down as she says this. Her steps falter. Her breathing gets more labored. She thinks of her mother, stroking the piano keys, of her father, the way he'd look at her mother when he thought no one was paying attention. How deeply childlike their slumber was at night—it was a family joke that nothing could rouse them after 10 PM. How cheerfully they greeted the day. Like people with clear consciences. Like people with nothing to fear.

"Aren't you being a little narcissistic?"

Anna is growing angry. Like her father, when she gets mad, she goes faster. She accelerates until Jim Fulson finally falls behind.

"Prick," she says over her shoulder. She is straining so hard she can barely force the words out.

He laughs and, seemingly effortlessly, catches up to Anna. "That I am," he says. Anna clenches her teeth and runs on, refuses to look at him.

They're nearing the high school now. It's growing dark, but cars are still in the parking lot. Anna had forgotten that for most people it was a day just like any other. Coaches and athletes finishing practice, and teachers going home after prepping for the next day. Both Jim Fulson and Anna see Ms. Thadeous at the same time. She's getting into her car, one haunch already on the seat, when Jim Fulson calls out.

"Clara!"

She turns, too quickly, upon hearing his voice. And although she doesn't exactly smile it's as if the sun has risen.

Then she sees Anna and the light is swiftly tamped down. She gets out of the car, and practically runs toward them, stumbling a little in her heels. "Anna," she says. "Annie." And holds out her arms. Anna goes straight into them. She is so tall, and Ms. Thadeous so diminutive, that Ms. Thadeous's head rests on Anna's shoulder as if she is the one requiring comfort. But Anna feels Ms. Thadeous's body's warmth even through her thick cotton layers, and with it such an outpouring of kindness that she is utterly humbled, for it is more than a sinner like Anna deserves. By the grace of God only is she able to accept it. Jim Fulson makes a point to look elsewhere. Somewhere during that timeless interval the sun sinks behind the Santa Cruz Mountains, the air turns chilly, and Anna's tears cease. She continues holding Ms. Thadeous. Some gifts are too precious. Praise the Lord.

28

THEY ARE SITTING IN MURPHY'S Tavern on Maude. Ms. Thadeous orders Anna a glass of white wine and a gin and tonic for herself. Jim Fulson sticks with plain tap water, no ice.

Anna is no stranger to alcohol, as her parents—her father in particular—were of the school that giving children early exposure removed its mystique and potential for abuse. But she's never cared for the taste. She takes only tiny sips yet somehow the glass is quickly emptied. Ms. Thadeous orders her another. Drink this one more slowly, she cautions. She gets her own drink refilled as well, but Jim Fulson continues to nurse his glass of lukewarm liquid, still three-quarters full.

They are all calm. A jukebox is playing some eighties Madonna song. At the next table, a man and a woman in their twenties are talking quietly.

"What happens next in the valley of death?" Jim Fulson asks.

"Jim," says Ms. Thadeous.

"I'm just saying," he says. You'd think he was the one drinking, his manner is so strange. "All paths seem to lead to the same place. It's like one of those mazes, you think you're going one way, you think you've been clever, and fooled everyone, and then suddenly you're back where you started."

"What is he talking about?" Anna asks Ms. Thadeous.

"Ask me yourself, prophetess," Jim Fulson says, without looking at Anna.

His words trigger something Anna hasn't thought of in years. Paths that lead back to the beginning. Getting lost, and increasingly frightened, and then finding a way out. Endless rows of mature corn bathed in a golden light. The salty smell of the nearby sea. Pumpkins glowing orange against stacked bales of pale straw.

Anna speaks slowly to keep from losing the vision. "Did you ever go through that corn maze? The one in San Gregorio? The one they always mowed in the field there? Off Route 84—the first one, before the other pumpkin farms started imitating it?"

Jim Fulson sits up straight. "Wait a minute," he says. "Just wait." His forehead wrinkles.

"We went every year," Anna says. "My father and I. It was our Halloween ritual. Dad refused to go to Half Moon Bay for the Pumpkin Festival, he hated the crowds. But we'd go to San Gregorio and pick our pumpkins there, then sneak into the maze because he said it wasn't worth paying five dollars each to get lost in some goddamned failed corn crop. We'd go in through the exit and do it backward, find our way to the entrance where the farmer took the entrance fee. That was my father's idea, anyway. But we never beat the maze. Every year we ended up cheating and broke our own way out of the corn into the pumpkin field. It was just like you said: you'd go down one path and find yourself back where you started. We tried everything, breaking off bits of the stalks to mark the paths we'd been through, digging little holes in the ground, but nothing worked. I was terrified by it, year after year. My father persisted; he wanted to teach me not to be afraid. The maze always won."

"The maze always wins," says Jim Fulson.

Anna is smiling, Anna is crying. "Once we mistimed it, went in right as the sun was setting. The sun went down while we were still lost, so we couldn't even cheat because we didn't know which way was east or west. My father just stood in the middle of the maze and bellowed. The farmer came in a panic, but refused to lead us out until we paid. My dad only had a twenty. The farmer took it, refused to give us change. We never went back."

"Goddamned farmers," Jim Fulson says.

Ms. Thadeous signals the waitress for another refill of her glass, shakes her head when the waitress offers to bring another for Anna.

"When was this?" Jim Fulson asks.

"Ages and ages ago," Anna says. "But I've missed it. Parkfield couldn't compare to the corn maze. Not even close."

"Parkfield," says Jim Fulson. "Yet another path that leads straight to the heart of the matter."

Anna is having trouble following him. She realizes how tired she is.

"And what exactly is that, Jim?" Ms. Thadeous asks. Whatever glow Anna had imagined she'd seen on Ms. Thadeous's face earlier is gone. Her glass is now empty. She tips it to her mouth and starts crushing the remaining ice between her teeth.

"Annie knows," says Jim. "Let's have Annie tell us. For someone so young, Annie's figured it all out."

"Jim, you're talking about a very mixed-up young girl, a girl who's just experienced a terrible loss," says Ms. Thadeous.

"Still," says Jim Fulson, "she's got her finger on the pulse. Don't you, Annie?"

"I do," Anna says. The wine has sharpened, not dulled, her wits. She suspects that if she gets up she might stumble, but her brain is agile. It's doing cartwheels. She can read Jim Fulson's mind.

"Give us one of your quotes," he says. "Let's put that wonderful photographic mind to work."

"Jim," says Ms. Thadeous.

"No," he says. "Let's have it. Let's have a little fire and brimstone."

"Okay," Anna says. "You asked. You shall receive."

Anna clears her throat. *"That terrible day of the LORD is near. Swiftly it comes—a day of bitter tears, a day when even strong men will cry out. It will be a day when the LORD's anger is poured out—a day of terrible distress and anguish, a day of ruin and desolation, a day of darkness and gloom, a day of clouds and blackness, a day of trumpet calls and battle cries. Down go the walled cities and the strongest battlements!"*

Anna's proclamation silences every conversation within ten feet of their table. Over at the jukebox, Tammy Wynette croons through a full chorus of *Stand by Your Man* before Ms. Thadeous speaks.

"Where on earth did you dig that one up?"

"Zephaniah 1:14-16," Anna says. "But there's more. *Because you have sinned against the Lord, I will make you as helpless as a blind man searching for a path. Your blood will be poured out into the dust, and your bodies will lie rotting on the ground. Your silver and gold will be of no use to you on that day of the Lord's anger. For the whole land will be devoured by the fire of His jealousy. And He will make a terrifying end of all the people on earth."*

Saying the words is less satisfying than usual. Something has shifted. Anna feels less certain. She wonders if her earthly loss has turned her into a coward, if this is why Lars looked so frightened at her parents' memorial service. To speak of death figuratively is one thing. To apply the word *dead* to her mother, her father, is enough to make a stone weep.

"That's what I'm talking about," says Jim Fulson, and Anna gets the feeling he understands something she doesn't. He's rolled up the sleeves of his shirt. In the dark room his long scars glow white. Marks of beauty. Beauty marks. Anna does something she's always wanted to do—reach out a tentative finger and trace one of the scars all the way up his arm, from his wrist to the crook of his elbow. Jim Fulson shivers.

Ms. Thadeous is watching them. "You two," she says. Her voice comes out thick. Her hands tighten around her empty glass. "What on earth have I taken on?"

29

MS. THADEOUS DRIVES ANNA HOME. Jim Fulson walks her to the
door. He opens it for her, then hesitates before letting go so
that it slams shut. "Damn it," he says, and gathers her into a hug.
Anna feels awkward, doesn't know what to do with her elbows,
but allows herself to be held for a moment. It doesn't feel like
Ms. Thadeous's hug earlier; it does not feel safe. Jim Fulson releases her, and then returns to the car without saying anything
else. Anna watches him get in. Ms. Thadeous says something
that makes him throw his head back in laughter, and then his
arm goes around her as she steers the car away from the curb.

Anna's Aunt Ginny is waiting. "I've put fresh pajamas on
your bed," she says, and then, half fearfully, "Where were you?
We didn't know whether to call the police. But someone saw
you leave with that boy across the street. They say he's okay."

"Very okay," Anna says.

Aunt Ginny looks worried. "Your mother never mentioned a boyfriend," she says. "I'm not sure she would have let
you go off with him like that. You're only seventeen. You're a
minor. They said he was older, out of college. He could get into
trouble for . . . anything . . . that might happen."

The slight buzz from the wine is wearing off and Anna realizes how tired she is. She hasn't looked at her watch since setting off on her run with Jim Fulson. She checks: it's been forty-five hours. Terror ignites in her chest. She brushes past Aunt Ginny to go upstairs. Aunt Ginny follows. At the landing Anna turns left into her parents' room, where she had slept the last two nights.

"No," Aunt Ginny says, and she grabs Anna's arm, an offense so heinous that Anna is speechless. "Your uncle and I decided. You'll be sleeping in your own room, your own bed. It's not right, you spending time in there."

Anna stops in the threshold of *in there,* her parents' room. The bed has been stripped. All the drawers are open. Empty. Photographs and lotion bottles and quarters and dimes and other miscellaneous items have been cleared from the tops of the dresser. Nothing more than a hotel room, ready for the maids. And the odor, the reek of air freshener and furniture polish, not the same, not the same at all.

"The smell," Anna says.

"Yes, there was that funny odor."

Her father's mineral and dirt samples. He'd forget and leave them in his pockets, empty them on the dressing table. Anna's mother hated it, used to make him leave his clothes outside the room and shower before he got into bed, but still the smell lingered.

Anna sits down on the bare mattress. That rich heady scent of earth and metal mixed with Lysol, her mother's attempt to cover it up. Gone. Replaced by the smell of artificial violets.

"You had no right," she says. Something that was hers, something precious, has been taken.

"We felt it was necessary," her aunt says. "You were getting morbid."

"We'll go to bed and discuss this in the morning," Anna says. She knows she sounds like her mother, down to the irritated inflection that clearly communicates to her aunt how tiresome she is being. Anna's mother told her she'd never gotten along with her little sister, bullied her, and her sister took it until she married a bigger bully. Once the younger sister, always the younger sister.

"Go to your room," Anna's aunt says, trying to sound firm. "You'll sleep there tonight."

"I'll sleep where I'll damn well please," Anna says. "In my new bed."

"That would be in Columbus," a male voice says. It is Uncle Bob. He has entered the room and stands behind Aunt Ginny. Anna doesn't know them well. She rarely visited her mother's childhood city. Anna's mother had loathed it, so Anna learned to hate the north side of Columbus where Uncle Bob and Aunt Ginny live, around the corner from where Anna's mother grew up and from where she fled immediately after high school. Anna had been ten the last time they'd visited, for her cousin Kenny's high school graduation. Their red brick house was in disrepair, a drainpipe hanging off the corner, stones missing from the façade above the front door. The backyard had been paved over with cement to create a basketball court for Kenny, and it being late May, dirty snow still lay in patches on the ground. A gray city, landlocked, stale air, stale food, even the songs on the radio were last year's hits.

Aunt Ginny's resemblance to Anna's mother is extraordinary, the same thick wavy hair, small but strong physique.

"Peasant stock," Anna's mother would say. "Never sick. We drop the babies in the field and keep working. Our type lives forever."

Aunt Ginny looks frightened. "Bob, we were just discussing that," she says. "No need for you to get involved." She gestures vaguely around the room, at the still-full walk-in closet, at Anna. "We're going to start sorting through the rest first thing in the morning, aren't we, Anna? In the meantime, Anna needs to sleep. She needs her rest."

"I'm staying here," Anna says, not moving. She finds that her fists are clenched. "And you're not touching anything else. Don't you dare go into that closet."

"Oh dear." The words escape Aunt Ginny's lips involuntarily. Strange to see someone who looks so much like her mother so terrified. Whatever she was feeling inside, Anna's mother projected fearlessness. Just recently Anna had begun to understand how fragile that façade was, how easily she could permeate it with a mere look. Had she only known. Had she only tried harder.

"Out!" Anna shouts suddenly. Then again, "Out!" Her aunt Ginny appears near fainting with alarm. Anna's head is clearing; she is gathering the strength that her aunt is losing.

Uncle Bob takes a step in her direction. He smiles. He is anticipating conflict. He is enjoying this. Anna picks up the lamp from the top of her mother's dressing table, pulls the cord so the plug comes out of the wall socket.

"Anna!" says Aunt Ginny, and her voice is thin; she is beseeching now, she sounds positively desperate. "You don't know what you're doing. What could happen."

"Fuck that," Anna says.

Her aunt winces and steps back, nearly colliding into Uncle Bob, who has taken another step toward Anna. Aunt

Ginny looks at his face and what she sees there almost un-hinges her.

"Oh my God," says Aunt Ginny, and retreats all the way to the doorway. Her hands go up in the air, wave excitably.

She is so much like Anna's mother, Anna experiences a sharp hiccup of pain, and involuntarily glances at her watch. Still forty-five hours. Only minutes have passed. Cold perme-ates her stomach, rises to her chest, too much time is gone now, and the brutal *unreasonableness* of it bubbles into her head and turns into rage. She is standing close to a window. She is holding the lamp in her hands, and then she isn't. What. Have. I. Done. After the initial shocking crash through the window-pane, they hear a muffled thump as the lamp lands on the lawn below.

"I would have thought you'd have enough of broken glass." Uncle Bob doesn't speak much, but when he does, it wounds. *He holds everything inside until it hurts him, and then lets it out in a way that hurts others,* Anna's mother told her once, after a long and weepy call from her aunt. A sullen mountain of a man. Anna's parents had despised him.

"Get out of this room," Anna says to him. She shivers in the wind blowing through the window. "You. Now."

Anna's uncle has a disconcerting habit of taking his time. Just swinging his large head around to get her in view takes him a good three seconds. Aunt Ginny retreats farther, into the hallway, her hands still waving, but silent.

"What's that you said?" asks Uncle Bob.

"You heard," Anna says.

"I don't think you quite understand the situation," says Uncle Bob. Anna wonders if there's something physiologically wrong with him, the way he moves his head to address her, then looks at the broken window, then back to her.

"Honey, go easy," Aunt Ginny calls from the hallway. "She's just a kid."

"Maybe," his head swings to the right, toward his wife. "Maybe," he repeats. "But I've had enough." He moves into position to get Anna in view again. "You. Hey. I'm talking to you."

The room is now quite chilly. Uncle Bob is slowly advancing and Anna is backing up, stepping away from him and closer to the window, and for a lunatic moment even wonders if he intends to push her out.

Words come to her. "You are cursed," she says. This stops him from coming any closer, he appears astonished that she would speak, that she would still have the power of words. The arrogance of bullies. But Anna has seen her share in school. She knows how easily spooked they can be. *"For by strength shall no man prevail,"* she says. *"But the wicked shall be put to silence in darkness."*

"Whatever that's supposed to mean," says Uncle Bob; Anna has his full attention, his bull-like head bowed as if about to charge. "Sticks and stones. Don't forget, I'm your guardian. Doesn't that wacko religion of yours say anything about honoring your parents? Well, I'm your parent now. And don't look at your aunt. This is not about her, this is between you and me. As far as authority goes, I'm it, baby."

"Is that a fact," Anna says. Her uncle is several feet closer, but approaching her more slowly, like she is a rabid dog. Anna picks up the top book from her father's bedside stack, weighs it in her hands. Her uncle takes another step. With both hands she lifts the book above her head and heaves it with all her strength through the second window. Another loud crash, another thump. Both of them are sprayed with flying shards of glass. Anna's uncle involuntarily backs out the door, covering his eyes. Aunt Ginny screams. Anna seizes her chance. Before either of them recovers, she's across the room, slamming the bedroom door.

"When you're reasonable we can talk," Anna says, and turns the lock.

Pounding, and obscene threats from the other side of the door.

"Quiet," Anna says, to roars of outrage. She sinks onto the bare mattress, hugging herself to keep warm.

The pounding on the door continues, gets louder. Anna ignores it. Taking armfuls of clothing from the closet, she makes the bed as well as she can, using her father's shirts to cover the mattress, and her mother's dresses and long skirts as blankets. She improvises a pillow out of one of her father's sweaters that she finds in the laundry hamper, and lies down. Minutes pass. Perhaps hours. She can't sleep. The wind whispers through the broken windows. A harvest moon has risen, implausibly large and orange, and has fixed itself in the sky just above Jim Fulson's house. His red truck is in the same position on the street as it was earlier. His rec room is dark. Whatever is happening between him and Ms. Thadeous is happening elsewhere.

Still cold, Anna rummages through the closet again and puts on her father's robe as a sort of jacket. Through the pocket she feels something that makes a noise when she moves: her father's lucky coins. He always had change in his pockets, felt naked without it, he'd say. Even in his bathrobe, he didn't feel secure without a few dozen pennies or nickels or quarters.

He liked the dull clang as they hit each other, the feel of cold metal at his fingertips. Anna has seen him steal from the Take-a-penny-leave-a-penny bowls at cash registers if he felt what he was carrying in his pocket didn't have enough weight or make a sufficient jingle. Anna is suddenly overwhelmed with a sense of what she has lost. She reaches into the pocket and brings out a quarter. A talisman. Although a superstitious act and therefore against His will, she kisses the coin and is finally able to sleep.

30

ANNA DOESN'T HAVE TO GO to Ohio right away after all. She—or rather Martha—wins a reprieve. She can stay until the end of the semester, until Christmas. As it turns out, Anna has enough credits to graduate a semester early. Then she goes to Columbus, where she will be under the care of her aunt and uncle until her eighteenth birthday in May. Until the end of the fall term, however, she'll stay with the Goldschmidts.

Weeks after the memorial reception, the pans of lasagna, plates of cookies, tossed salads with the notes *please return the bowl when done* are still coming, left on the Goldschmidts' front steps with discreet knocks. Anna can't force anything down; she is losing weight, vanishing. A wraith. She misses more school than she attends. The notices from the school district pile up at the Goldschmidts', but they are as uninterested in opening them as Anna is.

Without Anna, Lars is making better inroads at school. He's managed to gather together a growing cadre of outcasts. Now in the cafeteria Lars is surrounded by a table of admirers, spends time with them at church, even down in the Goldschmidts' rec room. His own ministry. His own disciples. Anna was merely a test case, the opening act for the soon-to-go-platinum Lars show. Anna doesn't care. She is quickly fading from the world.

A *For Sale* sign is staked into the lawn of her former home. Mail is still being delivered. Martha swings by several times a week to pick it up, to sort through anything important related to the estate. Anna says nothing to her. She has plans. She'll be eighteen in May. She'll have money from the house and her parents' retirement accounts. But she tells Martha none of this. She has decided to keep her own counsel. She is corresponding with Fred Wilson weekly now.

Dear Anna,

Yes I am looking forward to you joining us as an intern next summer when you're of age. I hope you are continuing with your Bible reading and studying, for there is much to make sense of in these times. You strike me as a particularly sensible girl, however, and your devotion to our cause warms my heart. Let's continue corresponding about this opportunity. We have some months before your birthday in May.

Affectionately,
Fred

Anna ramps up her workouts, is running three, four times a day. She runs faster and faster, punishes the earth by strik-ing a blow with each step. She spits the bile out of her mouth onto the sidewalk and still it comes, a font of poison. Street-lights flicker when she passes, trees wither, children wince, dogs whimper. She realizes she is not mourning, she is murderous. She squashes a fly flat with her palm on her thigh, so fast are her reflexes, so hot is she for blood.

In the safe-deposit box Martha had found a gold and opal rosary with Anna's grandmother's initials engraved on it. Anna finds it a useful device. For each of the pink translucent stones she repeats one word ten times as her feet pound the ground. Any word. A way of acknowledging the permanence, the intractability of her despair. For again she is descending. She is trying to protect herself, trying to stay afloat, only allowing herself to realize how much she has lost: a little every day, a little is all she can bear. Compartmentalize. That's what Dr. Cummings used to say; for once, useful advice. Anna separates memory fragments. Her father bent over one of his geological maps, colored pencil in hand. Her mother listening to her beloved Hindemith. But there is pain even in such small moments. Why didn't He give her some hint, some sign of what was coming?

Anna holds the rosary in her hand as she runs, counts off the beads as she sees things in His world that she knows are worth praising, even though nothing now is either useful or beautiful. This morning: *fence fence fence fence,* ten times. Then, in succession, *window window window window* and *rock rock rock rock rock.* And because the harvest moon has not yet disappeared despite the fact that the sun is almost overhead, *moon moon moon moon,* a sort of brain aesthetic that relieves her of the need to think. She forces herself to seek meaning, resonance in the words themselves. As she nears the Goldschmidts' house, she cycles back to the first word: *fence fence fence fence fence.* A resting place for blue jays, a support structure for bougainvillea. It keeps such things that must be contained, contained. It has its place in the world, and therefore it must be good. She must have faith. She must continue to have faith, as difficult as it is. Praise the Lord.

She goes straight to the spare room in the Goldschmidts' house. Her bed is a pile of sheets and blankets on a thin foam mattress, but the fabric is too soft for her rough skin, she throws all the bedding into the corner and lays down to sleep on the bare cold hardwood floor, but it still isn't enough to cool her body. A malignant growth of flesh surrounding a handful of bones. Adam's rib. Evolve or die. She isn't sure which will happen to her.

31

MOST PEOPLE SPILL INANITIES. KIDS at school she barely knows approach her, say how sorry they are, some even have tears in their eyes. Anna believes that most are sincere, most are sincerely trying. But most start their sentences with *I:* I *am so sorry.* I *can't believe what you must be going through.* I *wish there was something I could do.* I. I. I. I. Putting themselves in her place, guiltily relishing that they don't have to stay there for too long, feeling virtuous that they tried. Anna doesn't listen, but not out of rudeness. It's that she can't stand the proximity; the kids stand too close, some even touch her.

She's been spending more time with Ms. Thadeous, a surprising source of comfort. A surprising source of wisdom.

They're in the chemistry lab, between classes.

Anna had always loved this room. Sometime in the years before Anna took her class, Ms. Thadeous had papered the walls with posters, newspaper headlines, scientific articles cut out of magazines, colorful diagrams, and charts. She'd printed out pieces from online archives that delved into the history of scientific discoveries Anna had never heard of. Anna could read about the launch of Sputnik and the invention of the birth control pill as if they were happening now, feel the excitement and skepticism of the era. Anna first learned about Rachel Carson's *Silent Spring* from Ms. Thadeous's wall, about the first cancer-causing gene being discovered in a chicken retrovirus. She could dive into that wall for months and not reach bottom. It is a window into the teacher Ms. Thadeous was when Jim Fulson first knew her.

"When you lose a parent, you grieve. But the world, although changed, is still recognizable," Ms. Thadeous tells Anna. "But when you lose your second parent, you lose your way, and you never get it back. Not completely."

"How do you know this?" Anna asks, but Ms. Thadeous ignores the question. Anna is perched on the corner of one of the sinks, Ms. Thadeous is at her desk, grading lab reports.

"You see a shadow fall across the face of a ninety-five-year-old woman in a wheelchair," Ms. Thadeous says, "you know what she's thinking? That she misses her daddy. It never goes away, that particular ache."

Ms. Thadeous says there are really only three types of people in the world. People with both parents, people with one parent, and people like Anna. Orphans. This marks the most important difference between individuals. "Not whether they are male or female, or Buddhist or Muslim or Jewish, or rich or poor, or what country they were born in," says Ms. Thadeous. "No. The single most important thing is whether they still have two parents, one parent, or none."

Anna feels shy, but she asks anyway. "Which category do you belong in?"

Ms. Thadeous says she belongs in a special fourth category, so small it doesn't bear mentioning. Then she changes the subject. "What's up with you and Lars?" she asks. "You don't talk. You hardly even look at each other."

"There's just no need," Anna says. "Nothing's wrong. There's simply nothing to say. We understand each other. We have an understanding."

"It doesn't feel like that kind of quiet," Ms. Thadeous says, but lets the subject drop.

Anna doesn't mention the real reason. She's confused about it herself. Seeing Lars at her parents' memorial party, his fear. He failed some essential test.

Besides, Lars doesn't seem to need her. Now, in the cafeteria, Anna sits alone. She quietly consumes what little her stomach can take and goes to the library for most of the lunch hour.

Ms. Thadeous says, "Can I ask a basic question?"

"Of course," Anna says, but she is nervous. Ms. Thadeous has a way of sneaking up with questions you're not prepared to answer. It serves her well in the classroom: She can smoke out fakery among students in a heartbeat.

"Why are you in such a hurry for it to happen—whatever you call it, the Apocalypse, Tribulation, End Days, whatever?" Ms. Thadeous asks. "Why can't you let everyone enjoy themselves a little longer? Allow them to party themselves into oblivion without all the Sturm und Drang? Or maybe just lead quiet, decent lives until the supposedly inevitable happens?"

"Because the sooner it happens, the sooner we can see His face." Anna repeats what she has said many times, to others. But here, in this room of science, to Ms. Thadeous, her words sound false. She thinks of the Bosch painting, of the bloody fight ahead, but feels only a pinprick of her former longing. Her parents. Their earthly bodies burned and discarded—she never asked Martha what happened to the ashes—and Anna feels a rare stab of uncertainty. It is quick, but goes deep, and she feels a twinge of terror.

"I don't buy that," Ms. Thadeous says. "No. For Lars, maybe. For the Goldschmidts, definitely. They genuinely want to rise up to heaven and the rest of that twaddle. But you? You're after something else." She gets up from her seat and goes over to her wall of clippings. She tears off a piece of paper, crumples it, throws it in the garbage can.

A moment of silence. "Then, of course, on some level I understand perfectly," Ms. Thadeous says. She is staring at her wall but doesn't appear to see it.

"You do?" Anna asks. Ms. Thadeous tears down another article, one with a complicated diagram. Nuclear fusion. The wall underneath glows a purer white than the rest of the room. Ms. Thadeous rips off another, this one from *Science,* an article about the *Australopithecus sediba.* Then another. She is dismantling the evidence of the old Ms. Thadeous, the one that Jim Fulson remembered. Anna understands that she is in the presence of an unstable element, one that could react in a number of different ways depending on the stimulus. She gets that feeling, which she often gets with Ms. Thadeous, of ground shifting under her.

"Who doesn't want to be a hero?" Ms. Thadeous asks as she steps onto a chair to reach the clippings higher up on the wall, pulls off a paper illustrating the chemical transmission of nerve impulses. "Most people don't take their fantasies to the length you have, of course. I had my dreams, too, you know," she says. "If anyone told me I'd end up in a chemistry classroom in a suburban high school I would have been appalled." She pauses. Her dark hair pulled back in a tight chignon, she could be a heroine herself: fierce, straight-backed, unyielding. "Actually," she says, "I *am* appalled," and indeed she sounds so stricken that Anna tips her head back to see Ms. Thadeous's face. On it: shame, deep and raw.

Later, in her room in the Goldschmidts' house, Anna recalls Ms. Thadeous's words. They resonate. They sting. She is lying on the floor in the dark. She has taken the sheet off the window to welcome the moon in. Occasionally, the headlights of a car flash through the room. Otherwise soft ambient moonlight. And suddenly Anna gets one of those sharp aches of grief that are so piercing she has to hold both hands to her chest with as much pressure as she can, like pressing on a wound that will bleed out without a tourniquet. And for the first time she questions the mission she has chosen: to help Fred Wilson bring a pure Red Heifer into the world, to bring about the end of everything. Why is she doing this? Why would she want anyone else to undergo this type of loss? Why would she actively work to make millions suffer the way she is suffering? *My God forgive me, for I know not what I am doing.*

32

ANNA GETS IN THE HABIT of going to the science room even when Ms. Thadeous isn't there. If Ms. Thadeous had made overly aggressive overtures to deepen their intimacy Anna would have stayed away. But she has somehow made this a safe place.

Ms. Thadeous is careless: she left the lab while still logged in to her PC. Anna sits at Ms. Thadeous's desk, goes through her computer files, sees the grades she's giving the other kids, what she's saying about them in her reports. She doesn't look at what Ms. Thadeous says about her, Anna. She doesn't want to know. Her online search history is unremarkable. No news. No blogs. Overstock.com. Amazon.com. Drugstore.com. She demonstrates no obvious curiosity about the world. More telling are the letters she composes and stores in a folder called *Never Send*. They are variously addressed to *Dear Mom, Dear Ted, Dearest Janice, Dear Grandad.*

Dear Mom,
Never. Never. Never. Never. Never.
Clara

Just at this moment, an email arrives from Jim Fulson. *It takes two.* What does this mean? Praise or condemnation? Affection or criticism? Anna answers it. *Yes it does.* She waits, but no reply comes. Anna goes back to the *Never Send* folder.

Dear Megan,
It is true we have unfinished business. But I am currently starting other business that I do intend to complete. You will have to be patient and wait your turn.
Clara

There's a tentative knock at the door of the chemistry lab. Lars, poised delicately in the doorway as if loath to enter without her permission.

"Hey there," he says, "I thought I'd find you here."

"And here is where you found me," Anna says.

It comes out sounding hostile, although Anna doesn't intend it that way, not much anyway. They are rarely alone these days, despite living in the same house. In school Lars and Anna have tacitly agreed to go their own ways. Death has separated them.

Lars has changed his tactics, has decided to go native. He applied, and was granted by the school administration, the right to form a legitimate club for the Pre-Rapturists. He calls it The End Days Committee and now has the official use of an empty classroom after school on Wednesdays where he carefully arranges his leaflets and photographs on a desk and attempts to interest whoever wanders by. He's managed to attract a small but growing band of followers. All male. A freshman who blundered in looking for the chess club and discovered much more interesting mental puzzles were to be found in Revelation. A sophomore clearly more enamored by Lars than by His message. A pair of Seventh-day Adventists looking to do a little converting of their own. Lars even sets up a card table with information and pamphlets outside of the gym during basketball games. He and his disciples are in fact surprisingly successful at engaging people in what look like serious conversations. Lars is no longer teased or tormented. The world has matured in the last three weeks. Everyone is suddenly more reasonable. Except Anna. She has lost her bearings.

Lars sits himself on the edge of Ms. Thadeous's desk. He has grown taller and gained weight. His jeans, previously loose, are snug around his hips. His hair is longer and curls around his ears, reaches his collar. Lars is coming into his own. Anna sees with a shock that he may grow into a handsome man.

Anna passes her hand down the back of her neck, restrains herself from scratching. She hasn't shaved her head since the night her parents died. Her hair is perhaps half an inch long and her scalp itches, a constant irritant.

A flash of movement on Ms. Thadeous's computer screen catches Anna's attention. An IM has popped up. *I'll be there.*

No, Anna types back, and hits *Enter.*

"This isolation isn't good for you," Lars says.

"What isolation?" Anna asks. "I live with your family. I go to school. I'm a productive member of society." Again, her voice is rougher than she intended. Anna is unsure where this hostility toward Lars is coming from, is dismayed at how little control she has over her emotions.

"Anna. Look, what happened to your parents was a tragedy . . ." Lars begins.

"It was God speaking more directly than usual," Anna says. She doesn't realize the truth of this until the words are out of her mouth. God was speaking to her. Pushing her in His direction.

Another message pops up. Jim Fulson again. *Why are you being so difficult? Why now?*

Anna replies again, simply, *No,* and sends it.

"I don't believe you are following the path God wants you to take." Lars's words so closely mirror Anna's thoughts that she is startled.

"You are no longer my guide in that way," Anna tells Lars.

"Nevertheless," he says. "You're off track. You should see Reverend Michael, talk to him."

Another message pops up: *Is this about last night? I thought we'd settled it.*

No, Anna types. *We did not settle anything.*

Another message, quicker this time. *I'm coming there—now.*

No! Anna types.

Just as rapidly the reply comes. *Yes. Signing off now.*

Anna is thinking of Jim Fulson, barreling over here in his red truck. She is thinking of the secrets between him and Ms. Thadeous. She is thinking of her night ghosting, and how she misses seeing Jim Fulson start off on his daily runs at dawn. She looks for his truck out the window every morning, but more often than not, these days, his truck is not there. His room is dark. Words rise in front of her eyes. She speaks them aloud: *"And the sun will be darkened, and the moon will not give its light; the stars will fall from the sky, and the heavenly bodies will be shaken."*

Lars allows himself a smile. "You've kept up with your reading at least. That wonderful memory. You should make better use of it."

"A habit," says Anna.

"More than that. A gift. Don't waste it."

"You sound like my parents," Anna says. She can't help it. The words just come out.

Lars has nothing to say to this.

The bell rings, and students begin to file into the room. Anna gets up from Ms. Thadeous's desk, grabs her backpack, and moves toward the door.

"Don't you have English now?" Lars asks. "I'll walk there with you."

Anna doesn't want this. Spending time with Lars these days makes her feel unwholesome. She shrugs. "I don't think I'm going," she says, trying to sound casual. "I don't like the book. It pretends to be profound, and misses the mark. But fools some people."

"Sounds like what you think of me," Lars says, and his smile isn't pleasant.

Anna doesn't comment, and her silence hangs heavy between them. "I've got to talk to Ms. Thadeous," she says. "You go on."

Ms. Thadeous wanders into the room at just that moment. Her hands are free, her step light. She is not in a hurry although the second bell has rung. She seems irritated to see Lars and Anna. "Get to class," she says. "Both of you," but her glance is mostly directed at Lars.

Lars gestures to Anna to come with him. She shakes her head. She doesn't belong in the class that is about to begin, yet takes a seat at the back of the room anyway. A couple of students look at Anna curiously, but no one challenges her.

Ms. Thadeous stands by her desk, picks up her attendance book, begins calling out names. Every thirty seconds or so she gazes out the window into the parking lot, then continues taking roll. She makes it to *h* when she spots what she's looking for outside. Anna realizes with a shock how beautiful Ms. Thadeous is, how very very beautiful. How could Anna not have noticed? She is too much. The next time Ms. Thadeous turns to glance out the window, Anna slips out of the room.

Anna isn't sure what she intends to do, just that she can't bear sitting in Ms. Thadeous's room, watching her grow more desirable the longer Jim Fulson waits outside. Her first thought is to join him in his truck, break the connection that is causing Ms. Thadeous's loveliness to blossom. But at the last minute Anna turns in to the girls' locker room, opens her locker, and dresses in her gym clothes even though she doesn't have PE until next period. When she emerges, Ms. Ingels nods at her benignly and gestures for Anna to get in line and rotate into the volleyball game in progress. Like everyone else, she's cutting Anna a lot of slack.

"Hey, Anna." Paulina and Joan. Nice girls, Anna sees now. Two years ago, when she was more tuned in socially, she wouldn't have been able to get past the one's lumpy bottom and the other's underarm hair. Three weeks ago, she would have nurtured a malevolent secret satisfaction that the two most popular girls in school, making fun of Paulina and Joan, would be eternally damned for their trivial ways. She finds herself simply grieving for them, for everyone.

"What is it, Anna?" asks Paulina. Anna must have made a noise. She seems genuinely concerned, is holding out a tentative hand, as if she's going to put it on Anna's shoulder.

"Nothing," Anna says, backing up slightly to avoid the touch, but in fact she's feeling peculiar. She's worried that she's about to suffer an episode. She hasn't had one since her parents died. Anna makes a smile for Paulina, puts her hand against the gym wall for support. It is reassuringly solid. Yet the vermillion aura slowly materializes, begins tingeing the edges of the gym, blurring Anna's vision. The smell. The dizziness.

"Paulina!" calls Ms. Ingels. "Get in there!" Paulina gives Anna one slow last look and runs to take her place in front of the net.

The floor begins to roll beneath Anna's feet. The wall she is leaning against undulates against her shoulder. Is this it? Did her father miss it by less than a month? Is this the Big One? There will be much rejoicing in Parkfield tonight. Anna falls to her knees, places her palms flat against the hard gym floor. Nothing is solid, nothing is still; like this she can't keep her balance. She carefully lowers herself all the way to the floor, onto her belly. No one else seems affected. The game is proceeding, an intense volleying back and forth. Girls on both sides of the net leap high into the air, swat the ball. The gym reverberates with violent slaps. *Boom. Boom.* Outside, the sun disappears behind a cloud and the rays dim through the small windows high above. In the dull light the girls' skin seems to glow. But their movements slow, and the noises of the game begin to fade. A mist forms over the volleyball net. No one else notices, they continue to leap and slap. Yet it is growing and spreading, putrid and dark. Something is terribly wrong, something is coming. The volleyball is practically suspended in the air, inching upward, peaking, and then moving down toward the adoring faces that are worshipping it. And now the walls of the gym disappear, blown apart by dark clouds that continue to expand, and Anna can see that the grasses of the football field and the track and the yards of the houses surrounding the school are scorched and brown. In the distance, from the west, rising from the sea, appears a giant wave, arcing higher and higher, towering over the Santa Cruz Mountains, hundreds of feet high, a terrible and beautiful wall of deep green-blue water. When it breaks, it will engulf all of Silicon Valley, turn the former Valley of Heart's Delight into a giant churning whirlpool.

Anna is lying on her back, surrounded by faces. Ms. Ingels is bending over her.

"Anna," she is saying. "Anna, wake up. Gaby, get a wet towel from the locker room. Quickly. Beth, run to the office, get the nurse. And you, Jenny, go get Ms. Thadeous, tell her Anna's had some sort of fit."

"Not a fit," Anna begins, but a rough damp cloth is being pressed onto her face. For a moment she can't breathe, begins to panic. She struggles to sit up, is restrained, keeps trying. She finally manages to pull the towel off her face and can again inhale.

"Just lie there," says Ms. Ingels. "You're not well."

The cloud is still there, hovering above Ms. Ingels's head. Cracks are appearing in it, dark tendrils dropping down, writhing and twisting.

"*My God,*" Anna says.

"What?" Ms. Ingels asks. "Anna, I can't understand you. Speak up." Then, as the bell rings, Ms. Ingels calls, over her shoulder, "Everyone! To the showers!" She turns back to Anna. "Anna? Are you okay?"

"*Why hast thou forsaken me?*" Anna manages to ask before the cloud subsumes her.

33

THREE AM. ANNA AWAKE, AS usual, wandering from nearly empty room to nearly empty room throughout the Goldschmidts' house. Living without the comforts of an ordinary home has been surprisingly difficult. The Goldschmidts don't possess a single comfortable chair. In the kitchen, molded plastic stools are grouped around a pressed pine table. The living room holds four metal folding chairs, a hard, unwelcoming couch. The only soft materials are the blue-and-gold embroidered throw pillows Anna brought from her parents' house. Her grandmother's handiwork, elaborate loops and curlicues fray at the ends. Anna's mother had used one as a cushion for her piano bench.

Anna had mistakenly thought the austerity of the Goldschmidts' home would focus her mind, force her into a purer meditative space. The Goldschmidts seem inspired by the lack of amenities, the discomfort. They can sit for hours at their kitchen table arguing minute points of scripture. Anna used to listen in awe. No longer. Informed by her own reading, she finds their discussions vacuous, based on erroneous information and full of illogical or outright silly conclusions. It has been a sad awakening. She refuses to go to meetings at Reverend

Michael's church any longer. Tired of his bombastic grand-standing, she instead spends hours researching on the Internet, reading everything she can find, drawing her own conclusions.

His servants have turned out to be poor specimens indeed. Although she still has confidence in Fred Wilson, in what he is doing. That is something she can hold on to.

Anna's dreams are as vivid as ever. The less she sleeps, the more she remembers. Rich canvases teeming with fantastic images. She dreams endlessly about her parents' accident, understands now that it is her fault, her fault only. Anna's parents come to her room, but will not speak to her, their tears fall, wet her pillow and blanket. Who are they crying for? Sometimes she sees them naked, sitting calmly in their old living room, the sunlight streaming through the windows. Her mother's breasts, her father's genitalia fully exposed. No fig leaves, no modesty. Anna wakes up deeply ashamed.

For the first time in weeks, Jim Fulson's rec room light is on, a light in the wilderness. He has been neglecting his parents. Anna had watched his mother pulling the garbage to the curb, his father warily climbing a stepladder to change the porch lightbulb. Yet the more flaws he reveals, the more beautiful Jim Fulson becomes.

Anna steps outside and closes the door quietly behind her. She is not dressed warmly enough for mid-November. With no set plan, Anna walks toward the light in *C-A-R-O-L-I-N-E*.

She crosses the street, steps off the pavement onto the grass, walks around to the right side of the Fulsons' house. The California autumn night is so unseasonably cold that the grass is stiff, pricks her bare feet. The yard is no longer as well kept as neighborhood standards dictate. Jim Fulson has been letting it slide. Deep in the pleasures of his love affair. *Besotted*. Anna recognizes the bitterness of her word choice. Surely love is a good thing. Anna walks toward the rec room window.

Light slices through a gap between the curtains. Enough of an opening for Anna to crouch down and look inside. She's never seen Jim Fulson's lair before. It is very much like the rec room of Lars's house, its mirror image across the street. The furnace in the far right corner. Structural steel poles rooted in the cement floor at six-foot intervals. No remodel happened here. The only concession to improvement is that the rough cement walls have been painted a neutral cream. Nothing adorns them. Moving boxes overflow with clothes, books, and kitchen utensils. Electronics are stacked in another corner. The only light is emanating from a floor lamp leaning crazily at a 30-degree angle. The shadows it casts are not friendly. It is not a friendly room. On one side of it, a mockery of a bedroom: a dresser, a table with a lamp on it, a low bed. On the bed, Jim Fulson and Ms. Thadeous.

Ms. Thadeous's naked torso is surprisingly long and lithe for someone so petite. She is in fact beautifully proportioned, her clothed figure does not do her justice. The hollow dimples of her buttocks are deepened by shadows cast from the lamp. Jim Fulson, underneath, is mostly in the dark. This is a good thing. For the tableau is an awful one. Awe-ful. Do not worship false gods. A dangerous vision.

They are not looking at each other. Her face is turned to the side. Her eyes are open. He is staring unblinkingly, at the ceiling. Once he turns his head and appears to look right at Anna. She draws back, but his gaze continues traveling back and forth across the wall, as if reading a script. Anna would have thought they were just holding each other, torso to torso, except for the slightest movement of her hips, and flexing of her buttocks, the slight parting of her thighs. Anna does not want it to stop. She wishes she had the words to describe it. But the image is seared into her mind and will haunt her the rest of her life. That she is witnessing something holy and blessed by Him, Anna has no doubt. *His mouth is most sweet: yea, he is altogether lovely.*

34

ANNA HAS BEEN AVOIDING LARS. They pass in the hallway, Anna alone, but Lars accompanied by an ever-larger throng, girls as well as boys now, and no longer just the fringe. Lars is going mainstream. Usually Anna keeps her eyes down, avoiding any contact. But to her surprise, today he stops, waves his disciples to continue on without him, and pulls Anna out of the stream of other students to a quiet corner of the hall.

"Have you been corresponding with Fred Wilson?" he asks.

Anna is startled. She has said nothing of the email exchanges to Lars. "We've written," Anna says.

"Without telling me?" Lars asks. His tone is almost hostile. "I thought we had plans."

"We did," Anna says, then pauses. "We do," she corrects herself. But she has been thinking ahead to Christmas, to the pending move to Columbus, and how she will survive in her Uncle Bob's house until her birthday at the very end of May, when she'll be free to join Fred Wilson's outfit in Nebraska.

"Make sure to inform me of any developments," Lars says. "Fred is working on a matter of extreme importance. I need to be involved." He has grown grandiose, pompous.

Anna thinks about what Ms. Thadeous asked her, and asks the same of Lars. "Why? Why hurry things? Can't He be trusted to do things in His own time? Why does he need to be rushed? If the time is right, the time is right."

Lars is silent. He refuses to answer. When he does speak, his manner is stern.

"Have you changed your mind?" he says. "The Red Heifer was your particular interest. You thought you had a mission to fulfill. We've discussed all this at length."

"That's still true," Anna says. She doesn't say what she's thinking, which is that her parents' deaths have more than satiated her hunger for death. Lars is watching her closely.

"I am still as resolute," he says. "I will be ready to go to Nebraska on May 30th . . . I'm beginning to prepare my parents, and you'll be free of your guardians. That's still the plan?"

"That is the plan," Anna says. She adds, "Although I've always made it clear that you were coming with me. Fred Wilson insists on sending emails to me alone. He doesn't seem inclined to notice your involvement."

"That's not negotiable," Lars says. "I must be there too. Our work is bound together."

"Still?" Anna asks.

"I've been temporarily giving you time and space. I had other tasks to complete," says Lars.

"Your disciples," Anna says, and something in her voice causes Lars's face to become even colder. Is he taller than he was before? He seems more imposing.

The same deep voice, but it is less incongruous. He is growing into it. "My converts," he says.

Anna shrugs.

"Make sure you copy me on your next emails to Fred Wilson," he says. "Make sure he understands I'll be coming, too. That we will be working together to fulfill His prophecy." And Lars leaves Anna without waiting for a reply.

35

SATURDAY, NOVEMBER 24. MRS. GOLDSCHMIDT has obligingly called the attendance office every day for two weeks now to tell them Anna is ill. Anna sneaks into her old house to watch quiz shows. The cable has been shut down, but she can still get local channels, mostly soap operas and game shows. She learns many things from the latter. The thickest part of the human skin is in the palms of the hands and the soles of the feet. The coconut is a drupaceous fruit that Hawaiian women were once forbidden by law to eat. James Buchanan was the only bachelor president of the United States. Knowledge does not soothe. Anna switches to one of the few Christian channels in the Bay Area. Another quiz show. Moses was 120 years old at the time of his demise. A halberd killed Matthew the tax collector. A halberd? She looks it up. *A two-handed pole weapon that came to prominent use during the 15th and 16th centuries.* But surely the halberd didn't kill him? Surely an angry mob did? *Halberds don't kill people, Romans kill people.*

One morning she wakes to a perfect day. A gift. She thinks, *a beautiful day, wait until I tell Mom,* and the ache that inevitably accompanies such a thought is less than it has been. She is buoyed by possibility. The temperature is so mild she wears her summer workout clothes when she goes for her morning run. No need for jacket or sweats, feeling light as she runs through the streets. The lack of tree canopy is for once not a curse but a blessing, showering warmth and light upon all. Everyone is finding excuses to be outdoors. People are actually taking walks—something that never happens in Sunnyvale, the mechanical city—or biking, or basking in the sun. Even Lars's parents have dragged the molded white plastic chairs from their kitchen to the front yard, and are sitting there observing the scene.

For the first time in weeks Jim Fulson's truck is parked outside his house. Anna gathers her courage and knocks on the door. She remembers the run they went on the day of her parents' memorial party. She thinks about it often, enjoys the memory more than the actual experience. She wants a repeat, wants to pound down the sidewalk with Jim Fulson by her side on this beautiful, beautiful day. She wants to share it with someone. With him.

Jim Fulson's mother puts a finger to her lips as she unsteadily opens the door. "Still sleeping," she whispers. Two hours later, Jim Fulson emerges from the house. He stands on the small porch, stretches high, lifting his T-shirt up over his stomach, revealing a small paunch. Love has taken its toll. He glimpses Anna sitting with the Goldschmidts on their lawn and waves, but in a way that makes it clear he is not open to conversation. He has held himself aloof since the night of the memorial, the talk in the bar. This stings. Jim Fulson launches himself on his morning run. Anna prevents herself from running after him.

The *For Sale* sign in front of Anna's old home rattles slightly in the breeze. An insultingly low offer has come in from a childless couple. The realtor rejected it. Anna is glad.

Today, no place for morbid thoughts. Everything in Sunnyvale is shiny and new in the sunshine.

36

ANNA RUNS FARTHER AND LONGER than usual. Another Saturday to get through, not that weekends are any different from the weekdays now that Anna has pretty much quit school. Christmas is approaching. Just two weeks left to the term. Anna's aunt and uncle have already set the date for her to fly to Ohio. Just sixteen more days here. Then five months to endure until freedom.

Running back down her street toward *K-A-R-I-S,* Anna notices Jim Fulson standing next to his truck, one foot inside. "Hey," he calls in a friendly voice, as if they haven't been virtual strangers for more than a month.

"Hey yourself," Anna says, cautiously.

"I was thinking of going to the beach," he says. "Want to come along?"

"But it's so cold," Anna hears herself say. Why does she hesitate? After all, she'd be sitting thigh to thigh next to Jim Fulson in the tiny cab of his truck for the hour-long ride to the coast.

"No, it'll be great," Jim Fulson reassures her. "The coast is at its most beautiful on days like this." He hoists himself into the truck, settles in the driver's seat.

"Come on, keep me company," he says. "Clara has papers to grade."

Anna, displeased at being second choice, shakes her head, and starts into the Goldschmidts' house.

Jim Fulson shrugs, slams his door, and starts the truck. Then he hesitates. He rolls down the window, and leans out.

"Come on, it'd be good for you. Fresh air and all that. And you can tell me all your secrets."

"What secrets?" The question startles her.

"Why you and Lars are on the outs. What you think of going to Ohio. What will happen to the rest of us when you go," he says.

His upbeat mood is infectious. He is too charming. She climbs into the truck.

The drive to Half Moon Bay is quiet but not uncomfortable. Jim Fulson turns the radio on, occasionally leaning forward to push a button to a different station. The music he seems to like is what Anna has always despised—abstract jazz tracks without apparent key signatures or discernible beats. Yet today she finds herself drawn into the cool lines, feels the power in the dissonance, the shape-shifting of the notes and rhythms. When they finally reach the beach, and are walking along the shore, barefoot and slightly windburned, Anna asks Jim Fulson the question that has been on her mind.

"What you said before," Anna says. "Why do you care about my secrets anyway?"

Jim Fulson smiles at her with affection, much like Ms. Thadeous does.

"Haven't your ears been buzzing?" he asks. "You're a popular topic of conversation." He stops smiling. "Seriously. We've been concerned. Are concerned. We wonder how you'll fare in Ohio, living with that brute."

Anna doesn't want to talk about it. This time is too precious. She has learned above all things to savor those rare moments when the weight lifts from her shoulder, like now.

The coast is magnificent, Jim Fulson was right. The overcast skies cleared at the summit of the hills dividing the peninsula from the coastal plain. The wind is high, whipping the waves into white caps, but so temperate that many of the others on the beach have shed their coats and shoes, rolled up their sleeves and pants. Children are digging holes, trying to catch the seawater that ebbs to and fro with each wave. Dogs run free under the *Keep your dog on leash* signs, stealing balls from infants and carrying bunches of dripping seaweed to their owners. Everyone is taking care, however, not to go near the water. This beach is notorious for its steep drop-off, and for rogue waves that have pulled even experienced surfers out to sea. *Danger hazardous waves* signs are posted every hundred feet.

Jim Fulson and Anna walk without speaking, gazing at the expanse of blue and white.

Anna finally breaks the silence. "What about Ms. Thadeous?"

"What about her?" Jim Fulson asks.

"Are you getting married?" she asks. She doesn't know how to get this information other than by being direct.

Jim Fulson throws back his head and laughs, but it feels contrived, like he's been waiting for this question, and scripted a response long ago.

"When you're my age, love affairs don't necessarily end in marriage," he says.

"Is that what you have going, a love affair?" When what Anna really wants to ask is *so it's going to end*? What has blossomed between Ms. Thadeous and Jim Fulson seems stranger, more precious, all the more extraordinary because of its origins in high school chemistry classrooms and suburban rec rooms.

"She is the love of my life," he says, without a trace of cynicism or embarrassment.

Anna is startled. Whatever she expected, it wasn't this. She feels a brief rush of sadness, of longing.

"But isn't she awfully old for you?" Anna asks.

Another false laugh.

"You sound like my mother," he says. "Annie, she's exactly four years and one month older than me. She just turned twenty-nine and I'll be twenty-five in January."

"It just seems odd," Anna says.

"But I thought you liked Clara," he says. "She's very concerned about you, about your missing school, moving away."

When Anna is quiet, he says, "I know you haven't seen a lot of us lately. We've been ... busy."

A cry rises up. Jim Fulson and Anna see people pulling their children from the shoreline, rushing to put distance between themselves and the ocean. "Sharks!" a male voice shouts. Fingers are being pointed, everyone is straining to see. All other activities on the beach cease. About thirty feet out from the surf, three fins can be seen. They go under water, then come up again.

"Relax!" a man calls out. There's a moment of silence as everyone waits. "Those are dolphins," he shouts with convincing authority. "Everything is okay. There aren't many in California. This is a rare treat."

The mood rapidly changes to one of excitement. Dolphins! Their sleek curved backs and their snouts arc gracefully out of the water. Three of them, in perfect alignment, heading against the current and against the wind, pushing southward toward San Gregorio and Pomponio beaches. The miracle of sea creatures, everyone is pointing, still exclaiming. Jim Fulson is equally enthralled, he's taken out his cell phone like the others, is snapping photos, typing in an email. She has no doubt whom he is sending the photos to. She wants to hurt. She wants to inflict pain.

"You've been busy? How's the job hunt going?" she asks.

Jim Fulson stiffens as he finishes typing. He sends the message, puts the phone back in his pocket. "It's not."

"So who pays for everything?" Anna asks. She sounds spiteful. She feels spiteful. She wishes that the animals in the water had been sharks, bloodthirsty, looking for prey.

Jim Fulson walks away from Anna. He walks fast, and doesn't look back. A golden retriever that has been dogging their steps runs circles around him, thinking he wants to play. Jim Fulson picks up a piece of seaweed, throws it to the dog to chase, continues putting distance between himself and Anna.

Anna sits down. The sand is damp. She can feel it soaking into her jeans. Picking up a fragment of a mussel shell, she begins digging in the sand, trying to write her name, but the curve of the shell makes it impossible to do so legibly. Just chicken scratches. The tide is coming in, and the foamy water stretches a little farther up the beach with every wave. A finger of water touches Anna's bare right foot. It tingles. She watches the waves come closer and closer, waits until one covers her toes. Bone-chilling. Anna inches herself toward the water line. The next wave splashes her ankles, soaking the hems of her jeans. Anna closes her eyes, pretends it is heat, not cold, causing her skin to burn so. She takes off her red Stanford sweatshirt, throws it out of reach of the encroaching waves, rolls up her jeans to her knees, and moves even closer to the ocean. This time it takes just a few minutes before a surge large enough to drench Anna's legs breaks.

Anna stands, and brushes the wet sand from her jeans. Everyone else's attention is on the dolphins, still taking pictures. Jim Fulson is a tiny dot down the length of the beach.

Anna wades into the surf. The first breaker reaches only to her knees, but with such force that she staggers backward and falls. Before she can get back up again, a larger one crashes over her. She is now soaked through. This is not a friendly ocean. Anna is shivering as she pulls herself out of the water, but she has not yet had enough. She has some unfinished business here. Waves continue to slam against her, now to her waist, but she stands still for a few minutes, until the frigid water is slightly more bearable. Then she staggers in deeper. There's a sudden drop of the ocean floor and Anna is now chest deep, but the waves seem to grow more accommodating, molding themselves around her body. She has a revelation: If she plunges headlong into the surf, the cold will no longer be a problem, she will be at one with the sea. She prepares herself. Cries are coming from the shore, but Anna doesn't look back. Taking a deep breath, she plunges into the next wave, which arches well over her head, at least eight feet high. She emerges in the foaming turmoil following the break, but is unprepared for the next, even taller, wall of water that is curling above her, about to collapse. She is knocked over so hard that she bumps her shoulders, hard, against the ocean floor. Her head spins. She manages to find her feet but she must have drifted farther out because she's up to her neck and is hit almost immediately by another wave, and another. Anna is flailing, no longer in control of her limbs, being turned head over feet, tumbled in the rough surf, her head slamming against the hard floor again and again and then she surfaces and gasps for breath, but is quickly pulled under. Seawater forces its way into her mouth and up her nose and she chokes only to take in more. She feels His presence for the first time since her parents died, she understands that not since then has she truly believed, she is ashamed. She goes under, she is losing count, but it doesn't matter, she sees that she has until now only been going through the motions; she has not been truly honoring Him. She has been using Him for her own devices. She can see clearly. And a plan begins to form. She does have a mission, she will go to Nebraska, but for a different purpose than she'd thought. Her mission now is to stop Fred Wilson. To delay, not hurry, the Tribulation. To put off the suffering. To buy herself, and the world, more time. Ms. Thadeous is right. Let the earth continue to revolve around the sun, let people live out their lives, disaster and grief will inevitably hit them. Life is pain. No need to make it worse, even for the desire of seeing Him sooner. Somehow Anna's head is briefly above water and as she gulps air she glimpses a crowd gathering on shore. Two figures have plunged into the ocean and are heading her way. She tries to swim toward them, but is hindered by the waves, they are pulling her out farther, farther, just as Anna realizes that feeling the ground under her feet is what she wants more than anything. She goes under again and thinks *this is it, this is really it.* She feels human hands upon her. A man and a woman, one on each side of Anna, both panting heavily. Each takes an arm and pulls her toward shore. They are not gentle. Their faces, what Anna can see of them as waves continue to break over the heads of all three, are grim. As they fight up the steep grade, an especially powerful wave crashes into them, and the man goes down. The woman gives a cry and releases Anna's arm. Plunging in near where the man last stood the woman frantically sweeps the area with her arms, searching, and when the man reappears five feet away, clearly dazed, she swims over to him and lifts him from under his arms until he can stand on his own. With powerful strokes the woman is again at Anna's side and grabs her by her shirt. "You little fool," she says.

"You don't understand," Anna counters, but the woman continues to pull her forward. Her grip on Anna's arm will leave a bruise.

They join the man in the shallows, all three of them breathing heavily as they stagger onto dry sand. They are immediately surrounded. Towels envelop them, are used to vigorously rub them down.

"What was that about?" asks an older man. A small child, perhaps four years old, is holding his hand, staring. "A suicide attempt," someone says, softly. Others are gaping. Everyone is too close. Anna wants to protest, but she can barely breathe. Then she gets a push from behind; it's the woman who retrieved her from the water. She has a towel around her shoulders and one over her head. Before Anna can register any more the woman slaps her hard across her right cheek. "That," she says, "is for nearly drowning my husband." She raises her hand again, but someone grabs it. Jim Fulson. His face is unreadable.

"I've called 911," someone says.

The woman turns to Anna. "I hope you get a lot of therapy for that little exploit," she says. She is still breathing heavily, and is shivering. "Next time, act out your little suicide dramas in the privacy of your own home."

Anna is finally able to speak. "Exploit?" she gasps. "Suicide? Is that what you think?" She wants to laugh, but is still so winded that she can barely make a noise. She looks at Jim Fulson, forces out a denial. "It wasn't that at all."

"Where are your parents? I want to speak to them before the paramedics get here," the woman says,

Anna is finally able to give a real laugh. "Yes, by all means talk to my parents," she says, and turns to Jim Fulson, "don't you think that's a great idea?

"Anna," says Jim Fulson, he is studying her face for something. Whatever he sees reassures him, because he is now smiling. His face shows relief, he even begins laughing himself.

The woman looks from Anna to Jim Fulson. "What's going on here?" she asks. "Who are you?"

Jim Fulson tries to stop laughing, but can't. Anna can't either. "A friend," he finally says.

"A friend," the woman repeats. "A grown man with a minor *friend*. Interesting. Do your parents know about this, young woman?"

This sets Anna, who had started calming down, off again, but she sobers up after looking at the faces surrounding her. A pinprick of fear shoots through her. She whispers to Jim, "Let's get out of here."

Jim hesitates. "Listen," he says to the people around them, "this isn't what you think."

A siren sounds far away, is coming closer. Anna says, more urgently, "Come *on*." She doesn't want to be here when the authorities arrive.

Jim Fulson still seems indecisive. Then he gives a great shout, grabs Anna's hand, and pulls her away from the group, toward the parking lot.

"Come on," he says, and starts running.

Anna stumbles, but catches herself and tries to match his long strides. It's difficult in the sand; she is clumsy, but the few people who are halfheartedly coming after them are stumbling more and this sets her laughing again. "You should see the looks on their faces," she says.

Jim Fulson gives an answering laugh.

They somehow make it to the truck. Jim Fulson clicks it unlocked, opens the driver's-side door, and when Anna starts for the passenger's side, he grabs her and forces her into the cab. "No time!" he yells. Anna bumps her hip against the steering wheel. Another bruise. Then she's in and he's in and he's started the engine and they are off. As they exit the parking lot, a police car and ambulance scream past, lights blazing.

Once out of the parking lot, Jim Fulson steps on the gas. They reach the stop light at Highway 1 just as it turns yellow, but he screeches through, heading into downtown Half Moon Bay. Once across the street, he slows down. "What next?" he asks, he is still breathing hard.

"I'm starved!" says Anna. She is, for the first time in recent memory. The dousing in the chilled water seems to have awakened her appetite. "Can we get something to eat before heading home? There's never any food in the Goldschmidts' house."

Jim looks indecisive. "What if the police come looking for us?"

"They don't know our names," Anna says. "I don't think anyone saw your license plates. I think we're okay."

"What about your wet clothes?" Jim Fulson asks. "You can't stay in those things."

"It's not really a problem," Anna said.

"Okay," says Jim Fulson. He drives across Main Street, then into the full parking lot of a church having a rummage sale. He turns the ignition off, then faces Anna and says, "Okay, so it wasn't a suicide attempt. What was it, then?"

Anna has a flash of despair. The emptiness of the abyss beckons once more. Then she remembers. And then reveals to Jim Fulson what she would have found impossible to say to Ms. Thadeous, or Lars.

"I saw God," Anna says, shyly. She watches Jim Fulson for his reaction. It matters to her. "I'd lost Him when . . . but the beauty, the power, of seeing God in nature, seeing Him in the waves, in my parents . . . was wonderful."

"Oh yes?" says Jim Fulson. He pushes open his door, walks around the truck and opens Anna's door for her. "How exactly does He work, Anna? Do you really believe, after all that's happened recently, that you actually have a handle on this?"

Anna barely hears him. She is still radiant from the experience.

"I've been a fool, wasting all this time," she says. "I have a new mission."

"Oh no," says Jim Fulson. "Here we go again." He helps Anna out of the truck, and locks the door. They start walking.

They reach Main Street, join the weekend tourist crowd. The small boutiques that sell eclectic women's clothing and Tibetan furniture and designer kites are full of window shoppers, people fingering the silken robes, the worry beads, the old stone Buddha heads. People look but never buy, so the stores are constantly changing, from month to month the shops mutate into others that resemble them almost exactly and offer similarly doomed wares.

Jim Fulson puts his name in at the pizza place Anna's parents loved. The line snakes halfway down the block. When a police car cruises by Anna shrinks into the crowd, but it passes without pausing.

The fog is starting to waft overhead as the sun sinks lower in the west. Anna shivers in her damp clothes. Jim Fulson notices and takes off his windbreaker and puts it around her shoulders. "Why I'm acting like a gentleman I don't know," he says. "I seem to have gotten myself mixed up in a situation." But he doesn't look upset anymore. He even seems amused by it. "I have to admit," he says, "it's been an interesting half year."

"You mean Ms. Thadeous," Anna says.

"Yes and no," he says. "It's just that I feel more alive now than I did on high school graduation day. Which is saying a lot. And it's not only Clara."

He does look alive now, and strangely young. "You are gentle and humble in spirit," Anna tells him.

"What?" he asks, clearly disconcerted.

Anna doesn't answer.

They finally get a table. When their pizza arrives, they are so hungry that they devour it within minutes. Jim Fulson orders another. "We have time," he says.

They both jump when his cell phone rings, so intent have they been on eating. He looks at the screen, and can't seem to select answer fast enough. "Clara," he says. Anna looks elsewhere, pretends not to listen.

"Yes," he says. "We're here, safe." He rolls his eyes at Anna. "Yes, all that really happened. Everything's okay, though. But how did you find out?"

He listens, and then, "We're finishing dinner at It's Italia. We'll probably be here another twenty minutes. Then we'll come home ..." A silence. A long one. The waitress comes and goes from the table several times, clearing the dirty dishes, pouring more water, before Jim Fulson speaks again. "Oh. Oh fuck." More silence. "Oh shit, okay. Okay, we'll see you soon."

He hangs up. He stares at his phone. He doesn't look at Anna when he speaks.

"We have a problem," he says. "Your little ... escapade ... got the attention of a lot of people, including the state's child protective services. Someone took photos with a cell phone, sent them in. You were recognized. They're looking for us."

"So we'll just explain what happened. The Goldschmidts will understand. As my temporary guardians, they'll be fine with it."

"It's not as simple as that." Jim says. He has his hands over his face. His shoulders are slumped. "They're talking about child endangerment. Police got to my parents, to Clara, asked why a twenty-something male had a young girl at the beach, and allowed her to nearly drown herself."

"Well? It's all easily explained, like I said. And it's not like I'm eleven. I'm almost eighteen!"

"You might not get this, but that almost makes it worse," says Jim Fulson. "A twenty-four-year-old with a seventeen-year-old raises eyebrows."

Anna whacks Jim Fulson's arm. "Stop worrying," she says. She hears the bitterness in her voice. "You'll survive this. You and Ms. Thadeous will live happily ever after."

"Ah, Anna," he says. "That's where you're wrong." He stares at his hands. "I could be facing charges of contributing to the delinquency of a minor. The police told Clara that technically they could get me on charges of kidnapping. I took you, a minor, away without knowledge or permission of your guardians. While you were under my care you nearly drowned. Then we ran away. That was a very stupid thing to have done."

"So, let's go straighten it out," Anna says. "I'm okay. I'll explain everything. The Goldschmidts aren't going to say anything bad about you."

Jim Fulson is silent for a moment before giving a small shake to his head. "Clara already talked to her old roommate, now a law professor at Berkeley. It won't be that easy. Remember, I'm just some pervert who lives in his parents' rec room. A jobless, penniless former mental patient."

He leans forward until his forehead is pressed against the tabletop.

"God almighty," he says. "Can't I catch a break?"

Anna puts a tentative hand on his arm, but he shakes her off.

"Look, I know you're a mixed-up kid," he says. "But this happens to be my only life. Things were improving, I thought. But then I fuck up as usual."

Anna is puzzled. "I don't get why it's so serious. This isn't anything we can't explain."

"That's because you don't know about my record," Jim says. He speaks slowly, pausing between words.

"Your . . . record?" Anna asks. "Your hospital record?"

"Yes and no," he says.

"What's the 'no' part?"

Jim Fulson doesn't answer at first. Then he says, "I have a police record."

Anna is dumbfounded. "You?"

Jim Fulson lifts his head from the table and nods. "The first time, it was just really stupid. I got drunk with a bunch of fraternity buddies and we decided to lift a statue from an estate in Malibu and put it in front of our frat house. Only turns out the statue was worth a couple million dollars. So given that we were all above eighteen and of sound minds, we were arrested. We pleaded guilty and were sentenced."

"Did you have to go to jail?"

"No. We were given community service. But the charges weren't dismissed, so it went on my permanent record. They said the statue was too valuable, the owner too irate, for them to dismiss the charges, even for a bunch of privileged white boys."

Anna doesn't know what to say. "What does that have to do with what happened today?" she asks.

Jim Fulson rubs his head. The waitress has delivered the check, so he pulls some bills out of his pocket and throws them on the table. "It's really the second offense that was the serious one," he says. "It was when I was deeply depressed the second time. In LA. I'd already had one stint in the mental hospital. I had no intention of going again. So I locked myself in the bathroom with the intention of . . . doing things right this time."

Anna is quiet. She understands despair. She understands the urge.

"My girlfriend came home. When I wouldn't open the door, she used a bobby pin to get in. There I was, naked as a jaybird, holding the biggest sharpest knife from the kitchen. I was crazy. I'm not excusing what I did, but I was crazy. I lunged at her, I only wanted to scare her, honest to God, to get her out of the bathroom, but she thought otherwise and ran screaming out into the lobby of the apartment house, someone called the cops, and I was arrested for the second time. I pled guilty again, and given that I was already committed to the hospital, they commuted my sentence. But they warned me that another incident, specifically one that was violent or put anyone else in danger, was going to be taken seriously."

He sighs heavily. "Clara's lawyer friend says my record is going to be a problem. A real problem."

He looks at Anna. "And then there's you."

"What about me?"

"According to Clara, you'll be sent to a hospital for observation. To a psychiatric ward. Standard procedure for teens who attempt suicide."

"But I didn't . . . !"

"Annie," he says. "There isn't a person on the planet who will believe that wasn't your intent. Not with all those witnesses."

"Okay, okay," Anna says. "What then?"

"You'll be shipped off to Columbus," he says. "Your aunt and uncle have already been notified, and will be here tomorrow. Clara's on her way. She says not to go home just yet, there's a police car parked outside my house, waiting. She wants to help us get our story straight before talking to them."

Anna sees that Jim Fulson's hands are trembling. For some reason that enrages her. Her exuberant high has vanished.

The waitress comes, takes the bills, gives Jim Fulson change.

"Clara will be here soon," he says. His voice is expressionless.

"Let's not go back," Anna says.

"What?"

"Let's leave," she says. "Why stick around? I don't want to be *observed,* or go to Columbus. You don't want to get in trouble. Why don't we just hit the road?" She is tentative at first, tasting the idea.

"Three reasons to start with," he says. "Money, money, and money. I haven't got any."

"I've got five thousand dollars. And Lars has plenty. We've been planning to leave anyway," says Anna. The more she talks, the better this sounds to her. "We were waiting until my birthday, that's all."

This gets his attention.

"How does Lars have access to money?" he asks.

"He controls his parents' bank account. They have more than a hundred thousand dollars in it. They don't even know how much they have. They won't miss it. They would even give it to us if we asked."

"So this is what Lars and you have been up to," he says. "Unfortunately, that's stealing. More trouble to get in. More fucking up."

"It's a necessity," Anna says. "This is bigger than we are. It's been predestined. Lars, me, you . . . We have a mission to fulfill."

"Go ahead, I'm listening," says Jim Fulson.

"Listening to what?" asks a woman's voice. It's Ms. Thadeous. She is wearing sweats and a T-shirt and sneakers. Her face without makeup. She's also breathing heavily, as though she's been running. She pulls another chair to the table, and nods at the waitress to come over, orders a glass of white wine.

"So," she says. "Let's talk about this mess you two have gotten into."

"I was just explaining something," says Anna.

"Well, continue," says Ms. Thadeous. "Don't mind me."

"Lars's minister talks about this a lot," Anna says. "About the dispersal of the godly into the wilderness immediately before the Tribulation."

"Cut the Tribulation crap," Jim Fulson says. "I don't have a lot of patience right now. Stick to the practicalities."

"We borrow some money from Lars. We head out, go to some remote area in, say, Oregon," Anna says. "You help me get settled, help me buy a car, get a temporary place to live. Then leave. You'd be under no obligation. You could kick around a bit until everything has died down."

Anna thrills at the thought of Jim Fulson and herself, driving northward, up over the Golden Gate Bridge, up through Santa Rosa, Sonoma, Mendocino, across the border and beyond to the Lost Coast. Jim Fulson letting her take the wheel at night on the long stretches of empty road. And then, after lying low for five months, officially an adult, she'll head for Nebraska.

Jim Fulson interrupts her thoughts. "And what about Clara?" he asks.

"Yes, don't mind me," says Ms. Thadeous.

"I'm sorry," Anna says, and means it. A long silence.

"Let's get you back to my place," says Ms. Thadeous. "We can decide what to do from there." She pauses a moment, then, "I should just let you two take responsibility. Let the chips fall."

"Clara," begins Jim Fulson.

"Don't interrupt!" she says, loudly. "I don't have a lot of faith in the judgment of either of you. Anna isn't stable enough to live on her own at this point. And you, Jim, the police don't easily forget an incident like this. Kidnapping and child endangerment are not parking tickets, for God's sake! You'd be facing a felony charge when you came back. So what are you going to do, wandering far from home with no money? A ridiculous thought. Utterly!"

Anna and Jim Fulson are quiet throughout her tirade.

"Anna has been traumatized enough. Placing her in lockdown mode for a suicide attempt . . ."

"But I wasn't . . ." interrupts Anna.

"Shut up, Anna. I was going to say, putting you in lockdown wouldn't be the best thing in your current state. And Jim, you're not in the most stable place yourself."

More silence.

"For that matter, I don't understand my own behavior of late," says Ms. Thadeous. She turns then and puts her hand on Jim Fulson's knee. "This won't be easy."

Anna gets it first. "You mean," says Anna, "that you're coming, too?"

37

MS. THADEOUS IS CALM. NOT the detached, bored way she acts in class, but humming with suppressed energy. She has typed up a to-do list. "The three C's," she says. "Car, clothes, cash." They're in her house, packing essentials.

"But what happens if we can't reach Lars?" Anna asks. She had tried to call the Goldschmidts on the drive to Ms. Thadeous's house. A strange male voice had answered, and Anna had hung up without saying anything. Afterward, Jim Fulson took her phone away, turned it off, and threw it onto the highway. "They can trace you using these things," he says.

"Why would we involve Lars?" asks Ms. Thadeous. "Isn't spiriting away one minor enough?"

Anna looks at Jim Fulson, who shrugs. "He's got the money," Anna says. "A lot of it. He'll help us out."

"I have enough," says Ms. Thadeous.

"Clara," says Jim Fulson.

"Not another word," she says.

"Won't the police be looking for Jim's truck?" Anna asks.

"Yes, but they won't be looking for my car," says Ms. Thadeous.

"How can you do this?" Anna asks. "Just leave? The two of us don't have anything holding us here, but you have a job, a house, and responsibilities. You can't just walk away!"

Ms. Thadeous's face is aglow. "Just watch me," she says. She is bursting with savage energy. How many years had this been bottled up? "I think I've been waiting for this moment," she says. "Here I am. Falling in love with indigent rec-room dwellers. Being lectured by demented seventeen-year-olds. You bet I'm coming."

Anna looks at Jim Fulson. "But where are we going? She wasn't part of my plan."

"Somewhere safe," says Ms. Thadeous. "Utah," she says. "I know a place in Utah."

She rumples Jim Fulson's hair as if he's a small boy.

That night, after Jim Fulson and Ms. Thadeous close the bedroom door behind them, Anna takes the keys hanging on a hook in the kitchen and steals out to Ms. Thadeous's car. The engine erupts on the quiet street, the tires squeal as Anna pulls away from the curb too fast, and she is sweating by the time she's gone two blocks. She seems to have gotten away with it. No commotion, no one is following her. No traffic. The roads are so empty she's tempted to ignore the red lights, but instead waits at vacant intersections, nervously checking her mirrors. One cop car passes, but doesn't give Anna a glance.

Anna parks in the street behind Lars's house and climbs over the yard fence. She quietly lets herself in through the unlocked back door. Although the house is dark and silent, Lars is wide awake. He's lying on his bed fully dressed.

"Lars," begins Anna. "I need some money." Lars puts a finger to his lips, points to his bulging backpack, and a couple of paper bags from Safeway. Anna looks inside. They're full of her clothes.

"I had a feeling," Lars says. "Is there anything else we need?"

"There's no *we*," Anna hisses. Having Lars along would ruin her plans.

Lars shakes his head. She knows that look. "I come along, or no money," he says. Anna could scream. She should have known Lars would be one step ahead of her.

She picks up the bags of her clothes and begins walking out of the room. Lars scrambles to keep pace.

"Where are we going?" he asks.

"East," Anna says.

"Where east?"

"To Utah. Ms. Thadeous knows a place. Do you have the checkbook and the bank card?"

Lars nods. Then he takes Anna's arm. "Look at this," he says. He guides Anna to his bedroom window, lifts the bed sheet tacked there, and points. In front of Jim Fulson's house is a squad car, two shadowy figures in the front seat.

"He's in a lot of trouble."

"It's not his fault," Anna says.

"What exactly happened?" Lars asks. "The police say you threw yourself into the ocean, tried to drown yourself. I was concerned." Despite his words, his voice reveals no emotion.

Something perverse prompts Anna to ask, "Why?"

"Annie, we've talked about this. It isn't death per se that is the problem," he says.

"So you wouldn't have minded hearing that I was dead."

"Don't take it the wrong way," he says. "It was your soul I was concerned about. You were doing so well. Then there was that ... setback."

"Setback," Anna says. "I guess that's one way to describe it."

Lars starts for the back door, takes a few steps. "Tell me," he says. "How is your faith?"

"Stronger than ever," Anna says. She follows him slowly. "Reaffirmed, in fact."

Lars looks at her. "So you have turned to Him again?" he asks. His smugness is infuriating.

Anna gives the briefest of nods.

"I'm glad to hear that," Lars says. *"For if you sin deliberately after receiving the Truth, a fury of fire will consume you."*

"Right," Anna says, and then stops before she says something she regrets. She thinks of the money they need, the money Lars controls.

"What's the plan, then?" Lars asks.

Anna goes out into the yard and beckons him to hurry. "Ms. Thadeous wants to get on the road by 5 AM, to get over the bridges before rush hour." She leads Lars toward the fence, throws the bags containing her clothes to the other side, and starts to climb over it.

"I think this actually helps our plan," Lars says, throwing his backpack over. "It's God's work that matters, after all, and this is clearly preordained. We'll go east with Jim and Clara, but will wait our chance. When we can, we get away. We head to Nebraska. It's sooner than we expected. But clearly meant to be."

"I haven't thought that far ahead," says Anna, although she has. The last thing she wants is Lars trailing her to Fred Wilson's ranch.

"He'll recompense you for your suffering, you know," Lars says when he is finally on the other side of the fence.

"This is not about getting extra credit on a test," Anna says, openly losing her temper. She unlocks the car door and gestures for him to get in.

Lars's face closes up. "I've been praying for you," he says.

Anna almost tells him not to waste his time, but is afraid to trust her voice, so she changes the subject. "Clothes. Money. Are we ready?"

"The Lord has a plan for everything," says Lars. In the dim light he looks impossibly young. Anna softens. She walks around to the driver's side of the car and gets in.

"What will your parents think?" she asks, turning to Lars.

He hears her change of tone, and pulls a crumpled piece of paper out of his pocket and hands it to her.

"I wrote a note—see, here's the rough draft," he says.

Dear Mom and Dad,

I'm taking Reverend Michael's suggestion and joining our church's ministry in Las Cruces. As you know, he put me in touch with his brethren there already. One of them has agreed to find me a place to stay. You may be contacted by school authorities, but it is your legal right to give me permission to leave school at sixteen. You will simply have to sign a form. This has nothing to do with Anna. I will send you my contact information once I reach New Mexico.

Your loving son,
Lars Goldschmidt

"That's a good idea," Anna says. "Really good."

Anna would have thought him inured to compliments, but these small words of praise cause him to blush.

"Let's get out of here before the police catch on," Anna says. She starts the car and drives back to Ms. Thadeous's house as slowly as she had on the way over.

When they arrive, all the lights in the house are blazing in the otherwise dark street. A dog from the next house over starts barking the moment Anna pulls the car into the driveway.

"I'm not going to say a word," says Ms. Thadeous as they enter the house. In fact, she doesn't. Her packing is finished— Anna sees some sleeping bags and a suitcase. The refrigerator door is open and Ms. Thadeous is throwing everything into a large black plastic garbage bag. Jim Fulson comes in from the garage where he has parked his truck. He doesn't look at Anna or Lars.

"We brought money," Lars says.

Without responding, Jim Fulson picks up Ms. Thadeous's suitcase and takes it out to her car. Lars and Anna follow, helping Ms. Thadeous carry the bags of food to the curbside garbage can.

Ms. Thadeous then locks the front door, takes a moment to contemplate the sagging structure. "It was just a rental, but I liked it," she says, and then, to Jim Fulson only she says, "the end of an era."

When everyone is settled in the car, Jim Fulson says, "Well, Lars, I see you've thrown your lot in with us, too."

"Yes," says Lars. "It seemed to be the right thing to do. Given that this little ship is rudderless."

"I beg your pardon?" Jim Fulson looks tired, but alert. His eyes never leave Ms. Thadeous.

"Spiritually, I mean," says Lars. "We are meant to sojourn into the wilderness. You had the right instinct. But you require a leader."

It takes Jim Fulson a moment to realize what Lars has said. "You pompous little ass," he says.

Lars looks surprised. "What did I say?"

"Jim," says Ms. Thadeous, "remember who you're speaking to."

"What did I say?" repeats Lars. He looks genuinely anxious.

Jim Fulson rubs his eyes and sighs. "Nothing you haven't said about a million times previously," he says. "I'm sorry I snapped. We're all under quite a bit of stress."

Ms. Thadeous turns to Jim Fulson. "We should go," she says.

Dawn is close. It's already lighter in the eastern sky, and the morning paper has been delivered. The hum of traffic from nearby 101 has grown noticeably louder since Lars and Anna pulled up just twenty minutes earlier.

"It's going to be a little tight," says Jim Fulson, and turns around to face Anna. "How are you feeling, Little Man?"

Anna finds herself smiling. Despite her weariness, she is warmed.

"No more need to go into the light?" he asks. Anna realizes with pleasure that he is teasing her. Ms. Thadeous has turned around and is also looking at her. Anna can't read her face.

"Yes," Anna says, "quite done with that for now." A little white lie.

"Well then," says Jim Fulson, "I guess we're ready to get this circus on the road." Ms. Thadeous puts the car into gear, and they're off to parts unknown.

PART IV

Buying Time

38

THEY SHOULD BE ANXIOUS. THEY should be scared. They should be uncertain. Lars and Anna, uneasy conspirators. Ms. Thadeous, ex-teacher, ex-respectable citizen. Jim Fulson, rec-room escapee, suicide survivor, possible jailbird. But Anna feels only muted excitement. Still dark and too early to be slowed by rush-hour traffic, they sweep swiftly north on 101, past the airport, past the dim humps of South San Francisco and Brisbane, and onto the lower deck of the Bay Bridge. During the 1989 earthquake, when a 50-foot span simply dropped out of the upper deck of the bridge. Someone heading east had the extraordinary presence of mind to pull out a camera and videotape the car ahead accelerating toward the gap, caught the heroic attempt to soar over the breach, the epic fail and fatal plunge into the frigid water below. Or was it a resigned determination to go out with bravado that motivated that doomed driver? Anna guesses no, not bravado. No one wants to die on the Bay Bridge. No one jumps off its dull gray metal rails. Instead they travel six miles north to the Golden Gate, which provides not just an end, but a glorious means to a glorious end. Who would choose this dour construction when that magnificent red steel frame could be their platform for jettisoning this earth? From her quiz shows Anna knows certain statistics. Seventy percent of Golden Gate suicides jump facing the open sea, their backs to the city and their fellow humans. *Maybe,* Anna thought more than once while driving across the bridge with her parents, in her previous life, before Lars, before the accident. *Maybe.*

Traffic catches up to them when they reach the tangle of highways that separate Oakland and Piedmont from Emeryville, and they move excruciatingly slowly past Berkeley, past the industrial stink of the refineries and tank farms at Richmond. They get their first tedious view of the Central Valley at 8 AM. So far, so good.

My ministries are getting excited about this latest generation, Fred Wilson had written in his last email, another mass mailing. *The cows of Generation 7 are about to give birth. We hope to have worked out the strain of white ears that rose in Generation 6 by retreating back to eggs frozen from the dams of Generation 5, and fertilized with semen from Bull Q.*

It is a long and tedious process, but in the end we will prevail. Our Lord has endowed us with scientific knowledge and we have used them in ways that are in His service and beyond reproach.

I have been in constant touch with the good souls at the Third Temple Commission. They are preparing a storage facility in an undisclosed location in Gaza where we can store embryos for generations to come. We will leave nothing to chance, for every time a purification rite is needed, an embryo can be unfrozen and implanted, and a pure Red Heifer birthed. Give praise to God.

On the road, Ms. Thadeous does not appear to be worrying. Any resemblance to Ms. Tedious is long gone. She looks young, alive, her skin clear and taut, her dark hair loose around her shoulders. She has one hand on the wheel, her right hand intertwined with Jim Fulson's, who is leaning so far into her side of the car that another adult could fit in the front seat between him and the window.

Anna hasn't shaved her head since the night her parents died. At this point, more than a month, it almost covers her ears. The evening before they left, Ms. Thadeous had run over to the Gap at Valley Fair shopping center and bought Anna a pair of jeans and some striped pullovers, the sorts of clothes that normal teenagers wear. With her kitchen scissors she feathered Anna's hair so it more softly framed her face. Anna is now distinctly a girl in her new clothes and new hair, might even be taken for one who cares about style. Neither Jim Fulson nor Lars commented.

Every mile they put between themselves and the bloody intersection at El Camino and Page Mill, Anna feels a little lighter, a little more human. She even sees herself in the rearview mirror, and manages not to flinch. This time her mission will end in hope, not destruction.

39

ANNA MUST HAVE DOZED, BECAUSE now they're in the no-man's-land of Sacramento, formerly rich farmland eventually deemed too valuable to plow and now desecrated by row upon row of identical houses, constructed along straight lines that run parallel to the freeway all the way up to and over the skyline. Barracks, not homes. Many have *For Sale* signs tacked to their garages. The cramped layout of the encampment not even allowing for any patches of grass.. Huge billboards line the highway advertising easy-win casinos, exotic pole dancers, places to sleep, places to eat, real estate agents who can sell the depreciating properties of the desperate and help the enterprising find bargains. Anna can feel Lars is energized by what he sees, emboldened by this vision of a people indifferent to beauty, who have clearly rejected their stewardship of His earth. That they have fallen so far from His grace is a sign that the End Times are coming. Anna might have felt the same way twenty-four hours ago. But she now possesses a different attitude, the scene evokes her pity rather than her scorn, and she wants to beg for His mercy rather than his sword. *Give them time. Just give them enough time.*

They take the bypass and circumvent Sacramento's toy downtown, with its handful of skyscrapers and motley collection of ships anchored in the muddy stream of the Sacramento River. A long dreary stretch then, before Route-80 begins rising up into the Sierra foothills and Gold Country, where the financial crash had frozen new construction before any ground had been broken.

California hasn't had significant rainfall for more than three years, and the reservoirs they pass are dangerously low. By this time in their journey they should be seeing resplendent snow-capped mountains, fields freshly green from autumn rain on the lower hills. Instead they get gray fields with telephone wires strung on poles reaching eastward in perpetuity, and, in the distance, dull brown piles of dirt. They pass the first sign for Tahoe resorts, for Truckee and Reno and for a museum honoring the Donner Party's infamous cannibalism.

Ms. Thadeous and Jim Fulson switch seats, and he takes the wheel. She settles down to sleep with her head on his shoulder, the picture of young love.

Jim Fulson catches Anna's eye in the rearview mirror, switches on the radio and finds a news station. KFBK. Class warfare, unemployment, the dismal business climate. A slow news day.

He pulls over at a gas station outside Dutch Flat to refuel. Although the pump is self-service, a bored attendant in his mid-fifties wearing a gray jumpsuit offers to fill up the tank. His thin frame swims in the denim folds.

"Not many people heading up to Tahoe this weekend," Jim Fulson says to him.

"No reason to. No snow."

"Yeah, we didn't bother bringing our skis," Jim Fulson says. He sounds casual, nonchalant, but his hands are shaking.

"Smart decision. Enjoy the nice weather. The resorts are hurting, of course, which means folks around here are, too. A good snow season, a chain monkey can make a thousand dollars a day easy," says the man. He looks at Ms. Thadeous, then at Lars and Anna, openly curious.

"So, here to do some hiking? Hitting the casinos? Although"—here he stooped down, gestured at Lars and Anna—"those kids seem a little young. Likely to get carded if you try to sneak them in."

"No, visiting relatives. Death in the family." This is Jim Fulson's first attempt to vocalize the story they agreed on, and it stinks of falsehood, the four of them as far from being a family as anyone would imagine.

The man doesn't blink, though. "Looks more like a honeymoon trip," he says, pointing to the sleeping Ms. Thadeous. He's right. Even sleeping, she looks like a bride. Jim Fulson blushes.

Jim Fulson pays and takes off. Ms. Thadeous promptly opens her eyes. "I thought we'd never get out of there," she says, sitting up. Jim Fulson smiles and pulls her toward him again as he maneuvers the car back onto the empty highway. Anna distrusts the tenderness. After years of witnessing her parents' hard-edged courtship, she finds a relationship that exhibits this much mildness implausible.

40

THE ROLLING HILLS SOON GIVE way to pine forests rising high on either side of the divided highway. Noon has come and gone and Anna is hungry, but doesn't feel comfortable asking to stop. At one point Lars has to go to the bathroom, so Jim Fulson pulls off the highway. Lars disappears into the bushes for five minutes. Otherwise, they drive in silence as they climb to two, three, five thousand feet, and plunge into the shadows of the Sierra Nevada.

Anna's father hated the mountains because they reminded him of his despised West Virginia upbringing. But Anna's mother often missed the snow of her Midwest childhood. At least once a winter they drove the five hours to Tahoe so Anna's mother could get her fix of snow and Anna could become a passable skier. About thirty miles before Truckee, well before the turnoff to the Donner Pass, they'd see the signs for the Rainbow Lodge. Anna had always begged her parents to stop. The name evoked magic.

Once, Anna's mother relented and they stopped at the Rainbow for lunch. Anna has a vague recollection of rich brocaded upholstery and paneled walls, and of pitchers of cold water that were constantly being filled from a large spigot in the corner of the dining room. The Rainbow owned the clearest and purest spring of drinking water in California, and for each meal they put pitchers of this clear good water on the table. No ice, no fuss.

Anna has just one photo from that trip; she must have been eight, her hair in two braids, standing next to a snowdrift three times her height, her mother smiling and looking young. Anna remembers her father telling her that the men standing at the bar in the Rainbow saloon, leaning against it as they talked, holding glasses in their hands, were the *hard drinkers.* "You can tell a hard drinker by whether he needs a surface to put his drink down on," he had said. "If he does, he doesn't qualify. Not really."

Anna only had to say "The Rainbow!" with a pleased voice for Jim Fulson to brake slightly. "Do you want to stop?" he asks.

Ms. Thadeous shakes her head. "It's too early. We should get to Reno tonight."

"I don't know," Jim Fulson says. "It's almost 2:30 and I'm beat." He smiles at Ms. Thadeous.

"I'll take my turn. We need to keep going. We'll find plenty of cheap hotels in Reno," Ms. Thadeous insists.

"Let's make a quick stop, then. I'll bet the kids are hungry," says Jim Fulson. Anna thinks, what an indulgent father he would be. "Besides, Reno is so sleazy. Everything smells of smoke, and all the food is deep-fried."

"I'll feel better when we reach Utah," she says.

"I get it," says Jim Fulson, "But it's a long haul, and taking a break now won't make that much of a difference. We're not on a fixed schedule." Ms. Thadeous shrugs.

They pull into the Rainbow's gravel parking lot.

"We don't open for dinner until 5:00, but you can get snacks in the saloon," a young woman tells them as they enter the hotel, motioning them into the very room Anna remembers so vividly, where she'd sat sipping hot chocolate, her parents on either side of her. Everything deeply red with undertones of royal purpose, the dark wood paneling and lack of natural light making it into a sort of Aladdin's cave. Safe and warm. A womb of possibilities. Anna takes off her shoes and rubs her bare feet across the uneven floor boards covered with patterned rugs, sinks down into a brocaded chair. The others join her around a low oak table; Jim Fulson also immediately slips his shoes off and puts his feet up on a small embroidered footstool.

They're far from alone. A local crowd is already gathered, under the inevitable gazes of stuffed deer and bear heads on the walls, and, less conventionally, an assortment of mounted wildcat heads. Each of the cat faces wears a distinctly human expression—one with its mouth open in a round O of surprise, one looking sly with half-lidded eyes and a definitive upturn to its mouth. A frowning cat wears a Tyrolean hat with a feather in it. Anna is delighted.

"Let's stay here," Anna says. "Please?" She's surprised at the strength of her desire. Lars appears indifferent. One night's stop doesn't matter. He will reach his destination, will fulfill his destiny. A look passes between Ms. Thadeous and Jim Fulson. They are calculating costs, and logistics.

"I can pay," Anna says, but they hurriedly say "no, no," just as Anna's parents would.

"It's a small place," says Jim Fulson. "I'll have to ask if they have rooms."

As it turns out, one room is available. Third floor, no elevator. Bathroom down the hall. Two double beds, barely enough space to walk in between them.

"I'll share a bed with Anna, Jim and Lars can take the other," says Ms. Thadeous. This nod to convention makes Anna smile.

Lars brings his backpack and they haul up Ms. Thadeous's suitcase to make it seem as though they are honest travelers. Lars comments on the smallness of the room and goes to read in the lounge until dinner.

Anna grabs a change of clothes and retreats down the hall where she takes the longest hottest shower she's had in recent memory. The aging pipes wail and knock as she lathers herself with the peppermint soap, the apricot-scented shampoo. Her body a mixed bouquet.

She turns off the scalding water. She takes a soft white towel—softer and whiter than any she's ever felt against her body—and dries herself, briskly rubs her short hair. She dresses in clean clothes and walks back to the room, realizing immediately upon entering how obnoxious her scent is, how it overpowers the space. The second thing she realizes is that she's interrupted an embrace between Jim Fulson and Ms. Thadeous. It is Anna who is self-conscious. The visuals go into some kind of infinite loop inside her head, and she is condemned to witness that embrace, that open mouthed kiss disrupted by her arrival over and over again. That she disturbed something more important than a kiss is clear. Some tender thread prematurely snapped. Anna hurriedly leaves the room, joins Lars in the lounge. They wait more than an hour before Jim Fulson and Ms. Thadeous descend.

Dinner, served in the formal dining room, is superb: thick brown onion broth, rich Gruyère cheese coating the fresh French bread that floats on top of it, the miraculously clear crisp water. The waitress fills and refills the pitcher. Even Jim Fulson and Ms. Thadeous forgo stronger drinks; this is heady enough stuff.

Lars isn't paying any attention to them. Anna sees him actively calculating, looking around the room, eyeing in particular a middle-aged couple sitting morose over their roast duck and taking no pleasure in the room, the food, the warmth. Anna marvels at Lars's ability to relinquish pleasure in the here and now in pursuit of some more cerebral object.

Anna is alert to every move Jim Fulson makes. How his fingers accidentally brush those of Ms. Thadeous while reaching for the salt, how he puts his hand on the back of her chair, caressing the worn wood because it holds her body. Love by proxy. Ms. Thadeous has showered also; the ends of her hair are still slightly wet, her face shockingly bare. Ms. Thadeous's eyes are smaller, less prominent, less obviously soulful as when they're surrounded by kohl and thickened lashes. Her complexion is ruddier. Perhaps Ms. Thadeous considers the rosy tint of her cheeks, nose, and forehead coarse, but to Anna, it suits her, contrasting nicely with her black hair, which she must ordinarily straighten, because now it curls chaotically to her shoulders. No earrings. No shoes, either, Anna realizes. A child of nature. Jim Fulson can't take his eyes off her.

Anna is honored to be a part of this magic circle. Even the indifferent Lars is indispensable; he is the neutral element that prevents the system from short-circuiting. For the air is too charged, the rug too soft, the food too flavorful. It is all too,

too much. Anna is the only one who seems to realize that they are in a bubble, and that it has stretched as far as it can to accommodate them. Anna wants to savor this because it will not last, that the intensity of the evening is only possible precisely because it can't last.

More time, thinks Anna. *I can buy the world more time.*

41

"A HAPPY MARRIAGE. YOUR PARENTS had one, I think. And yours, Lars, I believe they have one, too."

"Yes," Anna says.

"Perhaps," Lars says.

They have finished dinner, are in no hurry to leave the table. Ms. Thadeous has apparently taken on the role of hostess. She is asking the questions, directing the conversation.

"They seem content," Anna says to Lars.

"*Content* is a good word," says Lars. "So is coexist. That's what they do. They thought they should conceive a child and so they did. Otherwise, the relationship is a matter of convenience. And companionship. The members of our church who live alone don't do as well."

"Your congregation doesn't tend to attract happy people," Anna says. It comes out more challenging than she intended.

"No," Lars says. "People seldom reach out to us because of excess happiness."

"Is it your church's goal to attract unhappy individuals in particular?" asks Ms. Thadeous.

"Let's say we keep our eyes open for the ones that will be most receptive."

"Like me?" Anna asks.

"And unlike us?" asks Jim Fulson. Anna notices the use of the word *us* with a little shock. It's the one time he's spoken for Ms. Thadeous, talked about them as a unit. Ms. Thadeous hasn't noticed, is drinking more water. She's already had to excuse herself to the bathroom twice.

"I thought we had possibly misjudged you," Lars says to Anna. "I felt you slipping away. But now you're back."

"Give the girl a break," says Ms. Thadeous. Her arm goes around Anna. For the first moment all evening, Jim Fulson looks directly at Anna. When Ms. Thadeous lifts her hand to brush the hair off Anna's forehead, his eyes follow it, and for a second his eyes rest on Anna's face, but they don't linger.

Drunk on water, they stay up talking past 10 PM. When they eventually stumble to the room, no one bothers to find pajamas, they all fall into bed fully clothed. Lars seems to fall asleep the minute he lays his head on the pillow. Jim Fulson takes the far side of the men's bed, which is pushed against the wall. Anna thinks she won't sleep but she keeps dropping off only to be woken up by Ms. Thadeous moving past her to get to the bathroom down the hall. After her third or fourth trip Anna and Ms. Thadeous switch places so she'll be closer to the door.

Anna is awakened by a hand tentatively touching her shoulder. The thick velvet curtains have been drawn so tight that the room is black. She can't see who it is.

"Clara?" Jim Fulson's voice.

Anna holds her breath, doesn't speak.

"Clara? Wake up." He is speaking softly, but Anna wants to hush him, she doesn't want him to wake Lars or Ms. Thadeous. She wants the hand to stay on her shoulder. But it doesn't. It starts moving, travels down Anna's arm, stops at her wrist, lingers there for a moment. Soon it will move again and he'll realize whose body he is caressing. Anna reaches out and stops his hand with hers. She presses it tight against her side. With her other hand she reaches up and strokes Jim Fulson's face, feels the bristles of two days' growth. Anna has never touched a man's face other than her father's, and that was more than a decade earlier, during their games of grab-the-nose. Anna feels Jim Fulson coming closer to her, his breath on her cheeks.

Then whispers, at first unintelligible. Anna slowly gets used to the cadence, begins to put syllables, words together. Jim Fulson has much to say. He doesn't seem to care if Anna can hear; he just apparently needs to say the words aloud.

"Clara. Clara. It hurts to be separated like this. I can hear you breathe. I know your breathing. Clara, I want you. Please say it. Just say my name."

He waits.

Anna's throat is dry. She pitches her voice low, whispers it as softly as she can and still force the word out.

"Jim."

Silence. Then, "Clara?" His voice is questioning. Anna's hand still on his face, the curve of his cheekbone against her palm. Oh holy of holies will she ever get this chance again? She can hardly breathe. His hand against her side stiffens. Anna thinks he's going to take it away. Then he stops, exhales, and instead tightens it around her waist. Holds her. A moment of pure bliss. Then Anna pulls her hand away from his face, slowly and reluctantly. He also detaches, removing his hand from her body. A pause. Then he suddenly grasps Anna's wrist. His face is close to hers; she can feel his breath again. Lars stirs on the other bed, barely eighteen inches away. "Jim?" he asks. Jim Fulson withdraws, quickly.

Anna hears him sigh, and feels rather than sees him walk away. The door opens, letting in a slice of light from the hallway. Anna shrinks under the covers but he doesn't look back. She hears him fumbling with his shoes and coat. Then he's gone.

Anna goes to the window, pulls aside the heavy curtains. Immediately the room is lit up by the bright moon.

The Rainbow Lodge is perched on the banks of the South Yuba. Unlike other rivers they've passed, this one is full, gushing and bubbling and catching the moonshine as it splashes over the rocks and logs. Anna waits, watches. Jim Fulson gets to the river less than one minute after he leaves the room. He simply leans against a pine tree, appears to contemplate the scene. He bends down, picks something up, throws it. A rock. His old habit. The river is so lively, so turbulent, the rocks he throws into it don't make visible splashes. He heaves each one harder and farther, easily bypassing the bank on the other side, sailing the stones into the air to land, invisibly, in the forest beyond. Even through the coat she can see his broad shoulders, the strength he puts into each throw.

Anna hears Ms. Thadeous wake for another trip to the bathroom. When she returns, she comes to the window. They watch in silence. "Just beautiful, isn't he?" Ms. Thadeous says, finally. Anna nods, but doesn't speak.

As if he could hear them, Jim Fulson turns around. He looks up at the hotel, examines it carefully. Anna shrinks away from the window. Ms. Thadeous does the opposite; she pulls the curtains back farther, unlatches the window, and with some effort pushes it open. A gust of chill wind. She leans out, almost too far. She waves. The longing in his body as he returns the gesture is palpable. Like the schoolgirl Anna is, she wonders when her turn will come.

Ms. Thadeous throws on her coat and leaves the room. After a few minutes she reappears downstairs, then, like Jim Fulson before her, looks up toward the room's window. Anna waves and she waves back. While she is watching, Anna deliberately draws the curtains together. But not completely. When Jim Fulson pushes Ms. Thadeous against a tree and presses his body to hers, Anna witnesses every tremor.

42

THEY'D INTENDED TO BE ON the road again by 7 AM, but they sleep too late and at 8:30 are finally finishing their breakfast. Outside, the green pines stretch high into an infinite blueness. Yet the waitress is gloomy. "No snow forecast this week or next week either," she says. "More of this goddamned sunshine." If the weather doesn't change, she'll be out of a job on New Year's morning, she says. Anna recalls that she also once thought of the sunshine as ominous, the brilliant blues and greens of the Northern California landscape as threatening. All that has passed. For He couldn't be sending Anna a more direct message. *Today is the day which the Lord has made. Let us rejoice and be glad.*

Ms. Thadeous gives Anna half her eggs and her toast. Anna is ravenous, eats it all, and then shamefacedly orders more, eats that, too. Ms. Thadeous and Jim Fulson are less affectionate this morning. Something was released in the woods last night, the fever has broken. They could be colleagues chaperoning charges on a school field trip. Lars eats methodically. His eyes go to the only other occupied table in the restaurant, the same middle-aged couple from the previous night. He is openly calculating. Then, while Jim Fulson goes to the front desk to settle the bill,

Lars decides. Without saying anything to either Ms. Thadeous or Anna, he gets up and approaches the couple. Anna can't hear what he says, but the couple's faces, raised dully to Lars, don't immediately reject him. "My goodness," says Ms. Thadeous, and she is expressing admiration, "so that's how he works these days. A little more sophisticated than his time at Sunnyvale High." Lars pulls out a chair and hitches himself up to the table. Ms. Thadeous and Anna leave the restaurant, but not before seeing Lars place his hand on the woman's arm. Both she and the man are listening intently.

It's 9:30 by the time they're able to separate Lars from his new friends. From the warm handshakes and fervent goodbyes Anna knows he's made two more conquests, walking away with names and phone numbers scribbled on a napkin.

In the car Anna falls asleep, exhausted after her sleepless night. When she wakes, it's after dark, a full ten hours later. She slept through three pit stops and a drive-through McDonald's, but she doesn't feel rested and the landscape is not reassuring. They have been transported to what looks like the dark side of the moon. Ms. Thadeous is driving on a narrow band of highway that slices through a dark sunken world of dubious aspect. In the distance, a city, dwarfed by the landscape but growing bigger by the minute, a city with a center that includes a small number of skyscrapers and some sort of large dome. Salt Lake City.

Unlike San Jose, Salt Lake City is not ringed with suburbs. Instead, the undeveloped flatland pushes all the way up to the city limits. Then the car crosses a line, and suddenly they have returned to civilization. Ms. Thadeous drives confidently past the Subways and Days Inns and McDonald's and Hiltons but after a while becomes confused. They pass the same Chinese restaurant at least three times. Finally, she pulls over, defeated. "I don't recognize any of this," she says.

"How long since you saw it?" asks Lars.

She doesn't answer for a moment. "More than thirteen years."

"Let me drive," says Jim Fulson. "You'll do a better job navigating if you're not behind the wheel." They switch seats and move into traffic again.

They're in a sort of downtown area, with some skyscrapers but also derelict stores and restaurants from earlier eras, many boarded up or vacant. Jim Fulson proceeds slowly, making constant detours that loop them around where they've already been, despite the fact that the streets are laid out on a grid. Construction everywhere. A city reinventing itself. Large, friendly signs with arrows pointing in different directions to municipal landmarks, but whatever street they try ends up blocked and forces another detour upon them. After twenty minutes, having driven past a Rite Aid more than a dozen times, Ms. Thadeous calls, "Turn here."

At first glance, it's just another block of gleaming and seemingly empty office buildings and new-looking condominiums with *Prices reduced* banners on them, but Ms. Thadeous gives a little cry, and the expression on her face is half triumph, half trepidation. Jim Fulson pulls over where she points. One of the few single-family homes left on the block, dwarfed by the grand edifices around it. A small bungalow, freshly painted. A neat front yard with gravel instead of grass. No trees. The driveway goes past the house to the rear, with a small backyard, also gravel, surrounded by a link fence. The curtains are closed.

"This is it," she says.

"It doesn't look like anyone is home," says Jim Fulson.

"She's probably still at work," says Ms. Thadeous. "Unless she's changed her habits, which I doubt."

"She's expecting us, though?" Jim Fulson seems anxious.

"She is. But we couldn't expect her to alter her routine," says Ms. Thadeous. "Even to greet the prodigal daughter."

"Where exactly are we?" asks Lars. He is gazing around with a skeptical air.

"Home sweet home," says Ms. Thadeous.

43

"BUT YOU HAVEN'T BEEN HERE for a while?" Lars asks the obvious question.

"No," says Ms. Thadeous.

"I take it that 'she' is your mother?" Anna asks.

"Yes." Ms. Thadeous is only giving information on a need-to-know basis. She gets out of the car. They all do the same, and follow her up the path to the front door where she gives a hard couple raps. No answer.

"What did she say when you talked to her?" Anna asks.

"I didn't actually talk to her," says Ms. Thadeous. She turns her back to the front door and faces them.

"What?" says Jim Fulson. His voice comes out like a shout.

"I left a message on her answering machine. It's the only way of communicating with her. She doesn't like the telephone. Never has."

"You said it would be safe," Lars accuses her. He is clearly displeased.

"Actually, when I said it'd be safe, I wasn't talking about here," says Ms. Thadeous. She doesn't look at any of them. "We're still one step away from safe. But this is the only way to get there."

Lars shrugs. It has gotten very cold. They are still standing next to the front door debating what to do next when they hear a vehicle approaching. A green Ford Escort, at least twenty years old, pulls into the driveway. The sound of an emergency brake engaging, and an engine shutting down. From the car emerges a figure so like Ms. Thadeous that Anna emits a startled *oh!* Her figure and the way she moves, languidly, but with a half jump in each step, are Ms. Thadeous, exactly.

"Mom," says Ms. Thadeous. In the silence that follows Anna can hear the murmur of traffic from the main road, a block over.

"When I saw the crowd, I expected you'd be at the center of it." The voice is most definitively not Ms. Thadeous's. Flat and nasal, with a buzz at the back of the throat. A smoker's voice, although everything about the neat little house and immaculate-though-aged car makes Anna doubt this is the case.

Ms. Thadeous's mother takes a bag out of the trunk of her car. Groceries. Jim Fulson moves forward to help, but she waves him off. She decides only now to acknowledge the rest of the group.

"You," she says, pointing to Anna. "What's your name?"

Anna tells her and holds out her hand. When Ms. Thadeous's mother doesn't move to take it, Anna drops it awkwardly to her side.

"Ruth," she says, using a curious flip of her free hand to gesture at her chest. "And you?"

"Lars," he says, in his deepest, most compelling voice.

She turns to Jim Fulson.

"Something tells me you're the reason we've all come together like this," she says.

To his credit, Jim Fulson holds her gaze for a good five seconds before turning his head away. "You're not far from the truth," he says.

"Well, come in. Here"—she now decides to hand the bag to Jim—"make yourself useful."

She fumbles in the dark at the door, finally gets it open, and gestures them all inside, pointing to a little kitchen for Jim Fulson to place the grocery bag.

"I'll unload our car," Jim Fulson says, and heads back out the gate to the street where he'd parked.

Ruth shrugs and leads the way into the hall. "Clara, you and her"—she gestures to Anna—"can have your old room. You'll find it unchanged." She turns to Lars. "You can fight with the other one for the couch. One of you gets the floor. I have some spare blankets."

Anna follows Ms. Thadeous to the rear of the house into a tiny bedroom with white walls, no pictures or hangings of any kind. Two twin beds, a dresser. Bare wooden floors. A nun's cubicle.

"She really exorcised you," Anna says, trying to inject some lightness, but Ms. Thadeous doesn't laugh the way Anna expects.

"No, I can see that she hasn't touched this room, except maybe to repaint," she says.

"But," Anna says, and stops. She's thinking of the science lab at school, the wall papered with articles from *Science,* the *New York Times,* the *New Yorker, Wired, New England Journal of Medicine.* The person who had a vision of that mosaic had a mind big enough to encompass much more than Sunnyvale High, or San Jose, or even California. Anna had thought of the person who created the wall as the real Ms. Thadeous, only now awakening after a fallow period. Yet peel back another layer and you had ... this?

"I took nothing with me when I left for Berkeley, nothing here mattered," Ms. Thadeous says. She opens the top drawer of the bureau. Neatly folded underwear and bras, all white. She is suddenly no longer the teacher, no longer the lover, but something fiercer, more primal. She pulls on the closet door and gestures. "My mother's idea of how a young woman should dress." A strapless pink prom dress is hanging on the inside. A frothy kind of pink fluff outlines the bodice, sequins adorn the skirt. "My father made me go," she says, pointing to it. "I was asked by an okay-enough boy, someone I didn't mind, and my father said I'd regret it if I didn't go. I don't think I would have, but my father was a big believer that we regret our sins of omission more than our sins of commission," she says. "I like the way you kids do it, now. Everyone just goes, girls and boys, you don't need a date, and you dance with your friends. Much saner."

"I assume your father is ... gone?" Anna asks. She sits on one of the twin beds. It is surprisingly hard. She tries to bounce on it, but there's very little give.

"You were lucky. You don't know this yet, but you will," Ms. Thadeous says. "A lingering death is the most painful kind. Once you've witnessed it, you pray that everyone else you love goes quickly." She opens another drawer—this one full of photographs—hesitates, and closes it again. "Death isn't *interesting*, Anna."

"It depends on what's waiting for you on the other side." Anna tries not to think of her parents.

"Oh, don't start that. Especially not here, in this house, this room. My mother drove me crazy with such stuff." Ms.

Thadeous puts her suitcase on the other bed, opens it, and be-gins unpacking. A couple pairs of pants. Some T-shirts, mostly white. A large manila envelope.

"What's in that?" Anna asks as Ms. Thadeous slips it into a drawer. Ms. Thadeous smiles, looking slightly chagrined. "My diploma from Berkeley. I was summa cum laude. I al-ways wished my father had lived to see it. I thought the least I could do would be to bring it back home. Although my mother blames Berkeley for turning me against her, and against God." Ms. Thadeous says *God* with a mocking distaste.

"Your mother is a religious woman?"

"She was excommunicated years ago, but it hasn't stopped her from going to services or worshipping," says Ms. Thadeous. "In her way. Always her way."

"Excommunicated? What does a Mormon have to do to be excommunicated?"

"She wasn't Mormon," she says quickly.

"Oh. Sorry. I just assumed."

"So does everyone. And she lets them. She was—is still, in her mind—a Christian Scientist. Strange, isn't it? She was from New York. Born into an upper-middle-class Presbyterian household. Her father was a doctor. Her grandmother was a doctor. And she chose to turn her back on everything they believed and to come to this remote enclave of outsiders, and then to be an outsider among outsiders." Ms. Thadeous shakes her head and gives a half laugh. "What a crazy family I come from," she says.

"How did your father . . . go? If you don't mind me ask-ing," Anna says.

"Pancreatic cancer," she says, folding her hands in her lap.

"That's supposed to be a bad one," Anna says.

"It was. And you can imagine the horror show if you don't treat it. Or even take palliative measures." Ms. Thadeous smiles but there is no amusement in her face.

"Not treat it?" Anna doesn't understand.

"Not with medicine. No. My mother was adamant," says Ms. Thadeous. Her hands seem fused together, they are so still. "And nothing for the pain, either. Just prayer."

Anna is shaken at the thought. She remembers Martha going through her chemotherapy treatments, her mottled skin and wigs that she and Anna's mother giggled over. Anna's mother even wore a wig, in solidarity, when they went out together.

"He was already so sick by the time they caught it that they probably couldn't have saved him. But he was also in so much pain. They could have eased his last months. She wouldn't hear of it."

"What possible reason would she have for making him suffer?"

Ms. Thadeous's smile is bitter. "She wanted as much pain as she could get. She ate his pain, she grew thick with it, you could see her thriving as he wasted away. As she prayed."

"How did your father take all this?"

"He was afraid. He was not a believer. But he couldn't stand up to her," Ms. Thadeous says. "Those last weeks, we'd joke about what was on the other side. 'A big black dog,' he'd say. 'A big black dog is on the other side, waiting for me.' He said the only question was whether it would lick his wounds, or gnaw at them."

They are both silent. Anna is unsure what to say. Ms. Thadeous doesn't seem to need comfort. Rather, she seems open to talking, an unusual opportunity.

"What do you think?" Anna asks. "About what happens, afterward?" She has never dared ask Ms. Thadeous about her beliefs before.

"I think he entered the void. Where we all go, eventually. Into nothingness." Ms. Thadeous says this without any feeling.

"A harsh fate for your father."

"It's a kinder vision for him than what my mother had." Ms. Thadeous looks down at her hands. "But you're right. He deserved better."

"As did many others," Anna says, thinking of her own parents.

"After he died, I had no reason to stay. Certainly not for her," says Ms. Thadeous. "As soon as I graduated high school I left."

Anna remembers something Ms. Thadeous had once told her. "You said that the world is divided into three categories. People who have their parents; people who have one; and people who have none. Then you said you belonged to a fourth category, but didn't tell me what it was."

"The fourth category would be for orphans of a different kind," says Ms. Thadeous. "Those who have thrown off their parents completely. Abandoned them. As I did."

"Ask for His forgiveness," Anna says. "He will listen."

"I've tried," Ms. Thadeous says. "But the lines of communication into the void seem to be down at present."

They hear Ruth's voice in the hallway outside the door. Ms. Thadeous visibly braces herself. "I see that this is not your safe place," Anna says.

"No," says Ms. Thadeous. "Not here. Never here."

44

DINNER IS SIMPLE. RUTH DEFROSTS some chicken breasts, pours a
can of mushroom soup on top of them, heats up a can of green
beans, puts a stack of presliced wheat bread, some margarine
and salt and pepper on the table. It tastes surprisingly good.

"You're too thin," Ruth observes, looking at Anna. "You,
too," she says, inclining her head toward Lars.

He's been noticeably quiet since they arrived. Taking
Ruth's measure. If he's smart, rejecting the possibility of making
inroads. In a minute he will do one of two things. Anna knows
him. When he feels he has a chance with someone, he turns
on his considerable charm. With people he has given up on, he
becomes stern, sometimes offensively so.

After dinner, Ruth brings out a gallon of vanilla ice cream
and without asking, spoons some into bowls. They all accept
silently. She is a formidable woman.

Jim Fulson is looking shy and uncomfortable. Despite
the heat in the house, he has his long-sleeved shirt buttoned
over his wrists, hiding his scars. He's combed his hair carefully,
slicked it so that it appears even darker than usual. He looks

large, uncouth, perched on a tiny chair, especially next to petite Ms. Thadeous and Ruth.

They are remarkably similar in the light. Fine-boned, with ruddy complexions. Ruth's hair is pure white. She sits erect, the skin of her hands free of the liver spots you see on others of her age, which Anna estimates to be around sixty-five. The demeanor of someone with no regrets.

"You are lovers," Ruth says. She is not asking a question. She has waited until they finish their ice cream, just as Jim Fulson started to relax. He stiffens up again.

"Of course," says Ms. Thadeous mildly. "And not my first."

Ruth nods, not apparently perturbed. A fact-finding mission.

"You are younger?"

"By four years."

"Your education?"

"UCLA, BA in business administration."

"Your occupation?"

"At the moment, unemployed."

Seemingly satisfied, Ruth nods at Ms. Thadeous. A curt *he'll do*. If he passed a test, it was a test with an odd rubric for success.

"You," Ruth says abruptly, talking to Anna. "You have the hands of a healer." And, when Anna looks down in bewilderment, she says, impatiently, "That's just an expression. We say that about people in Christian Science who have a more direct line to Him than the rest of us. A deeper intuitive understanding of the relationship between the physical and the spiritual." Then, without missing a beat. "You've been having headaches."

The statement startles Anna. She doesn't look at anyone else. "Yes," Anna says. She's been enduring one for two days now. *The altitude,* she told herself at first.

"That's the price the gifted often pay," Ruth says. "We will pray. Now."

"Mom," says Ms. Thadeous. "I will not allow this."

"I will," says Lars, abruptly, the first words he has spoken since dinner started. "Let us join hands." He reaches his left hand out to Ms. Thadeous, his right hand to Anna. Ms. Thadeous slaps it away. She stands, pushes her chair back, and leaves the room. They hear the front door open and bang shut. Jim Fulson leaps up, grabs their coats from the hook behind the door, and follows her out.

"Let us proceed," says Ruth, and so she, Lars, and Anna join hands and pray over the dirty dinner dishes. Anna shuts her eyes, but the only thing that comes to her mind is *please.*

"You're hungry," Lars says after a few moments. Anna opens her eyes to find Lars gazing at Ruth. "You desire things you are not getting." He releases their hands and looks around the pristine kitchen, the walls painted a bright, unrelenting yellow without a calendar or other hangings to break up the color. Anna has read that if you put a baby in a yellow room it will scream uncontrollably. "You are alone," says Lars. "You are lonely."

"As you well know, those are not the same," Ruth says. She places her hands in her lap. She certainly has dignity, Anna thinks.

"For you they are." Lars is his most certain, his sternest self. The Lars Anna saw toward the end at school, preaching in the cafeteria, attracting a growing number of followers. Anna begins gathering the plates together.

"Enough of this," Anna says. "Let's do the dishes and go to bed."

Both Ruth and Lars ignore her. "Don't overstep your boundaries in this house," Ruth tells Lars. "I see that you may well have a large ministry in your future. But I won't be a member of it."

Lars lifts his hands then drops them to his side as if to say, *so what?* Anna is a little shocked by his rudeness, but Ruth appears unperturbed.

"You slept the whole way here," Lars says to Anna. "You can't still be tired." Then, softer, only for her ears, "We need to talk."

"I am, and we don't," Anna says and begins running water in the sink. They wash the dishes in silence, the three of them working efficiently together. When they are finished, Jim Fulson and Ms. Thadeous still haven't returned. They didn't take the car—the keys are on a hook next to the telephone.

Lars takes the blankets Ruth set out and makes a bed on the couch. "Jim gets the floor," he says. Anna helps him, and is about to head to bed herself when Ruth exits the kitchen. She is rubbing lotion into her hands.

"It's been a while since I've had company," she says. "Forgive me if this evening was uncomfortable." She begins rolling up her sleeves, massaging the lotion into her arms, revealing deep purple bruises and some long scratches. Anna thinks she even sees teeth marks. Ruth notices what Anna is looking at. "The children where I work," she says. "I care for kids up and down the autism spectrum. They can hit. They bite. They scratch. Me more than anyone. But that's when they are still in control. They are merely playing a part. When they are truly out of control, I can tell when they've crossed that line. Then they listen to me. They don't have the language. But they understand bodies. Better than anyone. I believe in the power of touch. When they cross that line, I use that power. I'm the only one who can do it."

She finishes her ministrations, sits down in an armchair next to the couch that Lars is now lying on, blankets pulled to his chin.

Anna hesitates, then positions herself tentatively on a straight-backed chair next to the front door. "Tell us about Ms. Thadeous when she was young," she says, tentatively. She's not sure how Ruth will take this request.

"You admire her."

Anna is surprised, and even more so to find herself admitting, "Yes. Very much."

"But you also envy her." Another statement. This Anna doesn't answer.

"He's an attractive young man," Ruth says. "But not an ambitious choice. It won't last. She's like me, too strong, wanting a challenge always." Anna thinks back to how wrong she'd been about Ms. Thadeous, mistaking her boredom for not caring, for weakness. Her lack of interest as a lack of passion. She is suddenly worried for Jim Fulson. He is in over his head. He will eventually get hurt. But simultaneous with her concern a small voice whispers to her about possibilities.

Ruth starts talking again.

"The home I work in is up in the hills," Ruth says. "It has a large picture window looking out onto the Great Salt Lake, across that huge expanse of nothingness. I could ask, as so many of our visitors do, *What on earth would cause anyone to choose this godforsaken place to settle? Of all the bountiful lands, rich in resources, that make up America, who would choose this?* And the answer is, of course, that no one chooses this. One accepts it. And when I look over at what God has created out there, however loathsome it might appear to the untaught eye, I am grateful. You look at me and probably don't see a grateful woman. Yet I am. I stay close to home. I know what my limits are. I know what would happen to my soul if I wandered in the wilderness, as Clara has chosen to do."

Anna thinks of Clara's anonymous childhood bedroom and her equally nondescript house in San Jose, and she is quiet.

"You might not think of Clara and me as much alike in anything but looks," she says. "But she has iron in her soul. She will not stay with this young man. She knows she would destroy him if she did."

"She'll destroy him if she leaves," Anna says.

"Nonsense."

"You can be hurt by absence as well as presence," Anna says.

Ruth appears not to have heard Anna. "My children up on the hill. Conventional wisdom is to treat them softly, with compassion. Now I can summon as much compassion as the next person. I can play that game. But what these children need, what all children need, are boundaries, walls they can bounce off. It makes them feel safe."

Safe.

Then, a noise. The front door opens. Jim Fulson and Ms. Thadeous appear, both red-faced with cold, their breath coming fast from exertion. The small room is now crowded.

No one says anything for a moment. Then, "Where did you go?" Ruth asks.

"We walked," says Ms. Thadeous. She has something to say. Turning to Anna first, she begins abruptly. "You," she says. "You and your death wish. And you," she gestures toward Jim Fulson, but doesn't finish her sentence. He does not meet her eyes. Whatever happened out in the cold night, it wasn't a good thing for him.

"And you," Ms. Thadeous says to Lars. "God knows what you're up to, but at least it's not dying. You're after something else. That it appears to be something highly suspect is not my concern."

"Why did you come, then?" Lars asks. "And why did you tell us you were leading us to a safe place?"

Ruth leans forward. Her face softens. "Did you really say that?" she asks Ms. Thadeous.

"I wanted to bring you to the safest place I know," says Ms. Thadeous to Jim and Anna. She doesn't include Lars. "I thought I could protect you."

"Here?" asks Ruth.

"Don't be ludicrous," says Ms. Thadeous. "The cabin. I need the keys. We'll be leaving in the morning."

There's a moment of silence before Ruth sighs.

"Suffering," she says. "It certainly is a part of life."

"That's exactly right," says Lars. "We accept the suffering. For with that we become closer to Him."

"That's not what I said," Ruth says sharply.

Lars doesn't respond.

"Mom," says Ms. Thadeous. "We want the keys to the mountain cabin. No evasions."

Ruth says nothing.

"You do still have it? You haven't sold it?"

"Of course not. I rent it out as a holiday home. Or rather, an agency takes care of that for me. It's the best investment your father ever made. Winters have been slow, what with the drought. No skiing. But we manage to keep it rented in summer."

"It wasn't an investment. He loved it. So did I. And we need it. Tell your agent it's booked for the foreseeable future. Give me the keys."

Ruth leaves, goes into the back of the house where her bedroom is located. After a moment she returns with a key ring. "Sharper than a serpent's tooth," she says as she hands it over to Ms. Thadeous.

"Don't get me started," says Ms. Thadeous, and leaves the room.

45

ANNA IS AWAKENED BY A hand on her mouth. She is instantly alert. Of course she should have anticipated this. Anna nods to Lars, who is kneeling by her bed. He carefully takes his hand away. Anna sits up, trying not to rustle the bedclothes, places her bare feet on the floor, stands without making a sound. Ms. Thadeous is asleep, her mouth open. She snores, lightly. Her clothes in a heap on the floor, her bare shoulders gleaming in the moonlight. If Anna were Jim Fulson, the sight would have undone her.

Lars already has his backpack and Anna's two Safeway bags of clothes by the door.

Anna lifts the keys from the hook next to the phone, takes her bag and is almost out the door when she hears a noise behind her. Ruth, in a long white nightgown, but looking as perfectly groomed as when fully dressed, is standing in the hallway, her right eyebrow arched.

"It won't do them any harm to be stranded for a while," she says. "Bring down their pride." She smiles. "No, it wouldn't hurt a bit."

She holds out a map. "You'll need this, wherever you're going," she says. "I pray you are going toward Him, not away."

"Toward, definitely," says Lars.

"We hope," says Anna.

46

PEOPLE TALK ABOUT THE MAGNIFICENCE of the American West. Anna can appreciate that. A magnificent emptiness. A blank landscape for fantasies or nightmares. But when they leave Salt Lake City and head east on Route 80, the sun just rising in the east, she also wonders what mote in her eye prevents her from seeing what so many others have rejoiced in. The dawn sky is overcast, but no snow is forecast. Lumpy, lifeless land.

The Great Plains stretch for miles in all directions. The absence of fences, the fact that the landscape hasn't yet been despoiled by man, should make this a sublime experience. Yet the dull frozen dirt does not inspire. Neither does the bleached-out sky. Occasionally they come upon evidence of human existence amidst the flat gray terrain: slanting wooden shacks that seem abandoned save for the curtains in the windows, and vehicles in the yards. They also pass bright yellow, green, and red commercial buildings at strategic crossroads: modular gas stations with convenience stores attached. Subways, 7-Elevens, other places that discourage loitering, designed for quick ins and outs. Take your stuff and be on your way. *How do they staff these places?* Anna wonders. The clerks are young, about Anna's age. *Where do they live? Go to school?* Homes, schools, or other signs that people inhabit this landscape are nowhere to be seen.

"He designed this place to make you feel that improvement is necessary. Or at least possible," says Lars. "That you must do something to help." Anna just nods. She can't imagine any way the landscape could be improved, made more hospitable. "If not for Fred Wilson's operation, we could have gone in a different direction," he says. "Into the city, to San Francisco, to LA, witnessed the crowds and the despair there. A different kind of misery. But here is where He placed us. It is for a reason, I'm sure. My ministry is here. The heartland."

"The heartland? The emptyland," Anna says, but stops there. She is surprised at what she was going to say next. She misses Sunnyvale. She likes being in a valley, the enclosure of mountains on all sides, knowing the infinite waters of the sea are within easy reach. Yet these people, few as they are, survive in this landlocked place, blown about by winds, exposed as ants on a cement path.

"We'll help Fred Wilson in any way we can," Lars says. "And after he achieves his goal—after he breeds a pure Red Heifer—I'm going to look for a church in this region. A church compatible with our beliefs. A place we can serve."

Why you say "we," white man? thinks Anna, but she doesn't say anything.

They're now in Wyoming. Lars is stretched out in the back seat, the map on the floor beside him. They stopped consulting it hours ago. A long line almost to the edge of the state, then a left turn and north for another hundred miles. Nothing to do for hours except keep her foot on the gas. Steering is hardly necessary; the road is so straight and true.

They pass Rock Springs. Where the West Begins. Without Lars, Anna could easily imagine herself as the only living thing within hundreds of miles. This is not a pleasant feeling. Anna had always pictured this part of the country to contain developments like Columbus: neighborhoods of small brick houses. Cement instead of grass. Leafy trees growing out of squares cut in the concrete. Chain-link fences. More pit bulls than Labradors. Anna clearly suffers from a failure of imagination, because she could never have conjured up this wilderness.

No music on the radio, nothing but static as she drives. Reminders of the transience of life abound. White wooden crosses appear every so often, marking the spots of fatal highway accidents. Anna counts more deaths than the living people she's seen since Utah. Many of the memorials decorated with plastic flowers, roses and carnations. Some have stuffed animals next to them. At one intersection, a blossom of crosses, a whole busload must have perished. Anna stops and both she and Lars get out of the car to look at the names carved into the weathered wood. Some of the flowers are fresh. Yet the sign *May they rest in peace* is dated sixteen years earlier. "They would have been Ms. Thadeous's age," says Lars. They get back into the car and keep driving.

They approach a small town at 9 AM. In California it would be considered the height of the morning rush hour, the coffeehouses full and expressways clogged, but Crawford, Wyoming, appears deserted. All the storefronts say closed. The only sign of life is on Second Street, at the senior center, where a middle-aged woman is loading trays into the back of a van. A gas station is kitty-corner to it. Anna pulls up, stops the car and tries the Regular unleaded pump. It works. The office is unlocked, with a cash box on the counter. *Please only take exact change, we've come up a little short lately. Much appreciated!* Lars and Anna look at each other. Is this possible? Apparently, yes. Anna pays for the gas, leaves a twenty-dollar bill as a tip in gratitude, and they keep moving.

They drive on and on through the endless prairie. Finally, in midafternoon, growing tired, they agree to stop for the day. The left turn at 287 North, in Rawlins, Wyoming, takes them through the most upscale community than they've seen since leaving Salt Lake City. They pass a gleaming fifties'-style restaurant, Penny's Diner, but Lars shakes his head, and also at the glossy chain hotels planted in the center of town. No cars in any of the parking lots.

"We'd be too noticeable," he says.

"So weird," Anna says, "All these hotels, empty."

"Didn't you see that sign for the Frontier Prison Museum? I bet that fills the hotels during tourist season." Lars smiles. Anna has never heard sarcasm from him before. A first.

"It's people in transit along 80," Anna says. "Probably a lot go through here in the summer."

"Not the high season right now." Lars speaks with authority. "Keep going, I want a place outside the main junction."

The Rawlins municipal building seems to be a combination town hall and recreation center, with notices of executive council meetings posted alongside *Spin with Lynn* and *Jr. Rifle League*. There are the usual holiday decorations, only unlike the ones in California, they're fake. These green boughs look truly exotic after the miles of dirt stretching in all directions. They pass the Frontier Prison Museum, two cars in the parking lot, and then they are done with Rawlins. Anna is tired, so tired.

"I have to stop soon," she says, "I can't keep my eyes open much longer."

"Look for something small. Not a chain. A privately run place," Lars instructs.

"I'm not sure we're going to see anything out here," Anna says. "We might have to go back to Rawlins, find someplace off the main drag."

Lars shrugs. But a few miles down the road they see a motel so downmarket it doesn't even have a name. Just the sign *Motel*. One other car in the lot. Anna pulls in. Lars stays in the car while an elderly woman takes down Anna's name and accepts thirty-five dollars in cash. They are given no. 8, which has two beds and a chest of drawers. It reeks of skunk. Things skitter just out of eyesight. The bathroom pipes squawk as Anna showers. When she emerges from the tiny bathroom, Lars is asleep on the bed farthest from the door. He pulled down the shades and put the chain up. The shadows of bristles on his face are much more pronounced than when they left Sunnyvale. If anything, they make him look younger; they accentuate the soft whiteness of the skin on his neck. Sleeping faun. Deceptively innocent-looking.

Anna takes the bed nearest the door, and lies down. The next thing she knows, her eyes are open but she can barely see, the light is so dim. She brushes the curtains aside and sees that it's dusk. She's slept the rest of the day away. She looks over at Lars, who still seems to be sleeping deeply.

Taking the key, Anna unhooks the chain from the door and carefully closes it behind her. There are no newspaper stands in sight, so Anna walks to the office to ask if they have a paper. The elderly woman is gone. A young blonde girl, not much older than Anna, has taken her place. She's smoking despite the large *No smoking* sign above the register, and it's tough to breathe in the small space. Through a half-open door Anna sees a small room with an unmade bed. The girl looks at Anna curiously, but manages to find today's *Rawlins Sentinel.*

Anna thanks the girl, takes the paper, and leaves. The cold is shocking after the overheated room; she's only wearing Jim Fulson's threadbare UCLA sweatshirt and jeans. She considers going back inside, but the smoke-filled office doesn't attract her, despite its padded seats and vending machine. She leans against the motel wall and opens up the front section of the paper and reads it by the light over the office door. Nothing about a stolen car and two teenagers on the loose in Utah. Nothing about kidnappings in California. They'd passed Wyoming state troopers three times while driving, but none of them gave chase. Ms. Thadeous and Jim Fulson must not have reported them. Somehow they seem to be safe. Thank the Lord.

47

AFTER READING THE PAPER, ANNA is uncertain what to do next. Go back to the motel room and remain quiet, stare at the wall while Lars sleeps? No book. No iPod. Her stomach rumbles. They'd stopped at a Burger King in Rock Springs for breakfast, but hadn't eaten anything since. Anna curses Lars for forcing them to stay in the middle of nowhere, but then notices that at the far end of the street is a white aluminum-sided building. It is recessed from the road, behind a large oak tree, one of the few trees in the vicinity. A single lighted sign of a slightly tipped martini glass hangs out front, and under it, *Cocktails* and *Good Food* written in a cursive font Anna associates with the 1950s.

The room is mostly empty when Anna enters except for two kids playing video games and a man sitting at the bar holding a glass between his hands. It's insufferably hot, so Anna immediately sheds her sweatshirt. She chooses the bar rather than one of the tables, carefully taking a stool two seats away from the man. He's a burly type, with industrial-looking waterproof clothes and gear heaped on the stools between them. An emergency technician or fireman, Anna guesses. The bartender is younger, Anna estimates about Ms. Thadeous's age. Anna orders a white wine. The bartender doesn't ask for ID although Anna can't look more than fourteen, her short hair still wet from her shower, no makeup.

A boxy room, nothing picturesque or even barlike about it. A Formica-topped counter. No real wood anywhere. The floor is linoleum, the tables metal. Even the bar stools are just thin steel tubes with fake leather seats. It looks like a lunch counter. When she asks the bartender if he has anything to eat, he throws a couple bags of Doritos down in front of her.

"Sorry, that's all I got," he says. "You're lucky we're even open. We typically close down after Thanksgiving."

Anna is still testing her stool to see if it can bear her weight, it feels so rickety. "Why didn't you?" she asks.

"The weather," says the bartender. "No snow, no storms. We're seeing a lot more cars coming through here than usual. Trucks drive through all year but they prefer to stay in Rawlins, more stuff going on there. No reason to stay open for them. But people that don't know the route, they go past Rawlins, realize their mistake, and see us. Most of our customers stumble in here by accident."

"Like me," Anna says.

"Like you."

After giving Anna her wine, the bartender goes into the back room; Anna can hear thuds as if he's hoisting and stacking heavy boxes.

"So why you here?" asks the man, two stools down. The fireman. His voice is surprisingly high, almost a falsetto, but not unpleasant.

A thick yellow rubber coat and pants are hanging on the stools between them. He's kept his boots on; they are huge, he is huge, a Paul Bunyan of a man, with a cratered face. Hands. Big hands, with long, sinewy fingers. Hands that would save. Anna wonders how many chances he gets to be heroic here.

"Just passing through," Anna says, and braces herself for more questions, but he seems to have run out. He returns to studying his beer.

The bartender comes back, weighed down by a large crate marked *Guinness*. He heaves it onto the floor, starts loading bottles into the fridge. He's not bad-looking, a full beard but oddly, no mustache. It gives him an Amish look. His T-shirt is red with the words *Why Not* embossed on it.

Anna finishes her white wine and considers asking for another. She doesn't know if sufficient time has passed for that to be acceptable. She runs her hands over the curious marks on the bar top, as if someone has been chewing it. Anna's stool squeaks when she moves, even if she just shifts slightly, so she tries to keep still. Outside the front window, darkness. It's now 6:30 in the evening.

"Where you from?" The fireman again.

Anna considers her answer. "California," she says finally. The license plates in the motel parking lot would give her away, anyway.

"Long way."

Anna nods, but looks down, not wanting to encourage this kind of questioning.

The bartender is wiping down the bar. "So you drove all the way here in December? You couldn't have done that ten or even five years ago," he says. "Anyone who claims the weather isn't behaving strangely needs to pay us a visit."

The fireman orders another beer. He's constantly checking his cell phone, disappointed each time.

"Expecting something? Or just hoping," asks the bartender. Although the words are teasing, he asks in a respectful way. Anna likes that.

The fireman gives a snort that could mean anything. But he puts the silent phone away in his pocket.

"Don't you get worried about earthquakes there in California?" he asks.

"Don't you worry about fires here? Blizzards? Tornados?" Anna retorts.

"I saw this video on YouTube," says the bartender. "Apparently, all you Californians are wrong about what to do in case of an earthquake. A fireman was giving this talk on how getting under a table or in a doorway is a lot of hooey. You're sure to die that way, crushed by falling stuff. He said there's a better way. He called it the Triangle of Life. What you do is find the biggest object in the room and lie down next to it, not under it. There's a void there, a protective space, in the shape of a triangle that exists next to every big object in the room if the ceiling collapses. You have to get into that Triangle of Life in an earthquake or you're dead meat."

Anna shakes her head. No one can tell her about earthquakes. Her father taught her well.

"That theory's been proven wrong. Drop, cover, and hold on is still best," says Anna.

"That's what I've been taught," says the fireman.

"No, he showed pictures," insists the bartender. "Of a room after an earthquake. Next to the big dining room table and this huge china cabinet you could distinctly see the tri-angles—areas where nothing had fallen or been damaged."

"I'm not saying these voids don't exist," Anna says pa-tiently, the way she's heard her father explain it. "But depending on the architecture, the type of quake, and what's in the room, your injuries could be worse if you tried to find the triangle than just following the tried-and-true drill."

"You've clearly thought about this," the fireman says.

"Someone I knew certainly did." *Knew*, she said without thinking. The denial stage passed without Anna noticing. She understands now that her parents are irrefutably gone. "I'll have another white wine," she says.

"Not likely we'll have to worry about that anytime soon," the bartender says as he fills her glass.

"Not soon, but eventually. One day it'll happen," Anna says. "You've got the New Madrid Fault that runs through the Midwest, including parts of Nebraska. Then you've got the Fort Union Fault. That's part of the Mid-Continent Rift System, which is basically a gigantic, billion-year-old crevice under our feet. It's seven hundred miles long and forty miles wide in places. When that goes, hold on."

Everyone lapses into silence after this speech. The fireman leaves shortly after, gathering his gear and carrying it with him into a newish Ford Explorer parked outside the large windows. He sees Anna looking as he starts it up, and he gives a wave. She waves back.

Anna eats both packages of Doritos. She then devours a bag of pretzels the bartender finds in the back room. Fin-ishing her third glass of wine, Anna realizes she's traveled be-yond the pleasant point she'd reached in that other bar, that night from her previous life with Jim Fulson and Ms. Thadeous, but still she doesn't stop. She orders, and drinks, another glass. Then she has to pee, and slides off her stool and walks unsteadily to the door marked *Ladies*. On the back of the stall door is a poster for Miss Rawlins 2011 contest. The silhouette of a cowgirl on a bucking horse holding her hat above her head has been predictably defaced. Someone has drawn large breasts on her, and she is surrounded by a virtual cloud of disembodied penises. All the graffiti scratched into the metal walls of the stall are sexual. Who has done what to whom. That's always the issue, isn't it, Anna thinks. Who is getting the most love.

When Anna emerges from the bathroom, the girl from the motel office is occupying her stool.

"Saw you head here," she says. "Hope you don't mind if I join you. Finally got off work."

"Of course not," Anna says. She is rather, no, very, drunk. Anna takes the seat next to the girl, grabs her wineglass, only dregs in it.

"Stephen!" the girl calls. The bartender comes slowly out of the back room.

"Oh you," he says, and without saying anything else pours a shot of tequila and puts it in front of her. She downs it in one swallow and holds it out to him. He shakes his head, but pours another.

"That your boyfriend with you?"

"Just a friend."

"On the road together?"

Anna considers what to say. The girl had asked in an offhand way, Stephen isn't paying attention, and it doesn't seem to matter to either of them who or what Anna is. Was. She's reluctant to lie, so she just nods. "We took off."

"I was on the road myself last year. Got stuck when my ride dropped me here and I couldn't get another one. I started cleaning rooms for Greta, watching the front desk when she needs a break. She lets me crash in the back office, too."

"You don't mind being stuck in this place?" Anna asks. She's dying to find out the girl's age, but stops herself from asking.

"Everyone's okay," the girl says. "Actually, Greta sent me to find out the scoop. If you're runaways or whatever. Don't worry, I won't tell. It's not like Greta would do anything, she's only curious. She likes a good story. You could tell her the wild-est tale and she wouldn't pass it on. Just chew it over."

Stephen laughs. "You got Greta pegged right." He comes out from behind the bar and heads for the bathrooms. "Behave while I'm gone," he calls.

When he's gone, Anna opens her purse and gives the girl a hundred-dollar bill. "Tell her we're eighteen and pregnant and just got married in Reno but it's all legal."

The girl takes the bill, quickly pushes it into her jeans pocket, eyes Anna's flat stomach. "Pregnant?" she asks. "If I was a different kind of person, I'd tell you to ease up a bit." She nods at the empty glasses on the bar.

"Not really," Anna says. "That's only chewing material for Greta."

"Oh. Gotcha. But why are you drinking this terrible wine if you've got money? Why not have a real drink?"

"I've never had one," Anna says.

"Now's the time. What'll you have?"

"Vodka," Anna says. She's her father's daughter after all.

The girl glances quickly toward the bathrooms, then reaches behind the bar and picks a bottle up by the neck. She pours until Anna's wineglass is three-quarters full. "He's not as stupid as he seems, so drink this quick."

It burns into a hot little puddle in Anna's stomach. There's a moment when her throat rebels from the harshness, then a deep shudder, and the world looks slightly brighter. "Another," Anna says. The girl reaches down and has the bottle poised over Anna's glass when Stephen emerges from the bathroom.

"Caught you red-handed," he says. "And I told you to be good."

Anna reaches into her purse, and extracts another hundred-dollar bill. Monopoly money.

"Will this cover it?" she asks.

Stephen laughs. "I'll say."

"Can I pour now?" asks the girl.

"If that's what the woman wants, that's what she gets," Stephen says. He kisses the hundred and puts it in his wallet.

"It's what I want," Anna says. *I am my father's daughter. I am my father's daughter.*

"So why are you really here? Why'd you take off?" asks the girl.

Anna has to think about this. "Obsessions," she says finally. Images. Sounds. The Red Heifer. Bosch's depiction of hell. A rock hitting a tree. A rock splashing in a river. The flex of an arm attached to a shoulder throwing a rock.

"Give me a hint," says the girl.

Anna considers it. Drunk as she is, she tries to phrase her reply carefully. "He's not for me," Anna says.

"Oh, *that* kind of obsession."

"So what I want to know," Anna says, "is how you become un-obsessed."

She doesn't expect an answer, but the girl provides one. "You take action," she says. "You take control."

Anna thinks of her father's earthquake preparedness, his counting cans and noting expiration dates, her mother's repeated playing of Mahler. Rituals for managing obsessions. Acknowledging that they exist, and would always exist. Running them into the ground. Anna knows what she has to do. She finally knows. She slides off her stool, heads unsteadily for the door.

"Glad I could help," the girl calls after her.

48

ANNA TRIES THE DOOR TO the hotel room. It's locked. She knocks softly. When she doesn't get an answer, she fumbles with the key, manages to insert it into the lock, and opens the door with much more noise than she intended. No one there, the sheets and blanket on Lars's bed rumpled. The room is warm and moist and smells like soap, the window fogged. The heat and damp are coming from the bathroom, the door is open halfway. Inside, the light is on.

Lars is in the bathtub, lying with his eyes closed. Endearingly, he has used the tiny bottle of complimentary shampoo as bubble bath, and the tub is piled high with frothy white foam. His hair is wet and slicked back. The normally pale skin on his shoulders and neck is flushed. All else is submerged in the tub, under the bubbles. A tiny spider hangs on a thread from the ceiling right above Lars's head.

As quietly as Anna can, she crouches down, goes into a kind of kneeling position beside the tub. Although the water that has splashed out of the tub onto the floor is cool as it soaks through her jeans, the tub is warm to touch. The room is altogether too hot. Anna pulls off her shirt without unbuttoning it.

Now she's just in her bra and jeans. Lars still doesn't perceive that he isn't alone.

Anna tentatively touches the side of Lars's neck. His eyes fly open and he sits up, giving a tiny, almost imperceptible gasp. When he sees Anna, he looks relieved. Then he shrinks back into the bath self-consciously. Anna touches him again, the same spot, only it's more of a caress this time. He flinches.

"What are you doing?" His voice, unprepared, comes out several registers higher than usual. Anna realizes this must be his natural voice.

Anna doesn't answer. She keeps her hand moving downward, past Lars's shoulders, down his hairless chest, to his concave stomach. He tries to stop her, but Anna easily pushes his hands aside. She moves her hand past his stomach to his groin, cradles what she finds there in her hand, little seahorse. Lars starts struggling, pushing Anna away, but she presses him back into the water. Through this, neither of them says a word. Power games. Then Anna lets go and stands up.

"What are you doing?" he asks again, his voice closer to its usual dark timbre. Then he uses her name, "Anna?" first as a question, then "Anna!" But she is too far gone. She is in control, she is negotiating for some peace of mind, some sense of closure. Lars is small and pitiful. He arouses nothing in Anna but distaste. And she clearly has no power over him; he remains flaccid. Anna takes off her bra, slides out of her jeans and panties.

Except for Anna's slight breasts, she could be a boy herself, she's so thin. Even Lars has more meat than she does. Anna steps carefully into the tub even as Lars tries to get out.

"Stop fighting this," Anna says, and to her surprise he does. She maneuvers herself into a position where she is sitting astride his hips, her legs on either side of him. She bends and tries to kiss him, but finds her lips pressed against an unyielding wall, no air to breathe. Anna thinks of Jim Fulson and Ms. Thadeous, their open pliant mouths, and is ashamed. She and Lars, two pale sticks in a pool of tepid water.

Anna thinks, *I can do this.* She imagines a God above, manipulating the pitiful humans below. Here, you mate with her, and you with him, let's see what the result will be.

Anna's pubic hair is blonde and curly, and she hasn't shaved under her arms or legs in more than eighteen months. She is as He made her. Lars is studying her as though she were a specimen. His body still unaroused.

He is waiting for Anna to make the next move. She senses calculation. He is determining how to turn this to his advantage. Anna waits until the silence is unbearable, then says what she has been thinking for some weeks.

"I don't think I like you very much."

"You don't need to," Lars says. He is contained now, as tight in his body as a crustacean. "Liking is never necessary. You will still feel my power." Anna thinks perhaps she has misunderstood him, she is drunk. Surely he couldn't be saying these things. "My ministry will grow. I learned a lot from you, from the months in Sunnyvale. That was necessary, as were the missteps before it."

Suddenly anger explodes inside Anna, gets her up and off Lars. She stumbles clumsily out of the tub, dries herself with the too-small rough towel, grabs her clothes and leaves the bathroom, closing the door behind her. She dresses herself fully, then sits on the made bed and waits for Lars to emerge. He takes his time.

"That was odd," he says, "but then I smelled the alcohol."

"What you smelled was a moment of honesty," Anna says. She is close to tears. Appalled, not for what happened, but for what didn't happen. She failed to transfer this burden. Unrequited love. Anna has a rare flash of pity for herself, so cheapened now. Offering what no one wants. She slips under the covers, turns her back to Lars, and pretends to sleep.

49

ANNA OPENS HER EYES TO another blinding headache, worse than any she's ever experienced. Then she remembers the previous night, and is awash in shame. Lars is already up, dressed and packed. She can't look at him directly although he shows no sign he was impacted by what happened.

They get into the car. Unsure of the next time they'll find food or fuel, they double back to Rawlins, tank up, and buy coffee and breakfast sandwiches at McDonald's. They also stop at a 7-Eleven for some apples, bananas, water, and yogurt. Judging from the map, they have about seven hours of driving, and want to get into Valentine before dark. They are on their way, fed and provisioned, by 8:30 AM, with very few words spoken between them.

"Unless we have to stop for any reason, we'll hit Valentine by 3:30 or 4:00 at the latest," says Lars. He has been carefully studying the map. "We can find more gas in Douglas and then again in Chadron."

The day is clear. Still chilly, but the freshness of the air feels good. Anna rolls her window down halfway, enjoying the wind on her face as she drives. The clouds lift and the American West so glorified in song and stories finally shows its face. Vast distances, miles and miles without any sign of human inhabitants, muted but splendid colors.

"A man could be a man out here," says Lars, and, looking at Anna, laughs. A little self-consciously, but not much.

"Practicing?"

"A bit," he admits. "It's like a movie set," he says. The tension between them relaxes. They pass any number of decrepit wooden houses, their roofs and porches sagging, stripped of color by rain and sun, foils for the magnificent scenery. At random intervals, fences subdivide the expanse of earth, but no animals, and few humans, in sight.

Despite herself, Anna is impressed. "Big sky," she says.

"I think that's Montana, but yes, it most definitely is."

They fill the tank in Douglas. While the gas flows into the car, Anna stands outside and peels an orange. Everything at the junction is brand new. A Holiday Inn and a Sleep Inn & Suites so recently constructed that the earth around the parking lot is still raw. No one has attempted landscaping of any kind around the buildings. They just let the prairie run up to their doors. An unsettling mixture of earth and plastic.

They continue on. Lars dozes off about twenty miles out of Douglas. Almost seventy miles after that, Anna sees something white in the distance, something off the road. As she gets closer, she begins to understand the gigantic scale of the thing, whatever it is. Tall and shaped like an elongated teardrop. Its unnatural white glows against the surrounding flatlands. A radio tower of some kind? It grows as they approach it, rising to an incredible height, five or six times the length of one of the telephone poles that parallel the road.

Lars wakes as they approach it, still several miles away.

"What on earth ...!" he exclaims, sitting straight as he squints into the distance. It grows closer and larger. Lars understands before Anna.

"It's a statue," he says.

"Not possible," Anna says. "Not unless it's a statue six stories high."

Yet that's exactly what it is. Positioned around two hundred yards off the highway, they can soon distinguish a head, small in relation to the rest of the body, forming the top of the teardrop. From the shape of the bottom part of the statue, it appears to be wearing robes of some kind. At least sixty feet tall.

"Not pants, not a dress, at least not a modern one," says Lars. "I don't see any limbs, either."

"An angel? Moroni?"

Lars shakes his head. "No trumpet. Besides, we're a long way off the Mormon Trail. We left that when we turned off 80."

They're perhaps two miles away when Lars gets it.

"Mary," Lars says. "Mother of Jesus."

He's right. Anna can see it now, the same shape, the same hooded head, the clasped hands, the flowing robes, just as the life-sized statue in front of St. Lucy's, on Maude, back in Sunnyvale.

"Good God," says Anna.

"Yes," says Lars.

Although a large parking lot that can hold at least three hundred cars has been paved amidst the brush and sage of the countryside, no one is here except Anna and Lars. There isn't a visitors' center, not even bathroom facilities. Only a looming giant of a woman, smiling, a beatific smile on her face. *Our Lady of Peace* is carved on her base. *Our Blessed Mother.*

"I guess that out here in the middle of nowhere, people get big ideas," Lars says.

"They do in the middle of everywhere, too," Anna says.

They get out of the car and walk to the statue. Since no one else is around, Anna leaves the keys in the ignition, Lars's door half-open.

"An eyesore," says Lars.

Anna is surprised at the vehemence in Lars's voice. She sees that he is more affronted than she has ever seen him. Even the bullies at school didn't evoke this reaction.

"Mary worship is an aberration," says Lars. "Our biggest challenge for conversion are those that idolize her. *Thou shalt not bow down thyself to them, nor serve them: for I the Lord thy God am a jealous God.*"

Both Anna and Lars are then silent. Anna tilts back her neck and shades her eyes against the sun to see the statue's face. She has seen few things on earth as benign as Mary's expression.

Anna wonders how much of what she's thinking he can guess. She wants none of what he wants. She is thinking that their goals are not aligned. He'll find out when they reach Fred Wilson's ranch. Everyone will find out. She is a hypocrite, an activist directly opposed to Lars's mission.

"Look," she says. "What are those little spots of color on the base?"

Hundreds of pieces of paper have been taped to the bottom of her smooth stone robe. Some of what's written on the paper are illegible, washed out from the rain or bleached by the sun. Others are fresher, perhaps a day or two old. Some are carefully laminated, and thus preserved, and easily read. The ground is littered with scraps.

"I've heard you see this in Jerusalem, too," Anna says. "Against the wall of the Temple Mount. People write their prayers and put them between the stones."

"Idolatry," says Lars, nearly spitting the word. He grabs a handful of the papers, rips them off the stone, crumples them, throwing them to the ground. "Appalling."

Anna points to one that has been carefully drawn in crayon, clearly a child's handiwork, laminated and taped securely with electrical tape. "This person came prepared," she says. *Blessed Mother, pray for me,* it reads, the child's drawing of the statue, elongated and off scale, with the mountains in the distance only coming up to Mary's elbows.

"Let's go," says Lars abruptly, and begins walking back to the car. Anna doesn't follow. Instead she sits at the base of the statue, the cool stone against her back. The highway stretches out in either direction as far as she can see. Our Lady of Peace. Anna feels peaceful, almost as if she's found the safe place Ms. Thadeous was seeking. If the Tribulation is indeed coming, she would like to curl up at the base of this giantess and beg for her protection. Anna would call upon the souls of all the hopeful people who had left her notes and arm herself with their faith against the horrors to come.

50

THEY'RE BACK IN THE CAR and on the road for maybe thirty seconds when they hear a sharp crack. The car swerves to the right.

"Oh no," says Anna. The car is noticeably listing and with each rotation of the wheels they can hear a resounding thump. She swings the car off the road once more.

"We don't have time for all these stops," says Lars. "Not if we want to get to Valentine before dark."

They both get out and walk around to the back of the car. The rear left tire is flat against the gravel.

"Do you know how to fix a flat?" asks Anna.

"No. Do you?"

A slow hour passes before Anna sees a small dot traveling toward them. She hits Lars's arm. The dot grows bigger, reveals itself to be a blue van. Black letters on the side read *Elizabeth O'Malley, DVM*. Anna is barely on her feet when the van pulls over in a cloud of dust. A tall stout woman of about fifty-five opens the driver's door and steps out. She's dressed in blue jeans and a jean jacket.

"What do we have here?" she asks, then answers herself. "I see. You need some help?"

"Yes, please," Anna says while Lars scrambles to his feet.

"We can do that," says the woman. From the back of her van she takes out a canvas bag full of tools. Anna and Lars stand by silently while she expertly jacks up the car, removes the flat tire and puts on the spare from their trunk. "You're lucky, this is a real tire, not just a temporary," she says.

The woman eyes their California plates. She examines them more closely. "Awfully far from home," she says.

Anna falters. "Yes."

"You traveling alone? No adults?"

Again, Anna pushes out a "yes." She feels as though she's being scolded by one of her teachers.

"Shouldn't you be in school?" the woman asks. Standing there with her hands on her hips she actually looks like a disapproving teacher.

Trying to choose among all the lies they've been telling, Anna finds herself stumbling to say something sensible. For the first time, Lars volunteers a version that sounds reasonably coherent. "We're cousins. We have an aunt who's very ill," he says. "We're meeting our parents at her house. They're flying in."

The veterinarian nods, her face impassive. Anna sees her staring again at the license plate of Ms. Thadeous's car.

"Thank you," Anna says. She takes Lars by the arm, pulls him gently toward the car. But Lars has spotted something. She knows that look now, that puffing up of his shoulders, the look of gravitas that settles over his face. He points to the small gold cross the woman is wearing around her neck.

"Do you believe?" he asks. Then, getting no response, he says in his deepest, most reassuring voice, "We do."

Her face does not soften. "Perhaps."

"An odd answer," says Lars, his voice deepening even further, his eyes focusing on hers, beginning what Anna now thinks of as working his magic.

"Believing means a lot of things around here. Sometimes crazy things," the woman says.

Lars doesn't miss his opening. "Crazy as in implausible? Or crazy as in obviously not the right way of the Lord?"

She doesn't answer, but her eyes are sharper.

"Where you heading?" she asks.

"Valentine," Lars says.

Anna could swear something in her face changes slightly, and she curses Lars for telling the truth.

"Know anyone out there?" Lars asks.

"Valentine's only about a hundred miles away. That makes us practically neighbors. I know most of the farmers in the area. They have their own vets of course. But every once in a while they need a helping hand. What's your aunt's name?"

Anna and Lars are both silent. Then Lars says "Mrs. Fred Wilson. Do you know her?" Again, that slight shift in her face. Even Lars perceives it this time, Anna sees him pull back.

"I know of them," she says, finally. "Not the most neighborly of the ranchers in these parts, I'd say. Fred Wilson has a bit of a reputation with the ladies." Here she stops as if she's said too much. "His wife is active in politics. Very religious, both of them. But you'd know that, them being your relatives and all. Sorry to hear that your aunt is ill. I don't know her."

"Thank you," says Lars, in an agreeable voice, as if she isn't telling them anything they don't already know.

She hesitates for a moment, then says, "Follow me to town. Have a cup of coffee. You're still three hours from Valentine."

Anna again sees her looking at the license plate for longer than Anna would have thought necessary.

"No, we have to get going," she says. They say their good-byes to the vet, who gets in her car and drives off, and, Anna is convinced, will immediately pick up her cell phone to report two minors hundreds of miles from home in a car with plates 2MZA584.

"We need to get out of here," Anna tells Lars. Once inside the car, they get back on I-20 and after another twenty miles or so reach a major milestone: their destination's name on a sign. *Valentine 150 miles.*

"Almost there," Anna says, to break the silence. But Lars isn't talking. His failure with the vet is smarting. They make the final leg of their long journey without saying a word to each other.

51

THEY MAKE GOOD TIME—ANNA IS going more than 85 miles an hour on the empty, flat road, and so the sun is still low in the sky by the time they circumvent the unmarked turnoffs and roads around Valentine. They're forced to retrace their route at least half a dozen times before they locate the gravel road marked *Wilson*. The sign is hand-painted, the letters faded. The ranch buildings are perhaps three-quarters of a mile away, but the terrain is so flat, they can see them from the turnoff. The scene is not prepossessing. Whatever air of prosperity Wilson had projected at Reverend Michael's church, little of it has rubbed off on his property. Dry, unfertile-looking fields, beaten down fence posts with much of the wiring between them missing. As Lars and Anna drive closer, one of the buildings turns out to be a house. Not a classic farmhouse, but a rancher reminiscent of Sunnyvale, close to the ground, and, like all the dwellings they've seen in the state, not landscaped, but with dirt and scrub running straight up to the walls. A cracked pavement leading to the front stoop. No trees. The hills a long way off.

God painted this landscape using the same palette of browns and grays He'd used since they entered Wyoming.

Three satellite dishes are affixed to the roof of the house, and a telephone wire is attached to the chimney and strung on poles that run alongside the driveway. Substantial, physical infrastructure. What can Anna hope to disrupt about this, to put an end to Fred Wilson's nefarious scheme?

Her hands are shaking on the wheel. Here they are. At last. Close to the epicenter of an operation that would throw the world into chaos. Anna marvels that it's been under one hundred hours since her awakening in the waves. She has no plans. She has no idea of how she will prevent the End of Days.

"Must be one hell of a muddy place when it rains," Anna says as they get out of the car. Lars looks as excited as Anna is anxious. The bare earth that surrounds the house is dry with large cracks making a crazy sort of jigsaw puzzle. Approximately two hundred yards from the house are some buildings that look in better repair, and behind them, a larger structure that could be a barn. Then an enclosed space with perhaps twenty cows penned in. About half are lying down. The temperature has dropped precipitously with the sunset, cold enough to see their breaths.

Three pickup trucks and a late model Lincoln Town Car, all covered in dust, are parked next to the ranch buildings, away from the house.

"So what do we do now?"

"Take a deep breath, and let Fred know we're here," Anna says. She tries to steady her hands.

They approach the front door, and, after searching unsuccessfully for a doorbell, Lars knocks, first timidly, then louder. No answer. No sounds of anything within the house.

They look at each other.

"You know how loony he'll think this is, us just showing up?" Anna asks.

"It's His will," Lars says. "Mr. Wilson can't argue with that."

They walk away from the house, toward the first outbuilding. Inside they hear voices, one raised above the others. Lars cautiously pushes the door open. It's a sort of laboratory, with burners, glass containers on counters, cartons piled on shelves. In one corner of the long room, four large freezers. Stainless steel everywhere, like a restaurant kitchen.

Three men are gathered around a tall table. One of them has his eyes to a device resembling the microscope from Anna's biology class, but instead of just one eyepiece, it had two, one for each eye. The man is peering into the tubes and counting.

"Two, three, five . . . I count eight!" Fred Wilson, dressed in perfectly creased jeans and a button-down shirt, looking as dapper as he had in California. Incongruous given the setting.

At that, the other two men give whistles of admiration. "Great catch!" says the younger one. Unlike Fred Wilson, he's dressed for the farmyard, with work-worn jeans and a flannel shirt.

"Whooee!" says Fred Wilson, and pumps his fist into the air. "Most if not all of them viable, I'd guess."

"Not a bad haul," says the youngest.

"You said it," Fred Wilson responds, straightening up. "Okay, Richard, get these into nitrogen and labeled. Put them in 3a. I have high hopes for no. 3. Our friends in Jerusalem should be very happy. Good times are here again!"

He sees Anna and Lars and abruptly stops talking. The other two men swing around.

Lars is standing in front of Anna, and quick to take control. He sticks out his hand. "Mr. Wilson, Lars Goldschmidt.

I met you at Reverend Michael's church in California. The Preparing-for-Him congregation."

Fred is frowning. He catches sight of Anna. "You look familiar," he says.

Anna steps nervously forward. "We've been corresponding by email," she says. "Anna Franklin."

"Anna . . . Anna. The name's familiar. And I recognize your face," he says, and finally he relaxes into a smile. "Your hair's longer. It suits you." Anna tugs at it self-consciously, shrinks into her sweatshirt.

"So what are you kids doing out here?"

"We're here to help," Lars says.

"Help?"

Anna speaks up. "You said in your emails that He needs all the help He can get." When Fred Wilson looks blankly at her, she adds, "You mentioned couriers."

Fred Wilson glances over at the two other men, who have been listening quietly.

"Richard, go on, get these embryos into the nitrogen. Larry, take Betsy back to the barn. I'll check on her later."

"I thought we also wanted to flush Billie today," Richard says.

Fred runs his right hand through his hair. "Let's get to work, then. Larry, bring Billie to the flushing stall." He turns back to Anna and Lars. "You can watch, if you're interested."

Then, "Couriers, huh? You're awfully young. But that might work in your favor. We've had some trouble with paperwork lately."

He takes Lars and Anna into an adjoining room, empty except for a makeshift stall full of straw in a corner.

Larry comes through a back door. Before it closes, Anna sees that it leads to the cattle yard. He's walking in another cow. She's mostly red, but has white ears and some speckles of white on her back, as if she's been lightly salted.

"Billie is several generations away from where Betsy is today," says Fred Wilson. "But we're optimistic for her line. We think the generation will give us the results we're hoping for."

"You said in your last email that you're close," Anna says. She tries not to show how intensely interested she is in what he is saying.

"Very close. We'll keep two of the most promising of Betsy's embryos, transplant them into two of our healthiest incubator heifers. We'll send the rest to Israel. They'll be born there, but carefully tracked. If one or more is pure red and makes it to two years without any impurities, bingo, we'll have the genetic recipe we need."

"Your partners in Israel being the Third Temple Commission?" Lars asks.

"That's right. Strange bedfellows, aren't we?" Fred Wilson gives a short laugh as he prepares. He's pulling up a low metal stool and is hanging a clear bag of some kind of liquid on a tall steel pole on wheels. "Once the fighting ends, and construction on the Temple actually starts, they'll need many, many Red Heifers to cleanse all their workers. Our job is to provide them."

"You're doing His work," says Lars.

Fred puts on a pair of rubber gloves. The other two men are doing the same. "We're just a cog in the wheel. But an important cog, if I do say so myself."

"We agree. And we want to help," says Lars. "You should use us. We've been sent."

"Actually, you might be the answer to a little problem we're having with exporting," says Fred Wilson. He stops fiddling with the bag of liquid.

"What kind of problem?" Anna asks.

"We had a visit earlier this year, from the USDA," Fred says. "The Animal and Plant Health Inspection guys. The inspection was a bit of a surprise. They weren't too pleased with our setup here—the flushing of the embryos is supposed to happen in a different facility than the impregnation. So we've temporarily lost our certification that gets our shipments through customs."

"How could we help?" Anna tries to sound excited, but not overmuch. She is information gathering.

"Well, young persons like yourself, especially if you dress nicely and act real polite, you're not going to be subject to the same kind of scrutiny that an adult would be. Neither of you fit any risk profiles."

"You're saying we'd smuggle the embryos into Israel?" Lars asks. He looks thrilled. Anna tries to put a suitable expression on her face.

"Perhaps. For a while. That's the only way we can keep our operation going, keep the folks at the Temple Commission happy. Since they sign the checks, that's important. I need capital to build the requisite facilities. But they want to see how Betsy's progeny turn out. The embryos aren't much good to me here. If I can't get them to Israel, they're just a novelty. These cows aren't particularly good for either dairy or eating."

While the men are preparing Billie, Fred takes them back into the first long room, to where the large white containers are lined up. He's still wearing his gloves. "Here, the embryos are frozen, labeled. I've got a generator so that even if we lose power, we're safe," he says.

"This family"—he points to a section of the freezer labeled *2D: Great White Hope*—"we thought we'd succeeded in breeding out the white tufts on the ears. For some reason, the ears are always a problem. So we shipped the embryos, they implanted, and out of five embryos, we got one that looked like the real deal. Everyone was thrilled. But in her third year, some impurities showed up on her belly, some white patches. Big, big disappointment."

"When do you next need couriers?" asks Lars.

"Real soon. I want to get them Betsy's embryos that we just extracted ASAP."

"We're ready," says Lars.

"Whoa, cowboy. Just take her easy. One thing at a time. Right now we need to do another extraction, where we take the fertilized eggs, the embryos, out of the cow. Billie's waiting. It's actually a very simple procedure. Not surgical."

"What if you found the perfect cow and the perfect bull to mate and something happens to one of them?" Anna asks. "What do you do? Start over?"

"When we get what we think is going to be a genetically important cow or bull, of course, we get as much semen from the bull, and extract as many eggs as we possibly can from the cow," says Fred. "We freeze it all. Even if every cow in my stable died overnight, and I lost my bull, I'd be fine."

Fred gestures toward the freezers.

"What counts the most is stored here. And we have backup generators, of course. But we're also almost done putting together a disaster recovery plan that will make our operations fail-safe. I'm transferring half my stock to another ranch with freezing capabilities, in Texas. Another rancher among the faithful. He doesn't have the skills to do any of this, but he has the freezers. He'll have a mirror image of my stock."

"What about your records?" Anna asks. "From what little I know of genetics, you have to be careful to track everything."

"We keep meticulous records. For one thing, we need to for regulatory reasons. The other reason, of course, is that we need to precisely track the genetics of each embryo we extract, freeze, and implant."

"It'd be terrible to lose those records," Anna says.

"It'd be catastrophic. But every night they're backed up, off site."

An impatient voice calls from the other room. "Fred? Ready and waiting."

Fred Wilson leads Lars and Anna back to the adjoining room. "I palpated Billie's ovaries yesterday," he tells Larry, who is sitting on a stool next to a reddish cow with white ears. "I estimate only four corpora lutea, so we won't be getting the same volume as we did from Betsy."

Anna and Lars watch as Larry washes and then rinses the cow, then Fred Wilson takes a long tube and inserts it carefully into her hindquarters.

"This container has been coated with Teflon, like a frying pan, so the embryos don't stick together. There. You need to get the right mixture of air and water into the uterus," says Fred Wilson.

Fred's hands are surprisingly gentle, his face relaxed as he talks. The quick-pattering salesman has been replaced by a genial country doctor.

"We start by flushing the uterus and then—easy, now, Larry. Richard, calm Billie down, she's getting a little agitated," says Fred, lifting a bag of fluid and hanging it from a hook on the ceiling. "We then examine all the fluid that comes out of the cow's uterus under the stereoscope. Then it's a game of *Where's Waldo*." He grins, then starts stripping off his gloves. "Larry, do the cryopreservation. Richard, take care of the certificates. Don't miss any of the data. They're keeping a close eye on us. We have to do everything by the book."

Fred leads the way into the other room, to the microscope-like instrument, carrying the container of fluid extracted from Billie.

"How do you know that you haven't missed any embryos?" Anna asks. "Aren't they awfully small?"

"We put three pairs of eyes to examine each searching dish. Here, you be one of them. What do you see?"

Anna puts her eyes against the stereoscope. At first, nothing. Then she catches her breath. Floating in the pinkish solution are three tiny circles, one almost perfectly round, the two others bumpy around their perimeters. She sees tiny circles within those circles.

"I found three," Anna says.

"I actually saw four, but the fourth is quite small, and its shape is suspect. We look for thick membranes and even cleavage planes. We won't keep that one. Good job spotting three. You'd be amazed how much you can miss. It's a tedious job. That's why we need multiple eyes."

Fred claps his hands and gestures to Anna and Lars to follow him. They exit through the laboratory into a completely changed landscape. Black. Pitch black. Since they were last outside, the sun has set and a cloud cover moved in. No stars and not a light generated by man in sight. The already chill air has turned positively frigid.

"Here," Fred lights the way with a powerful flashlight. He picks out their car among the other three. "You kids staying at the Comfort or the Quality?"

"Neither," Lars says, and pauses. "We were hoping you might be able to put us up."

Fred runs his hand through his hair.

"I don't see why not. My wife's out of town, in Lincoln. She's in a spot of trouble due to some pro-life work she's been involved in. It's funny, she got interested in that from helping here, seeing the embryos so small. 'We think of them as cows already,' she said. 'Why don't we think of them as people?'"

Lars is yawning, and Anna's legs are aching from standing so long. "I'll get you kids settled," he says. "We'll discuss logistics for the long term later."

52

ANNA AND FRED ARE SITTING in the living room. She is still marveling at the deep darkness that surrounds Fred Wilson's stronghold. The light from the curtainless windows slices a bright five-foot beacon into the shadows, then ends abruptly, as if hitting a wall.

"In the summer that light would be thick with every type of bug you could imagine," says Fred. "But December's a sterile month for the flora and fauna around here. Thank God."

The room is comfortable. Not overtly luxurious, but money has been spent. A flat-screen television hangs on one wall, wired to speakers in each corner of the room. Fred Wilson is working on a tablet while sitting on the couch. A laptop sits on the dining room table, amidst a pile of papers. The phone rings periodically. Fred ignores it.

"You'll hear the phone really start ringing at about 1 AM, when Israel wakes up," he says. "Those are the calls I take. I'll try to keep it quiet, but don't be alarmed if you hear noises in the middle of the night."

Lars is in bed, which is surprising because he slept so much in the car. Without excusing himself, he went off to the guest room with the twin beds, decorated with staid blue and green plaids. Mrs. Wilson doesn't seem to have much of a decorative flair, favoring dark colors with busy patterns and the kind of Christian art Anna's parents had abhorred. Lots of crosses. The kitchen has three calendars from the Valentine Christian Assembly of God. One was marked *legislative,* one *community,* one *personal.* Many of the squares across all three calendars are full. Mrs. Wilson clearly leads a busy life. On today's date, she's written *Lincoln* and underlined it three times.

"We have to have a conversation, Anna," Fred says. He pulls up a chair and sits down. "Lars went to bed before I could bring it up with him, too. But we'll start with you. So tell me. What exactly is going on here?"

Anna doesn't answer.

"I'm sorry, Anna, but you need to come clean about what you're up to. I can't harbor two minors who simply show up on my doorstep. We agreed that you were going to come when you were eighteen. But Lars is clearly younger than that."

"I'll be eighteen in five months," Anna says.

"Well, you'll be welcome then," he says. "But you're not answering my questions. Do your parents know you're here?"

Anna ponders how best to answer. "No one knows we're here," she says finally.

"Where do your parents think you are?"

"Lars's parents think he's at a ministry in New Mexico," Anna says.

"Yes?"

Anna isn't sure she trusts him, so she tells him part of the story. About her parents, and about the original plan, that Lars and she had intended to join his operation eventually, that it happening this way was just an accident.

She doesn't tell him about her change of heart in the waves. She doesn't tell him that she is now, in effect, playing for the other team.

He is quiet for a long time after Anna finishes talking. Then he says, "You poor kid."

Anna squirms. She hates pity.

"But can we join you? That's the question."

Fred is still gazing upon Anna, his eyes wide, in an apparent attempt to communicate compassion, sympathy. An act, unskillfully played.

"Too risky," he finally says.

She smiles back at him, a smile so patently insincere it hurts her mouth. "But when I'm eighteen?"

"When you're eighteen. Yes. You can come back then."

"Are you kicking us out tomorrow?"

"No. No, I wouldn't do that. We'll wait until Mrs. Wilson gets back in two days and then have a discussion."

"You're full of common sense for someone who believes the End Days are near," Anna says. "How do you reconcile all this"—and she gestures around the room, at the entertainment, the gadgets, the electronics—"with the fact that you are actively trying to trigger the Tribulation?"

Fred considers. He takes his time before answering. "I'm a scientist," he says, finally. "Not by education, I barely finished high school. But at this point I know as much as any geneticist." He has a curious habit of patting his hair. He does that now. A mirror hangs on the opposite wall and he is watching himself as he talks, pats, talks, pats. He leans back and crosses one thigh over the other.

"Seeing those embryos was amazing," Anna admits. She thinks, this is what her parents saw, eighteen years ago. They looked at her under a microscope, counted her cells, measured the thickness of her membrane, looked at the evenness of her cleavage plane, and chose her out of all her potential brothers and sisters. For qualities that have nothing to do with her future virtues or vices. Survival of the fittest.

To be chosen. I was the chosen one. "We're so close to playing God, don't you think?" she asks him. "Perhaps too close?"

"I leave the bioethics to the boys with the big degrees," he says. "I have a mission, I just don't want to fuck that up. God picked me, and I'm humbled by that, and that's enough for me."

Anna can't believe she once thought him an important man. She tells herself, *I am gathering information.*

He doesn't look humble as he gulps down the last of his beer and stands up. "I'm going to go check on the cows, make sure everything's locked up," he says.

He's almost out the door when he turns and asks. "Want to come? I'll show you my prize animal, the one I'm pretty sure is going to be the answer to the Third Temple Commission's prayers."

"I thought that was Betsy," Anna says.

"She's the dame. I'm talking about the sire. I'm pulling so much semen from this bull, and it's pure gold. A single ejaculation can service hundreds of Betsys. I'm fairly sure he's the one."

Anna nods. She doesn't really want to leave the warm, brightly lit room. It reminds her of evenings spent with her parents, doing her homework at her father's PC, him at his laptop,

Anna's mother at her piano. The sight of lit computer screens as comforting as home fires. It feels safe here. She tells herself again, *I am gathering information.*

Fred Wilson hands her a large green coat that looks like it came from an army surplus store. "Put this on, it'll be cold in the stables." It reaches Anna's knees and well over her knuckles but she's grateful for its warmth when they head out the back door. The veil of low-hanging clouds from earlier in the evening is gone. It is bitterly cold and the heavens are clearer than Anna has ever seen. She thought she'd gotten used to the expanse of sky and the proximity of the stars over the past few nights, but it hits her anew. A curtain of stars down to the horizon. Because the house is slightly elevated, some stars even appear to hang below them. She follows Fred Wilson down the hill to the out-buildings, past the laboratory, through several stiles.

The cow barn is long and high, running about thirty feet wide and about two hundred feet long. Perhaps twenty cows in total. The floor is raised. Bright fluorescent lights overhead. The warm air feels balmy after the outdoors. Anna takes the coat off, hangs it over a railing.

"The winters here are pretty brutal," Fred Wilson says. "This year we've been lucky, because of the weather, they're getting much more fresh air and exercise than they generally would in winter. It's good for them."

Anna had expected a strong, and unpleasant, smell. But it's surprisingly benign, mostly an earthy mixture of hay and dirt. But she hadn't realized cows were so noisy. In addition to the occasional *moo* she hears a constant murmuring. Some breathy whistling. The barn is a warm, dry haven filled with the sounds of contented creatures.

"What a blessed place," Anna says, and she means it. She'd spend all her time here if she lived on the farm.

Fred is moving from stall to stall, speaking to the cows, patting their rumps. Some seem indifferent, but many move their dull large faces toward him, and low in response.

"They like you," Anna says.

"They're creatures of habit," says Fred. "If someone doesn't come in at 9:30 to check on them, they notice."

"They want to be tucked in," Anna says.

"Exactly," he says, smiling.

"If no one came to do it?"

"They'd be agitated in the morning. We'd certainly notice a difference. And you don't want to agitate cows. You want to keep them calm. Everything goes smoother that way."

He checks in with every cow, lying or standing, and then comes back to Anna.

"Now this way," he says. "We keep our bull separate. We're not really worried about trouble. Our cows have very gentle temperaments—they're bred for that in addition to color. But it's best to be safe." He continues to pat cows on the rump or the head as they pass stalls.

"Do they sleep at night?" Anna asks.

"Mostly they lie and eat. They need more calories the colder it gets, so I'll feed them again at 3:30 in the morning."

"When do you sleep?"

"In the middle of the day, I grab a few hours," he says. "And then again after dinner, until Israel starts calling. A rancher's life is not a particularly fun one. I'd typically be going to sleep right after I checked on the cows, without my . . . uninvited . . . guests." His smile doesn't quite take the sting out of his words.

As he leads the way into a separate enclosure, with a separate lock, Anna is startled to hear voices. Male and female. "I thought only you and your wife stayed on the ranch," Anna says.

"That's true," he says. "But cattle are social animals. They get lonely without companionship. The cows have each other, but the bull is alone. I leave the radio on for him.

The majesty of the creature takes Anna's breath away. The sheer bulk of his broad back. The flabs of flesh overhanging his haunches. His large muscled hindquarters, massive low-hanging sexual organs. His grandiose stupidity. *I exist*, his physical presence seems to say, *and I take up exactly as much space and air as I require.* No excuses. Anna would love to be as stoic and unapologetic about her own existence.

Fred is talking about the expense of keeping his ranch operational. "All in all, it's quite costly." His voice drones on. The space is enclosed enough for Anna to smell his breath. Sweet, like her father's late in the evenings. Sweetness from the beer. Anna's father. A hidden life, not what he seemed. Or rather, Anna just hadn't fully recognized all the ingredients that went into that complex mix.

Anna realizes Fred is talking and tries to pay attention. But her mind is on her father.

"I tried Red Angus, but went with French Limousin cattle for their ability to survive harsh climes," Fred is saying. He has turned into the bore he was when he first appeared at Reverend Michael's church. He's now talking about the various breeds. The room is getting hot. "I made a good choice, as it turned out." The space is so small both he and the bull are literally breathing down Anna's neck. She feels uncomfortable, the rampant sexuality of the bull combined with Fred's close-ness. He moves even closer and Anna begins to look for the exit when Fred's cell phone rings.

He reaches into his pocket, pushes a button. "Hello?" His eyes move to Anna as he says, "Yes, that's me." He then listens for what seems to Anna like a long time. She starts getting ner-vous. "We're on Rural Route 3," he says. "It's complicated. Best I email you directions from the airport. Yes. Well, I *was* wonder-ing what to do . . . All right, see you soon." He hangs up. His face is stern. "That was your teacher, The one you stole a car from." Anna feels herself flushing.

"What's going to happen?" she asks.

"You're lucky. She convinced the cops that it was all in the family. That she was your guardian." Fred Wilson gives a short laugh. "I can't believe the nerve of you kids. She's about to board a flight. They'll be here later tonight."

Anna is surprised to find herself frightened, not of what Ms. Thadeous will do, but what she thinks of her, Anna. The one thing Anna can do is pray that Jim Fulson won't be accom-panying Ms. Thadeous to witness her disgrace.

"I forgot your coat in the cow barn," she says abruptly.

Fred Wilson shrugs. "Don't stray," he says, and heads back to the house. Anna waits, then lets herself out the door. The moon has risen and she easily traces her way back to the first building where they had found Fred Wilson that day. The door is unlocked. Anna pushes into the room and turns on the light. The brightness blinds her momentarily, then she walks over to the line of freezers. There are four total: long low boxes that give off a faint humming sound. She traces her finger along the top of the closest one. It is cold to the touch. Her hands are shaking. She bends over and follows the power cord to a large, industrial-looking electrical box. All four freezers are plugged into it. One by one, Anna deliberately pulls out the plugs. One. Two. Three. The fourth one offers some resistance, but finally gives. The humming ceases. For good measure, Anna opens the doors of each case as well. The cold air wafts into her face.

Her job done there, Anna goes in search of the generator. Anna finds her way back to the cow barn, searches in the corners, then in every stall. Eventually she tries the door leading to the bull pen, wanting another look at the majestic creature, but the door is locked. Fred must have done that on his way back to the house. Going back into the barn, Anna hesitates. She is beginning to feel strange. Something is coming; she can feel it. Anna waits, and when the aura starts tinting the walls and ceilings with her lovely familiar friend vermillion she smiles. And then the buzzing and the smells intertwine and Anna is lying flat on the floor and her arms and legs are moving independently of each other as she flails out in every direction.

She makes a superhuman effort and rolls over. Her face is right next to a cow's pen, and the cow is emitting erratic deep grumbling noises in its throat. Then she flips onto her back again, and the cow is leaning over her. She sees its quizzical eyes, and all the metallic equipment in the room begins rattling and the roof undulates and as if in slow motion a window bursts and shards of glass fly. Anna hides her face in her arms to shield her eyes, then tries to get up on her knees and then stand, but is knocked to the floor as the shaking intensifies and she hears another explosion of glass. The cows are agitated, bumping against each other, panicking, their lows and moans getting louder and more frantic. And the rumbling becomes a kind of a roar, and then the ceiling above Anna starts to buckle and she finally knows.

"An earthquake," she manages to say. "A big one." And she hears her father's voice telling her to forget the Triangle of Life, forget trying to get outside, *do what you can: duck, cover, and hold on.* Amidst the shaking and the shuddering Anna crawls to the metal water trough in the corner of the room and with the last of her strength tips it over and gets under it. Anna is soaked but she is enclosed and then she is gone.

53

ANNA'S NEVER BEEN THIS COLD. But the night is so clear, and the stars so numerous and close, she doesn't mind. Her arms and legs won't obey her commands, and she lies, wet and chilled, looking up at the stars, a different kind of desolation, beautiful. And then Ms. Thadeous is gazing down at her. Taking off her coat and wrapping it around her. Anna hears words. *A trough. She was lucky.* In the distance, the noise of a helicopter reminds Anna that other humans inhabit this planet.

Jim . . .

His voice. His hand holding Anna's. "You're a one-woman destructive force," he says. "Did you conjure up this improbable earthquake on your own?"

"What about the cows?"

Jim Fulson shakes his head. "Not much chance that any of them survived. Or if they did, they'll be put out of their misery. This whole place is trashed. The epicenter was just five miles from here. A 7.1. Big even by California standards. But virtually unheard of here."

He is continuing, talking about luck and about the sparsely populated region and no lives lost as far as they know.

"Lars?"

"So I come after the cows?" Lars is there, too, his voice expressing concern. He leans over and places a warm hand against Anna's brow. "The house managed to remain standing," he says. "Fred Wilson is okay. But his lab and all his specimens have been destroyed."

A man in uniform is taking notes. He looks bewildered.

"I'll need names and addresses," he says. "We'll need responsible adults, your legal guardians since your parents are ... apparently unavailable."

"My aunt and uncle in Columbus," Anna says. "Where I'll be. Five more months."

"And after that?" asks Jim Fulson. He is still holding tight to Anna's hand.

"God only knows," Anna says. "But alive."

Epilogue

TWO YEARS, TEN MONTHS HAVE passed, so quickly that Anna has trouble comprehending it. She feels like the same old Anna. But people treat her differently now. Like the adult she is. Now she lives in the Pacific Northwest. In Port Townsend, a remote peninsula on the Puget Sound outside Seattle. She works for the state, taking care of elderly shut-ins. Sometimes that means just sitting and holding hands with them, like sweethearts.

Jim works on the boats of rich men. They get by financially. They more than get by in many ways. Anna doesn't like talking about it. Too much happiness is frightening. Don't look it in the face, or at least, not often.

Anna thinks of her mother often. *But I'm not ashamed of getting more than I deserve, for how else would I learn what I do deserve?* Unlike her mother, Anna feels shame at getting so much. She certainly doesn't need more. Where would she store a surplus of happiness? She spends what she has, possesses no residual when she lies down at night.

Jim Fulson never told Anna what happened between him and Ms. Thadeous. Just that she needed to do something big, something bigger than Sunnyvale High. She went to Africa as a volunteer, to fight AIDS on the Manzini-Mbabane Corridor. And Jim Fulson waited until January, waited until Anna had been eighteen for eight months, then followed her up to Seattle, the farthest Anna could get from Sunnyvale and remain on the same coast. Jim Fulson chose Anna. Anna herself had no choice, she never had. She never looks back.

Sometimes Anna goes into the state park on the edge of Port Townsend and sits on the cement battlements built during World War II in preparation for an attack from the west, from the Japanese, another long-awaited battle that never occurred. She dangles her legs over the Pacific, throws rocks into the surf from the cliffs above. Around two hundred yards away is a huge abandoned cistern. Where a tiny pebble dropped in reverberates with the power of a small bomb.

Jim Fulson still doesn't understand Anna's faith, but he tolerates it. For her part, she doesn't trouble him with her thoughts on the subject. She doesn't go to church, attends no formal services. All that is unnecessary.

Lars has a large congregation in New Mexico, in the high desert outside of Albuquerque. He is a force to be reckoned with, both politically and socially. Anna hasn't spoken to him. He has no more use for her, nor she for him.

Anna's headaches, the seizures, are not as bad anymore. When the aura appears, she takes 400 mg of Neurontin. This seems to forestall all but the very worst attacks. She refused to take the drugs for a long time, these fits being her closest connection to her past, to that wonderful and terrible year. She takes the Neurontin for Jim, and forgoes the falling, and the pain and ecstasy that would otherwise follow. Anna's highs and lows are now muted, contained.

A red calf was born in Israel. Not of Fred Wilson's stock, a fluke from a farm near Haifa. Fred Wilson disappeared into history.

Today is a sultry Monday in the beginning of September. An early chill. Each leaf that falls from each tree a reminder of little deaths. Anna had always loved autumn but never knew why. The early shrouding of day. The melancholy breathing of the wind. Summer limping to a close. Lars explained it to her all those years ago why it thrilled rather than saddened her.

There shall be no more death, neither sorrow, nor crying, neither shall there be any more pain: for the former things are passed away.

Decline is good. Such things signal He is close. It is cause for gratefulness. For ecstasy, even. *For I am passionately in love with death.* Some things never change.

The visions continue. They occur during the most serious seizures, the ones the Neurontin can't stop. Anna tells no one.

They are glorious.

Acknowledgments

MY THANKS TO MY BELOVED writing group and everyone else who read early drafts of this book and provided me with valuable feedback. As always, all my love to Sarah and David, who both inspire me and keep me sane. To Victoria Skurnick, friend and agent extraordinaire at Levine, Greenberg, and Rostan. And to the team at Grove Atlantic who made this a much better book than it would have otherwise been: Corinna Barsan, Elisabeth Schmitz, Morgan Entrekin, and Briony Everroad.

Coming of Age at the End of Days

Alice LaPlante

ABOUT THIS GUIDE

We hope that these discussion questions will enhance your reading group's exploration of Alice LaPlante's *Coming of Age at the End of Days*. They are meant to stimulate discussion, offer new viewpoints, and enrich your enjoyment of the book.

More reading group guides and additional information, including summaries, author tours, and author sites for other fine Grove Press titles may be found on our Web site, groveatlantic.com.

QUESTIONS FOR DISCUSSION

1. Reread the novel's opening paragraphs describing Sunnyvale, California. Do you agree with the statement that there are "no secrets, no mysteries, in this suburban enclave" (p. 3)? Even if the neighbors live in close proximity, how aware are they of each other's inner lives?

2. Against this canvas of normality, sixteen-year old Anna Franklin spirals into darkness, depression, and suicidal ideation. Look at LaPlante's deft descriptions of the physicality of mental illness and talk about how Anna's parents and friends react to her condition. Do they understand her? Why or why not?

3. Consider Anna's psychiatrist's diagnosis that Anna's "problem" is due to "a simple misalignment with her herd" and the suggestion that Anna should "hunt with the pack" (p.18). Do you agree with this statement? Does Anna? Identify examples throughout the text of the invalidation of Anna's illness, and discuss the ways that Anna reacts to it.

4. How sympathetic do you find Anna as a character? Identify ways in which her actions seem to alienate others, and consider how much of her behavior is within her control. Do you think she is aware of the way she makes others feel?

5. In the piercingly emotional scene on the golf course (pp. 29–32), Anna's mother asks her daughter if she will take her own life: "Oh, Annie, we're not going to lose you, are we?" Discuss the growing gulf between Anna and her parents, their helplessness and vulnerability, and their inefficacy in coping with Anna's turmoil. Did you feel that they could do more to help her, to reach her? Talk about your reactions to their parenting.

6. What are the consequences of her parents' pursuit of their own passions? What does music represent for Anna's mother, and how does it affect their relationship? Talk about Anna's father's obsession with earthquakes: What does he gain from his hobby, and how does it resonate with Anna?

7. When the Goldschmidt family moves in next door, Anna is immediately interested in them: "She understands that her world is now inexorably divided in two: before and after" (p. 44). Why is she so drawn to them? Later, when Anna and Lars miss the school bus, what endears him to Anna? What does he represent to her?

8. Anna's fascination with death—"for I am passionately in love with death" (p. 32)—pervades the narrative. Would you consider the book as mostly dark in tone? Discuss the ways in which the author balances the book's emotional intensity. Can you find instances of humor?

9. Anna is able to pull herself from the depths of depression through the help of the Goldschmidt's religious fervor. Analyze her attraction to the Tribulation at the End Days. What does she mean when she says, "I burn to serve" (p. 58) on her first visit to Michael's church?

10. Examine the ways in which faith is depicted in the novel. What does faith mean to Anna, to the Goldschmidts, to the other members of the congregation? How does it shape their understanding of themselves, of their world? Do they ever seem to doubt?

11. How does Anna's exploration of faith parallel her father's preoccupation with earthquakes? Consider this quote: "He is as enamored with the idea of widespread destruction as the bloodiest-minded members of Reverend Michael's church . . .

he delights in knowing he will be among the informed, among the prepared, among the surviving" (p. 119).

12. Discuss Anna's visions of the Red Heifer. Why are the visions so important in terms of her personal development, and what role do they play in her faith? What is your understanding of the visions from a medical viewpoint?

13. While Anna's coming-of-age is central to this novel, LaPlante has created other complex and memorable characters. What does Clara Thadeous mean to Anna? Chart Anna's changing view of her Chemistry teacher throughout the story, as well as Clara's evolution as a character.

14. Jim Fulson has fascinated Anna since childhood. What brings them together, enabling them to confide in one another? Talk about the ways in which LaPlante reveals their connection.

15. At the heart of the novel is an examination of the complexity of human character, the many ways that people can exist, and how little we understand each other and even ourselves. Find examples of secrets that the various characters keep— for example, Clara's relationship with her mother—and then discuss the dichotomy between their true selves and the selves they choose to present to the world.

16. LaPlante writes with insight and sensitivity about mental disorder and depression. What do you think the metaphorical imprisonment of Jim Fulson in his parent's basement says about society's attitude toward mental illness and suicide?

17. In light of this quote, discuss the impact of Anna's parents' death: "Anna is suddenly overwhelmed with a sense of what she has lost. She reaches into the pocket and brings out a quarter. A talisman. Although a superstitious act and therefore

against His will, she kisses the coin and is finally able to sleep" (p. 155).

18. At the beach, Anna nearly drowns—a baptism of sorts—and undergoes a sudden realization about the future. What changes take place following this incident? Consider the following quote: "But she now possesses a different attitude, the scene evokes her pity rather than her scorn, and she wants to beg for His mercy rather than His sword" (p. 214).

19. What do you think of the road trip that Anna, Clara, Jim, and Lars embark on? Does it add a level of suspense to the story? What were your expectations for their journey? Were you satisfied by the outcome?

20. The novel's epilogue depicts Anna and Jim living happily together. Are you optimistic about their ability to maintain their love and their mental stability? How has Anna matured during the narrative? What do you hope for her future?

SUGGESTIONS FOR FURTHER READING

The Last Days of California by Mary Miller; The Girl Who Slept with God by Val Brelinski; The Bell Jar by Sylvia Plath; Enduring Love by Ian McEwan